Praise for Jim Misko's Other Books

"Exhilarating"

"Incredibly entertaining...With keen commentary and descriptions of life in Nebraska, the author leaves readers contemplating the story long after its exhilarating conclusion."
—Review, *Nebraska Life*

"Unfailingly entertaining"

"An extraordinarily well written and unfailingly entertaining read from beginning to end, *As All My Fathers Were* showcases the impressive storytelling talents of novelist James A. Misko. Very highly recommended for community library General Fiction collections, *As All My Fathers Were*, it should be noted for personal reading lists that this outstanding novel is also available in a Kindle edition ($9.95)."
—*Midwest Book Review*

"Exciting . . . old-fashioned storytelling"

"In Jim Misko's exciting new novel, *As All My Fathers Were*, two aging brothers set out by horseback up the beautiful but endangered Platte River. Their odyssey into the heart of the contemporary American West is both harrowing and inspiring. Anyone who thinks that old-fashioned storytelling in the tradition of *Lonesome Dove* and *Cold Mountain* has gone the way of the Platte River buffalo herd must read this fine novel."
—Howard Frank Mosher, author of *God's Kingdom*

"Illuminating"

"In this tough but tender story of two estranged brothers—and their event-filled trek down Nebraska's Platte River—Misko simultaneously paints a memorable portrait, as incisive as it is illuminating, of America's disappearing past and its increasingly conflicted future."
—Robert Masello, author of *The Romanov Cross*

"A must read"

"What is extraordinary about Jim Misko's *As All My Fathers Were* is how he makes the land, Nature, practically a main character in his stories. You can't read his novels without feeling you've been in that world, and if you haven't, you envy those who have and still are. To do this, and still hold onto tension and the excitement of good storytelling with themes that have meaning to us, makes *As All My Fathers Were* a must read for anyone who wants to breathe fresh air."
—Andrew Neiderman, author of *The Devil's Advocate*

"Remarkable"

"*As All My Fathers Were* is a refreshingly unapologetic, environmental polemic—one with living characters and a pulse. But far more remarkable than the story of two Nebraska farmers on a quest to save their land, is its author: an 80-something self-described gun-toting political conservative. Jim Misko's condemnation of modern agribusiness bares an essential truth: Nature knows no politics, and we're all in this together. Off in the distance, you can hear Edward Abbey, Rachel Carson, and the Platte River itself applauding."
—Nick Jans, author of *A Wolf Called Romeo*

"Absorbing"

"If you want to know how the Platte River works, read James A. Misko's absorbing and rambunctious tale of Seth and Richard Barrett, who must complete a journey up the river from its confluence with the Missouri to its source near North Platte, Nebraska, and back if they are to inherit the family farm. In *As All My Fathers Were*, you'll learn the natural history of this once wild river that shaped the land and those who lived near it but in the past century has been broken by energy generation and the agricultural industry. Yet as Misko's novel bears witness, the Platte still has the power to inspire the imagination and fine literature.
—Lisa Knopp, author of *What the River Carries*

"Misko at his best"

"A passion play for the New West, *As All My Fathers Were* gathers momentum the way a river grows, gathering substance with every bend and merging channel, and shines in its descriptive writing. This is Misko at his best."
—Lynn Schooler, author of *Heartbroke Bay*

"A masterpiece"

"Jim Misko has done it again. *As All My Fathers Were* is a masterpiece. This novel has everything a reader searches for in pursuit of a fine book—strong characters, brilliant dialogue, exciting plot, tension that bounces off every page, conflict, high ideals and villainy. In addition, by the end of the book, the average reader is far better educated and informed of a real-life issue of which the vast majority is uninformed."
—Stephen Maitland-Lewis, author of *Emeralds Never Fade*

Other Books by James A. Misko

FICTION
The Most Expensive Mistress in Jefferson County
The Cut of Pride
For What He Could Become
As All My Fathers Were

NON-FICTION
Creative Financing of Real Estate
How to Finance any Real Estate any Place any Time
How to Finance any Real Estate
any Place any Time – Strategies That Work

The Path of the Wind

a novel

JAMES A. MISKO

SQUAREONE
PUBLISHERS

For information regarding special discounts for bulk purchases, please contact Square One Publishers at 877-900-2665.

Cover and interior design by Frame25 Productions
Cover photo by Honza Krej c/o Shutterstock.com
Tamarack, Oregon map created by Thomas Eley/Mapping Solutions

Library of Congress Cataloging-In-Publiucation Data
Names: Misko, James A., author.
Title: The path of the wind / by James A. Misko.
Description: Garden City Park, NY : Square One Publishers, 2017.
Identifiers: LCCN 2016053938 (print) | LCCN 2016055582 (ebook) |
ISBN 9780757004445 (pbk.) | ISBN 9780757054440
Subjects: LCSH: Teachers—Fiction.
Classification: LCC PS3613.I8447 P38 2017 (print) | LCC PS3613.I8447 (ebook)
| DDC 813/.6—dc23
LC record available at https://lccn.loc.gov/2016053938

ISBN 978-0-7570-0444-5

Manufactured in the United States of America

10   9   8   7   6   5   4   3   2   1

To the dedicated teachers
who work more for
their students than themselves.

ACKNOWLEDGMENTS

This novel is dedicated to the fine teachers I have known in my life, both living and dead. They did their best with me and with those who came before and after me. Some I never experienced in classrooms but have known as friends, readers, and authors. I salute the profession for their sincere interest in helping educate America.

William Nelson • Norman W. Hickman, PhD
Volney Faw, PhD • George Ennis, PhD • Andrew Neiderman
Howard Frank Mosher • Nick Jans • Kent Haruf • Pat Conroy
Sandy Bennett • Ted Bennett • Ashley Sinclair • Carrie Lassen
James Michener • Robert Penn Warren • Wallace Stegner
Irena Praitis • Don Rearden • Bryce Lambley • Lisa Knopp, PhD
James Alexander Thom • Mark Sanders, PhD • David Onofrychuk
Catherine Ann Jones • Willie Hensley • John Graves • Joe Cupl
Irene Auble • Alex "Pop" Cochrane • Ladd Cochrane, PhD
Eugene Dubach, PhD • Mike DeGeer • Larry Kaniut • Jack Potter
Les Rasmussen • William Stafford, PhD • Howard Morgan
Ken Jones, PhD • John Smelcer • John Claus • Thaddea Pitts
Cathy Bromley • Denny Bromley • John Bury, PhD
Susan Bury, PhD • Dan Holtz

Location of the Village of Tamarack, Oregon.

CHAPTER 1

THEY WERE HARD TO see, but one by one they emerged around Big Rock Corner, east of town on Highway 26, singing the fight song and passing the bottle. It was a warm August night in central Oregon and the moon was just creeping over the juniper-covered crest of Rooster's Knob, not enough to throw light on the sunken highway below.

School would start in a week, and it was tonight or never for a wild time before football season began. The five boys staggering over the dark roadway made up most of the high school's first team: young, strong, and creating some fun in Tamarack, a town of 200 people carved out on both sides of a valley. The town was named after the creek that ran from east to west, parting it like a furrow. The locals referred to it as Tam for short; the football team, the Tam Buffaloes.

The boys should have heard the car coming but couldn't have seen it before it came around Big Rock and smashed into them in the middle of the road. Two made it to the side and missed getting hit by the Oldsmobile that was straddling the centerline when it put three boys across the hood and into the windshield.

There is a cemetery in Tamarack. With no reason for autopsies and no funeral parlor within 60 miles, the three boys were buried in that cemetery on top of the plateau 100 feet above the creek. The school janitor was commissioned by the town council to construct

1

three caskets out of wooden siding material, and with almost the entire population in attendance, the boys were laid to rest before the blood was cleaned off the highway.

MILES FOSTER, NEW TEACHER, drove with his wife Eleanor, dog, and two cats up Highway 26 and into Tamarack two days after the accident, and three days before school started.

Driving past the sign welcoming them to Tamarack, population 200, Miles pointed at the rock walls of cliffs guarding the entrance to the valley. "Some fortress."

Eleanor followed his point. "Slow to catch the morning sun. I'll bet this canyon gets cold."

"Yeah, but what a commanding view from the top."

"Of what? Indians coming down the highway?"

"That's a good start. Probably windy, too. Cool air from the mountains moving to the valley in the evening."

"Drive on McDuff. We'll find our castle in this hamlet."

Past a gas station, and a restaurant, the grocery store had a sign in the window advertising the daily special. *Popsicles two for a quarter.*

Eleanor held up her hand. "Stop here, driver."

Miles tried the door but it was locked. A piece of black bunting hung inside the glass door and a hand-lettered sign said: *Gone to Funeral. Be back at 5:00.*

Eleanor pointed at a road. "Take that road up the hill. Let's see what's up there."

At the top of the hill they saw a two-story stone building they guessed was the school. Miles parked in the dirt parking lot, shut off the engine. They stared at the stone two-story structure sitting atop the high side of the valley.

"I'd say it was built in the 1920s," Miles said.

"Older than the pyramids, I'll betcha."

"Naw. Not that old. Look. It's got glass windows."

"A contractor upgrade." Eleanor unlocked the doors. "Are we gonna get out or just sit here admiring the architecture?"

A flagpole with a flag at half-mast stood twenty feet from the front door. The door was unlocked. Miles and Eleanor walked in.

"Wow," she said. "It is kinda like being inside a pyramid. You don't think we'll find a mummy in here, do you?"

A man stepped out of a doorway at the dark end of the first floor hall. He stopped, feet spread with only his legs visible.

Miles lifted his head, smiled. "I'm a new teacher."

The shadowed figure walked toward them and emerged into the light sifting in through the glass doors. He nodded, then smiled, and offered his hand. "I'm the janitor. Name's Roscoe."

"Miles Foster. I'll be teaching social studies and music."

"Good to have you," Roscoe said. "Haven't had a good music teacher in awhile."

"Don't know that I'm good. Could I see my room?"

"Sure can. Follow me."

"Where is everybody?" Miles said.

"Funeral. We lost three boys . . . good boys couple of days ago. I built their coffins but I couldn't bear to watch them go in the ground or I'd be there. Top athletes, too. "

"Oh boy, that's gotta hurt. I'm so sorry. And sorry I'll not get to know them."

Roscoe nodded, his head down, then turned and led them up a stairway to the second floor on treads polished like a mirror, turned right and pushed a key into the lock, swung the door wide, and stepped back.

Eleanor took Miles's hand and they entered together. The smile started at the edge of his lips and curled up to his eyes. He stood behind the desk, hands on the maple chair, and looked at the four rows of desks as straight as soldiers on a parade ground. Books on shelves across the back of the room had their spines even with the edge of the shelf. The windows gleamed. Shades all pulled to the same length. The floor looked like it had been spit polished. "I like it," Miles said.

Roscoe beamed. "I'll keep it nice for you."

Eleanor looked at Roscoe. "Do you know of any places for rent in town?"

Roscoe tilted his head. "Teachers has took up most of the rental places. There was one up the end of Hotpatch Road 'bout half a mile from here. Don't know if it rented or not. Sits on the bluff—kinda brown looking. You might'a seen it coming in."

Eleanor smiled at Miles, her eyebrows rising. "We might have seen it."

"Maybe. Who would we see about it?"

"I think Ralph Harrison down at the market is handling it for the owner. He's some kin of the owners. They wuz loggers here a few years back."

"Great. Thanks. We'll check it out." Miles said. He turned to go. "See you around."

"Yeah. I'm here all the time. You need anything, just let me know."

"Thanks, Roscoe. Good meeting you and see you soon."

Roscoe nodded. "Yup."

RALPH HARRISON WAS A lean man, wore a butcher apron over his clothes with two pens and a pencil stuck in the breast pocket. He came from the back of the store wearing a smile as wide as the aisle, his hand reaching out for a handshake.

"You must be the new teacher just come in. I heard you were in town. We count them as they come in and you're the last of the Mohicans. I'm Ralph Harrison."

Miles grabbed his hand. *Strong grip for a small man.* "My wife Eleanor and I'm Miles Foster. We were by earlier but you were closed."

Ralph nodded and let his tongue sweep across his lips. "We had a funeral for three boys killed by a car few days ago. Whole town was there." He shook his head.

"It was a horrible thing. You know . . . the kinda thing that shouldn't have happened but did? A body never likes to go to a funeral for a young person. Just isn't right."

Miles watched Ralph Harrison's hands as they wrung each other across the exposed veins, yellowed nails sliding over and over the skin.

It was silent a moment, then Ralph looked up and smiled. "Well, I'll set you up for a credit account right away so you can get stuff to start your kitchen. Where are you living?"

"We heard—the janitor Roscoe told us—that you might have that place up on the bluff for rent?"

Ralph nodded his head three times, "I do, I do. And it's a dandy. Great view, good water, a chicken house and root cellar and a small barn. And only $50 a month plus utilities." He frowned, reached both hands into his pockets, then pulled out a key and smiled like he'd found the last Easter egg in tall grass. "Got a key right here. You want to see it?"

THE HOUSE SAT just back from the cliff with views overlooking Highway 26 a hundred and fifty feet below.

"Wow," Eleanor said. "It's like Masada."

"Practically. We could hold off an army coming up the hill," Miles said.

Ralph shook his head. "We haven't been invaded for four hundred years, unless you count when the hunters come into town for deer season."

They walked through the house, looked out the windows, and ran the water in the shower. Ele pulled out all of the drawers in the kitchen and pronounced them clean.

"We'll take it," Miles said. He pulled out his wallet. "Here's a deposit. Let's get a lease signed so we can move in."

CHAPTER 2

RANCHERS SAID HELLO TO townspeople, they mingled, and then crossed the parking lot to the school gym to meet the teachers for school year 1957-58. Lined up like posts in a fence, the total contingent of nine teachers stood with their backs against the wall of the gym, smiling, greeting, and shaking hands. Black bunting hung from the backboard and basket, and photos of the three students killed the week before were on a table, a school annual open to each one's class photo under his picture. The men removed their hats when they got to it, pulled their glasses out of their coat pockets, and put their ranch-stained fingers on the legend, whispering as they read it. Women opened their purses, pulled out hankies, and brushed their noses.

Miles bent over to retrieve his nametag that had fallen off. As he straightened up, a sun-hardened smiling face with home-cut rusty hair, his muscled arm outstretched, greeted him. Miles shook his hand.

"Welcome to Tamarack," the man said. "I'm Earl Benson. Local rancher. You'll run into my kids in school." He let loose of Miles's hand. "Sure glad to see you here." He held the mimeographed teacher roster rolled up in both hands. "I see here," he shook the roster between them, "that you're gonna teach geography, history, and music."

"That's right," Miles said.

Earl's smile widened. "That's good. I like that. History is a great thing for young kids to learn. You gonna teach 'em or educate 'em?"

"There's a difference?"

"Oh you betcha," he said, shaking his head. "Teaching is imparting facts and expecting regurgitation of them at test time. Education is exposing them to ideas and independent research so they can assimilate information and make their own conclusions."

Miles crossed his arms. "Hadn't thought of it that way."

"Well—it's the way I think about it. They need to be educated when they step out of here. This is a small town and most likely few will stay here. When they get out to Portland or Salem or somewhere they need to be able to rely on their education."

"I get your point."

"Good. Good. We'll see more of each other. Come on out to the ranch and have a beer anytime."

Miles nodded and shook hands again. "Thanks for coming down, Mr. Benson."

There was that smile again. "Just call me Earl," he said. "I don't stand on any formalities, do you?"

"Not that I know of." Miles felt the pull in his face from smiling. "I hope none of those boys killed were yours."

Earl turned. "No. No they weren't. But two of them had worked for me putting up hay . . . building fence. They were good boys and we're gonna miss them. School's gonna miss them too. They were top athletes." His eyes glistened, as he looked hard into Miles's eyes. He looked around. "Their parents aren't here today."

"I imagine not," Miles said. "Are any of their brothers or sisters in school?"

Earl shook his head. "Just the boys." He covered his mouth with his hand. "There's the two that didn't get killed."

It was silent. Almost like nobody else had arrived in that room. Earl straightened up. Then he smiled, and the low murmur of the crowd came back.

Miles turned to the next person, a heavy-set middle-aged woman who looked out of the bottom of her glasses at him.

Must be bifocals. He pulled his lips back into a smile. "Hello. I'm Miles Foster. History and music."

"How do you do, Mr. Foster. My name is Mabel Kreneke. Did you major in music?"

"No Miss . . . or Mrs. Kreneke?" He tilted his head to one side. He waited for her reply and shifted his weight to the other foot. She stood, hands clasped in front of her, a brown faux-leather handbag dangling past her hips, feet planted, toes splayed. "Ah, no, Mrs. Kreneke, I majored in Human Development and took an education degree in advanced studies."

"I see." She took out a white tissue and wiped it across her upper lip. "I was hoping this time we would attract a real music major here. We have some wonderful players and singers and we would like to see them reach their full potential."

Miles nodded. "I'll do my best."

"See that you do, young man. See that you do." She raised her head, looked down her nose. "Are you good at following instructions?" She smiled and waited.

"I think so. What did you have in mind?"

"We'll be listening."

Miles nodded again and smiled back. "You'll be listening . . . that's good. That's a good one."

Mabel Kreneke nodded, turned 90 degrees, took three steps and addressed the next teacher in line.

Miles stuck out his hand. A tan-faced rancher with a white forehead clasped it. "I see you've met Mabel." His smile widened. "She'll be wanting a report every time you turn around."

"Report? On what?"

"Anything and everything. She about runs this place. On the school board, you know."

"Is she a Miss or Mrs.?"

"Oh, she just goes by Mabel. Don't think she was ever married." He turned his hat around and around in his hands. "Just stay on the good side of her." He nodded his head sideways. "She can be a bearcat, things don't go her way."

"Gottcha," Miles said. He turned to see Mabel moving on to the fourth teacher in line. One who had been there twelve years, wife of a local rancher, taught English and shorthand and home economics.

Twenty-three people came to greet the nine teachers lined up for Tamarack Public School, grades one through twelve. The townspeople drifted through the double doors and spread out across the parking lot, some walking, some driving home. It was Sunday evening and the ranchers headed home to do chores. The teachers wilted down and sat on the folding chairs that had been set up beside the memorial table.

"Hot dog," someone yelled. "We made it through that." It was Rodney Belker, new seventh grade teacher, freshly minted out of Portland State College and needing to make payments on a new Oldsmobile 88 he bought just before he signed a contract to teach in the boonies. He wanted to teach in Portland but, like Miles, had finished his certification at the end of summer school, and big schools with big budgets had their quota of new teachers.

Calvin Brooks, the principal and superintendent, came up the line, a frown lining his ancient face, lips moving and nodding his head as he greeted the new teachers. He bent forward at the hips, heavy with fat that had found its way to his once strong thighs. His right arm swung to balance each step and his eyes did not stray from the path ahead. Lurching, he moved down the floor, head up, eyes straight ahead, a half grimace passing for a greeting. He stopped in front of Belker. "I'd appreciate it if you would restrain from making any further outbursts like that." He kept nodding but moved on.

Miles looked at Coach Russell, who had his head down. "Yikes. That's a little over the top, isn't it?"

Coach Russell coughed in his hand. "Ol' Brooks has his own way of doing things but you don't get a play book. You won't know you've crossed him until after its done."

"Guess I'm assisting you with the second squad," Miles said.

"If we've got enough to have a second squad." Coach looked down at the table trimmed in black bunting. "With those three gone, we'll be lucky to field a full six guys who know enough to play this game."

Superintendent Brooks had turned around and now stood in front of Miles and smiled. "Did you find a house?"

"Yes sir."

"Good. Good. I'd hoped you wouldn't have any problem." He looked down at his feet, then back up. "Good to see you here. I hope you will enjoy it."

"Thank you. I'm sure we will," Miles said.

"The wife too?"

Miles nodded. "Yes. Getting settled in."

"The faculty is getting together tomorrow morning before start of school at 8 o'clock sharp at my office. Please be there."

"Sure."

"Fine. Fine. See you then."

ELEANOR HAD HER SLEEVES rolled up, shorts on, and was scrubbing the walls of the chicken house when Miles got home. "How'd it go?" she said when he found her.

"Fine. Met a lot of people. Met the other teachers. Good event." He looked around at the nesting boxes. "You planning on chickens?"

"Absolutely. Fresh eggs, organic meat, nothing better. Hand me that rag."

"I'm starting to itch," Miles said.

"Chicken mites. That's why I'm washing it. After this I'll spray it and kill every last one of them. Then we can get chickens and eat like kings and queens."

"How exciting," he said, his voice trailing off as he rolled his eyes.

Eleanor looked at him. "Get excited. You'll love them. We can have multi-colored chickens and even colored eggs if we want."

"I take it you didn't think a dog and two cats were enough for now?"

"Not on your life. If we're gonna live out here we're gonna have chickens and a cow and a garden. It's the least we can do for our budget."

"A cow? Like I know a lot about chickens and cows."

"You can learn."

Miles frowned and backed out the door. "I'll have my hands full at school, and we can't take the chickens and cow back to Portland with us, but I'm happy for you to have this wonderful diversion."

"I may have to charge you for eggs and milk if you don't assist, Mr. Big Shot."

"Honey—I have no idea what to do with a chicken or a cow. And I don't want to learn during the short year we'll be here. I know food goes in and comes out somewhat changed, and that they make a noise, but beyond that I didn't receive any formal education about them."

"I'll teach you so you can do it when the baby comes."

Miles stopped midway through the chicken house door. "What baby?"

"Our baby."

"We have a baby?"

Eleanor pointed to her stomach. "This one."

"Holy cow . . . when did that happen?"

"Well, you were there."

"I hope so. Wonderful . . . I guess. Great. When do we celebrate?"

"Now. Grab a broom and clean out the cobwebs on that far wall."

"Not till I get a hug and a kiss." He hugged her while she stood on a short stepladder.

We're going to have a family. A real, honest to God family. His face flushed and somewhere between his knees and hips the leg muscles twitched.

"Wow—what are we going to name it?"

"Don't know yet."

"Why didn't you tell me?"

"I just did."

"I mean earlier."

"It's only an inch long. I wanted to be sure before I spilled the beans."

Miles went inside, stripped off his tie, and sat in the rocker looking out over the canyon. Nothing moved as far as he could see. Even the clouds stood still as he contemplated being here while Ele was killing mites in the chicken house. The wind shifted and whispered past the woodpile and the side of the house and rustled the grass, urging him to reflect on how he had gotten here.

LEWIS & CLARK COLLEGE, PORTLAND, OREGON
January 1957

"The dean will see you now," the secretary said.

Miles Foster stood, smiled and walked toward the door upon which a walnut plaque stated, "Elwood Harrison, Dean of Education."

The dean stood when he entered and moved out from behind his desk. The lines in his face lit up, crinkled, his lips parted showing the lack of attention to his teeth. A smile took over his entire face, turning it into a greeting all of its own.

"Miles Foster," he said, his deep voice pronouncing it with distinction. "How good to see you back on campus." He clasped Miles's hand and with the other hand gripped his elbow.

Miles nodded his head and smiled. "Good to see you, Dean Harrison. And to be back."

"What brings you here today?"

"I would like to register for a degree in education."

Dean Harrison returned to his seat. "It would be stimulating to have a gold key winner and outstanding student like you in our program." He brushed some lint off his vest, lifted his head. "What brought you to this decision?"

Miles leaned forward. "I've had a couple of years to think about it and I have it set in my mind."

"Your undergraduate major was Human Development as I recall, not education."

Miles nodded.

"We don't offer that degree anymore. Has that degree worked for you?"

"No problem," Miles said. "I've been employed since graduation."

"Hmmm," Harrison mumbled. He stuck his lower lip over his upper, jutted his jaw forward, frowned, and said, "And now you want to teach?"

"Yes sir."

Dean Harrison swiveled his chair, his chin almost touching his tie, and looked out the window towards the Reflection Pool mirroring Mt. Hood in its still waters. He took a deep breath. "Miles . . . would you be willing to go to some of our remote communities to teach? I mean small schools without the glamour and budgets of Portland schools, where the pay is lower, the hours are longer and you really pay your dues with activities other than teaching?"

"I hadn't thought about it. I prefer to stay in Portland."

Harrison held up his hand. He turned and smiled. "Miles, this shouldn't just now come to you. It should have been your passion when you were here in undergraduate studies. I took time to look at your transcript when you made the appointment. You only took one education course during your four years here. We need alumni who are dedicated to teaching. To go out into the small communities of the state—show them what our graduates are made of. I see you as a big city person. Someone who will do well in the large schools," he hesitated, "but that isn't where teachers are needed."

"There are a lot of teachers in Multnomah County."

Dean Harrison looked at his watch. "Miles, it's good to see you again, but I'm afraid our department isn't for you. When you have this thing thoroughly worked out in your mind and can envision yourself really giving to the community, some small community, we can talk." He let his face light up again. "Right now I have a faculty meeting." He stood, shook hands and ushered Miles out the door into the reception area where the secretary looked at him with a bit of a smile, her fingers glued to the typewriter keys.

The deep carpet, cut velvet drapes, and soft furniture absorbed all sound in the reception area after the dean closed the door and left. Miles stood looking out the window. He had scheduled an hour for the interview and it had lasted ten minutes. Turned down by his alma mater. He couldn't believe it. Below to the right of the Reflection Pool was a clearing he had worked on when a student, cutting down trees, limbing them, and cutting them up to make room for a gazebo that had been donated by a wealthy alum. Memories stacked one on the other. He turned and walked out, closing the door behind him, letting his hand linger on the brass handle as he stood in the hall debating his next move.

HE FOUND A PARKING space in front of the administration building at Portland State College and walked up the stairs to the registration desk. A young woman looked up and smiled. "How may I help you?"

"I would like to get a degree in education. Is that possible here?" he said.

She nodded. "You bet your life. Do you know how to fill out forms?"

"I can learn."

"That's what we like. A good attitude." She opened a drawer, pulled out papers, stapled the sheets together, handed the package to him along with a pen, and pointed at a table in the corner. "Go. Sit. I'll be here when you're done. You will be allowed three free questions, after that I charge."

He snorted and rolled his eyes. "Does everyone get such high class treatment?"

"Only after they pay tuition. Did you bring cash or check?"

"I was just checking on the possibilities. I didn't bring either. How much is it?"

"I can't tell you until I see how much money you've got. We need all the money we can get. How much have you got?"

"Enough to take you out to the Carnival Drive In for a burger and shake."

"Ohhhhh. I don't get off until 6 today and I don't have a thing to wear."

"Good. I like naked first dates."

"I can see it is going to take a long time for you to finish your degree. You are a slick talker, impertinent, defensive, and unabashed." She smiled and looked up at him through long eyelashes.

"How do you spell impertinent?"

"You won't remember and I'm not getting paid to educate you. Please fill out the forms and pick me up outside at 6 o'clock sharp. If you're five minutes late I'll go with someone else."

He smiled, extended his hand. "My proper name is Miles Foster." She took it and shook it once. "Just call me Eleanor, like in Eleanor Roosevelt, but people I like call me Ele. That's like an L followed by an E . . . Ele. And I love the hamburgers at the Carnival."

MILES FINISHED STUDENT TEACHING at the end of spring term but he'd had two more classes to finish before he received his diploma, took the test, and was certified by the state of Oregon. In late summer he scheduled a conference with his advisor and started looking for teaching jobs.

Walking into Dean Severson's office, he couldn't help noticing the difference in décor and style from that of Dean Harrison's. The furniture bespoke public school: used desk, table, bookshelves. More clutter than he could enjoy, but Dean Severson thrived in it.

"Good morning, Dean Severson," Miles said.

Rising, Dean Severson smiled, extended his hand, and said, "Good morning, good morning. Have a seat, Miles. Unburden your feet and mind. Coffee?"

Miles shook his head. "No thanks."

"So you've finished? Certified and the whole ball of wax?"

"Thanks to you and Portland State. Now it's job time. What have you got in Multnomah County?"

"Ah, Miles. Those jobs have been gone for months." He leaned back in his chair and clasped his hands behind his head. "The spring grads snapped those up, you know. You might find an occasional job where someone got sick, changed their mind or moved. But not likely." He straightened up and pulled a pile of papers across his desk. "Here's one at the coast. Another on the Elk River." He looked up. "What's your minor?"

"Don't really have a minor."

"Could you teach music?"

"Probably. If I had to."

Severson smiled. "The principal of Tamarack is coming in this afternoon. He's looking for two teachers. You could teach high school history, geography, and music."

"Where is Tamarack?"

"Center of the state. Little town between Prineville and John Day . . . about 200 miles from here."

Miles shook his head. "Let's keep looking around here, say a 50-mile radius."

"I'll keep it in mind but don't get your hopes up. Most of the openings this year had two and three applicants and many of the newly minted teachers are in waiting positions, doing something else until one of them opens up."

Miles slumped in his chair. "I hadn't planned on being that far out of Portland."

"Best laid plans of mice and men . . . "

"Yeah, I know."

"Is there something else you can do if you have to wait?"

"I'll find something. I just don't want to go 200 miles in the middle of nowhere and start teaching."

Dean Severson leaned back in his chair again, threw his feet up on the desk. "Come by this afternoon and talk with the principal. Can't hurt. Give you a feeling for what an interview is like."

Miles nodded. "I could do that. And thank you." He stood. "Give me a call if anything comes in around Portland, will you?"

"You bet. Superintendent and Principal Calvin Brooks will be in the conference room at 3. And, Miles . . . take my advice as I said in class, get to know the janitor and befriend him. He'll get a lot more done for you than the principal."

"How many others are coming in?"

"So far, you're the only one."

"Great."

NOW, IN HIS FIRST CLASSROOM on the second floor of Tamarack High School, Miles stood in the hallway outside the room, arms crossed, watching the students come up the stairs. They gawked at him, the girls turning with smiles laughing and sneaking a peek at him as they moved away down the hall. He wasn't that much older than some of them—six or seven years, maybe.

A thin boy about as tall as Miles came clunking down the hall on cowboy boots with a half-smile exposing crooked teeth. He nodded.

"Good morning," Miles said. "I'm Mr. Foster."

The boy nodded again. "Billy," he uttered.

"Billy what?"

"Just Billy." His handshake was limp and cool. He seated himself in the last row farthest from the door.

"Billy, why don't you move up front here?"

Billy smiled, looked down at his books and pad of paper. "I'm okay." He spread his paper and books out on the desk, scooted forward and crossed his long legs in front of him.

Miles turned to laughter behind him. Three girls—*do they always hang out in threes?*—approached, arms clutching their books against their chests.

"You our new teach?" one asked.

Miles smiled. "I'm an educator from a land far away. Name's Mr. Foster."

"That's hot," one said and stuck out her hand. "I'm Carla. And this is Shelly and Brenda. We give new teachers fits." They all giggled.

Miles nodded to each girl; "Carla, Shelly, Brenda," he said. "We'll give each other fits and see how that works. Pick a seat up front and see if you can get Billy to come up there."

"Billy won't come up," Carla said. "He sits in the back of every room."

The girls flowed into the room, said "hi" to Billy who nodded in return, and took seats in the front row. Immediately behind them came two guys who looked like they could carry the school bus on its rounds. Jay Caldwell and Richard Kenkey barely fit through the door, dressed in Western snap-button shirts, Levi's, and cowboy boots. They took a seat close to the aisle behind the girls.

"Looks like everyone has the clothing down pat," Miles said.

The students looked at him but said nothing.

Miles waited. The bell rang, and like water running off a roof, the hallway was void of people. As he reached to close the door he could hear someone running up the stairs. Reaching the top of the stairs, the runner turned toward Miles and smiled.

"Sorry I'm late."

"Bell just rang. You made it under the wire. I'm Miles Foster."

"Tommy Jones."

For such a little guy he had a firm handshake and his eyes smiled when he talked. He took a seat in the middle of the row behind the big guys in front of Billy. Miles closed the door.

"Mr. Brooks said you all passed last year and are now the outstanding senior class of Tamarack High School. Be that true?"

"Of course," Carla said. "We're the best class; smartest, prettiest, and strongest."

"Good. Then I'll be expecting great things from such fine students. This is your homeroom and I am your class advisor. I'll also be teaching World History, Geography, and music."

There was a shuffling of feet. "Let's get acquainted by telling me a little about yourselves."

Carla looked around. "We all know each other. Been here since first grade. There isn't anything to tell."

Miles let that sink in. "Okay. Tell you what. Tell me all you remember about the three boys who were killed on the highway."

Every person looked at their desktop. Shelly's shoulders buckled, muffled sobs drifted out and Carla put an arm over her shoulder. Billy's long legs reached under the next row of chairs and he sat with his head in his hands.

Carla looked up. "Shelly was going steady with Darrell."

"I'm sorry. I wasn't thinking." He shook his head. "I'll tell you about me and you can ask any questions. Okay. I was born and raised in Portland, went to college there, graduated in 1955, and worked at various jobs until coming back to college to get a teachers certificate. I had planned on teaching in Portland where everything is bigger, brighter, and better. But this was the only job open when I got certified so I took it. I am married to my wife Ele, and we have a dog, two cats, and a baby coming next June. My wife is also thinking of getting some chickens and a cow. I know nothing about those things so I'll be leaning on you guys to help me there. I teach history, geography, and music."

He pushed his lower lip up over his teeth and looked at the class. None had moved. None moved now. The bell rang and he smiled. "No questions?" he said, as they filed out, letting the door close behind them.

IN THE CAFETERIA, CARLA plopped her tray down on the table, making the Jell-O jiggle. Brenda laughed and stuck her fork in it to stop the jiggle. Then she licked the whipped cream off her fork and sat down.

"Mr. Foster is nice," Carla said.

"He really laid everything out, didn't he?" Brenda said. "Choir should be interesting. Wonder if he knows anything about music."

"We'll find out," Shelly put in. "My piano teacher said he would check into his credentials. He sure doesn't know anything about manners. I could have died when he asked about the boys getting killed."

"He didn't know," Carla said. "It just popped out."

"I hope he knows something about vocal music," Brenda said.

"What if he doesn't know squat?" Carla said, putting a bite into her mouth.

Shelly shrugged. "He can't be any worse than old man Dutton."

"I could have done better than that."

MILES KNOCKED ON THE office door. He could see Principal/ Superintendent Calvin Brooks seated at his desk. Brooks got up and came to the door, a smile on his face.

"Yes Mr. Foster?"

"Could you spare a moment to check scheduling with me?"

"Of course. Come in please."

"The band is scheduled for fourth period—right after lunch. Could we move that to morning or fifth period?" Miles said.

Brooks stared at him. "Why would we do that?"

"Fourth period is right after lunch. The kids will be blowing food particles into their instruments."

"Have them wash their mouths out first."

"I can try that but the water supply is quite a distance from the band practice room."

"I'm sure you can work it out, Mr. Foster. Is there anything else?"

Miles stood a moment, heavy on one foot. "I would really appreciate if it you would reconsider the schedule? First period would be good. They will have come from home and have brushed their teeth after breakfast, and . . . "

" . . . Mr. Foster, I have a number of important things to attend to this first day and rescheduling classes is not one of them."

The bell starting fourth period rang. Brooks looked at Miles with unblinking eyes, his hands holding the door only halfway open. "Good day, Mr. Foster."

Miles turned his head to look down the hallway as students moved from the cafeteria to classrooms. He had arranged to meet the band in the auditorium. Nobody had informed him how many students were in the band or what their proficiency level was. He hadn't played in a band since high school. They would learn together, regardless of where they were in their musical education.

TOMMY HAD THE drums set up and was banging out a snappy march rhythm with a peculiar flourish at the end. Miles smiled. *So, we've got a drummer.*

Miles counted about eighteen people in the process of taking out instruments, setting up music stands and warming up. He found the director's stand and a baton with a broken tip. He set it up in front and crossed his arms. The room quieted.

"In case you haven't heard, my name is Miles Foster. I'm new to Tamarack and new to teaching music. But I've played in bands and sung in choruses for years. I can read music and tell when someone is off key. Let's just try a quickie. Do you have a favorite?"

"'Colonel Bogey's March,'" Tommy shouted.

"So take it out," Miles said. He knew the main theme from the movie *Bridge on the River Kwai*, but had never played it. He opened the director's score and raised the baton.

The familiar strain of the march coursed through the instruments, following the beat of his baton until he felt a rising pulse and a prickling sensation along his shoulders, neck, and face. *Great Scott—what a neat feeling to be getting this sound from this group in this place.*

Miles turned the page and recognized the transition from the main theme to the interlude. He glanced at the next four bars, then looked up as they entered that phase. His baton snapped out beats but everyone stopped. Instruments were placed in laps. Miles slowed, then halted.

"What's wrong?" he said.

"That's all we know," Tommy said.

"You've never played this part before?"

"No," they all said in unison.

"Well—we'll do it now. Trumpets first. Turn to the beginning of the interlude and in time with me, one and two."

Two of the trumpets got part way along and stopped. The third didn't try.

"Clarinets. Let's give it a go. Show them what it sounds like." He raised the baton. "One and two . . . "

There was the squawk of a dry reed and after the first two measures the clarinet section followed the trumpets' example and quit. They laid their clarinets in their laps and looked up at Miles, eyes half averted, a nervous glancing here and there. Miles laid the baton on the stand and looked down at the music. It wasn't that hard. He hummed a few bars to himself.

"Tell you what let's do," he said. "Split up. Brass section to the right; wind section to the left; percussion stay where you are."

There was a short chaos until they resettled. Miles went to the trumpet section. Three boys who looked similar sat staring at the music on their stands.

"What's your name?" Miles said to the first chair player.

"Ready O'Neil," he said.

Miles nodded. "Okay, Ready. Let's start with the first bar. You other two read along with us. By the way, what are your names?"

"I'm Willing O'Neil," the second one said. The third one, a mite smaller than the other two, chimed in, "I'm Able O'Neil."

Miles's head spun. *Am I being taken for a patsy here?*

Ready took over. "We only had one instrument in the house so we all learned to play it."

Miles nodded. "I see." He pointed to the first note. "Hit that one, Ready."

Ready hit it and smiled.

"Okay, now the next one."

He hit that one too. And the third one and was on to the next bar.

At the end of the fourth period the trumpet section could fumble through the interlude and play a pretty respectable main theme. The girls wielding the clarinets had followed suit. Tomorrow he would weld them together. The bell sounded.

"Thank you people. We're on our way to a great band," Miles said.

TOMMY WALKED WITH THE O'Neils over to the schoolhouse. "What'd you think about that?"

"He's fair enough," Ready said.

"I thought he might kill us," Willing said. "I was expecting to get kicked out of band, out of the auditorium, and out of school."

Tommy laughed. "They don't let teachers kill kids anymore."

"Yeah," Able said. "But when we all stopped he looked like he wanted to."

FIFTH PERIOD WAS WORLD Geography. Twenty students rolled in—half the student body. They sat in familiar seating arrangements, buddies and friends together, Billy in the back row.

Miles walked over to Billy and leaned over. "Billy, this is World Geography. You probably had this class."

"Flunked it."

Miles nodded, stood up and walked to the front of the room. His mind was churning. Billy was going to need some special attention, but not now. He clapped his hands together. "So this is the great senior class I've heard so much about."

"Absolutely," they boomed out.

"And bashful too, I see."

There was scattered laughter.

Miles set the large globe out in front of his desk. "Would one of you geniuses please come up and place your first digit on the country of Nepal."

Nobody moved.

"Oh come on." Miles looked around and clapped his hands together. "There must be a mountain climber amongst you. Who has been to the top of the Ochocos?"

One hand went up.

"How did you get there?"

"Drove a Jeep."

A titter of laughter drifted through the group.

"Well, you can't drive a Jeep to the top of the highest mountain in the world. What is that mountain?"

A girl held up her hand.

"And your name is?"

"Carol Denning."

"And the mountain is?"

"Mount Everest."

"Miss Denning, Carol, would you please come up and put your finger on Nepal."

She shook her head. "I just know the name. I don't know where the mountain is."

"I see." He sat down in the hard wooden chair provided to all teachers in the school, the kind of chair with solid arms, ribs along the back and a seat carved like a human's bottom. "The state has mandated that you learn certain items about this world's geography before you depart these sacred halls. The county has hired me to see that you become aware of the world around you even as far as Nepal. Together, we will hike the trails of Katmandu and other geographical sites until you can, blindfolded, touch this globe anyplace on Earth and know something about it."

Every soul sat glued to his seat. Miles let his eyes go from student to student. Few met his glance eye-to-eye.

"You've all had U.S. Geography, right?"

Some nodded.

"This is the same stuff, just different terrain." He thought about it a moment. "It is terrain, the kind of thing you don't even think of when you drive up this hill to the school house. You start at the creek level and rise up to what elevation?"

"Six hundred feet?" Nolan said. He smiled after he said it. Looked a lot like his dad when he smiled and Miles dug up the face and hair of Earl Benson from last Sunday's teachers meet-and-greet.

"Where did you get that figure, Nolan?"

"I don't know. Somebody said it was."

Miles sat on the edge of his desk and looked at the class. "How many know what an altimeter is?"

Nolan and Rebecca's hands went up.

"Rebecca."

"It tells you the height of something."

"Right. The height of anything above sea level or below sea level. So you are living in geography every day. You've noticed the hills and valleys and mountains around Tamarack. The earth was formed, and is still being formed, by volcanoes, rivers, wind, rain, snow, and ice. Not to mention mankind messing with it.

"Geography is the face of this earth. You've got a face—the earth has a face. And at the end of nine months you are going to know that face like the face of your boyfriend or girlfriend in the seat next to you in your dad's car in the dark."

Smiles and little giggles shot across the room. Several students looked at each other and chuckled.

"First assignment. Read the chapter on earth formation in the textbook and be prepared to tell us how you think the Tamarack Valley was formed. Dismissed."

CHAPTER 3

"This is a teachers lounge? Looks more like a closet," Coach Russell said.

"It was a closet," Marion Stillson said. "We chose it over the alternative—the furnace room."

"Good choice," Miles said.

The principal, Calvin Brooks, was not there at lunchtime. He took lunch with his wife, Winifred Brooks, the fourth grade teacher, in her room across the parking lot where she could keep an eye on the elementary school and her semi-blind husband. Plus, she prepared a sandwich, fruit, and a cookie for him every day that kept him lean and moving like a man ten years younger than his actual age.

Coach Donavon Russell, Marion Stillson (who was the English department), and Miles Foster sat on folding chairs, eating off ex-military aluminum trays.

Coach Donavon swallowed a bite of dumpling and chicken gravy. "Mr. Brooks tells me you are up for helping me with the coaching," he said to Miles.

Miles nodded. "I could do that early on."

"Did you play ball in college?"

"Couple years at guard."

"Good. I could use some lineman expertise. This is my first six-man experience. You had any?"

"No. My first year teaching. So we're both new at this business."

"Got you all beat," Marion said. "Been here for twelve years."

"Teaching English all the time?"

"English, speech, debate, and home economics." She put her tray on top of a chest of drawers being stored in the lounge. "What are you guys teaching?"

Miles spoke first. "I'm doing social studies, band and choir, and driving the school bus."

"That'll keep you out of mischief," she said.

"I'm math, science, and coaching," Donavon said around a mouthful.

"What's it like here?" Miles asked.

Marion smiled. "I think I'll let you find out for yourselves. It'll be different for you living here in town. I live out on a ranch twelve miles out of town and am not embroiled in the local scene."

Donavan smiled. "With 200 people, there's a local scene?"

Marion nodded. "Oh yes."

The door opened and Calvin Brooks stuck his head in the opening. "Mr. Foster, could I see you in my office for a minute when you are through here?"

"Of course."

Marion's eyes flashed. "That will be interesting."

MILES OPENED THE DOOR to the principal's office. Brooks was sitting at his desk. "Have a seat Mr. Foster. This will just take a minute."

Miles sat down and crossed his leg over his knee. Brooks stared at the crossed leg, then looked up. "Mr. Foster, I find that we have six or so students who want to learn typing. Can you type?"

"Yes, I can."

"Good. Good. I'd like you to teach it then. There will be two classes a week and I'll have Roscoe set up the room. I'm sure most of the typewriters work. We haven't had a typing class for several years, but Roscoe is the one to see about that."

"I know nothing about teaching typing," Miles said.

Brooks brushed it off. "Oh, that's not important. They'll learn it. Just need a teacher around for decorum purposes, you know."

"Is there any extra pay for doing this?"

Brooks looked him in the eyes, his face as stern as Miles had seen it. "Mr. Foster, it is only two classes a week and there is nothing for you to do but be there. You are already being paid extra for driving the school bus and assisting the coach."

"I see," he said.

Superintendent Brooks handed him a thick book. "This is the teachers' manual, although I don't think you'll need it."

"And what period will that be?"

"See Roscoe. He'll know when the room is set up and what periods it is vacant."

"So the janitor is doing the scheduling now? Will he move band class to first period?"

"We've already discussed that, Mr. Foster. Now . . . I've got lots to do . . . ."

MILES FOUND ROSCOE IN the boys' restroom replacing paper towels. "I hear by the grapevine that you setting up a typing room somewhere?"

"Yup." He closed the lid on the towel dispenser, pulled a towel down to test it and smiled, happy that it worked. "Be ready next week. I need to check out the typewriters and get the stuff moved up there."

"Where's it going to be?"

"That little room at the back of the English room."

"That isn't a room, Roscoe, that's a storage closet."

Roscoe smiled. "It works. I'll have it ready Monday. When's the first class?"

Miles nodded. "Super said you would schedule that."

Roscoe's smile widened. "Oh he did, did he?" He brushed his chin with a dirty hand. "I'd say fifth period when Mrs. Stillson is having volleyball."

"But the typing students are mostly girls. Aren't they playing on the volleyball team?"

"Yup, they are. That's true. Hmmm. I'll work on it."

"Great. Let me know so I can inspect it and get it approved by the State of Oregon Department of Higher Authority for a classroom."

Roscoe frowned. "There's a higher authority like that?"

"Always is," Miles said. "Especially on important matters like this."

Roscoe popped his gum and let the frown creep over his forehead. "I'll get right on it."

"Much appreciate," Miles said, smiling.

CHAPTER 4

MILES OPENED A CABINET in the kitchen. "Is there any Canadian Club left, honey?" Miles yelled.

"In the cabinet next to the coat closet. I haven't gotten everything put away yet. Pour me one too," Eleanor said.

"You can't have one. You're pregnant."

"I can have a small one. The baby needs to get used to those things."

"We don't want an alcoholic when he comes . . . "

" . . . She."

" . . . When she comes." He took two glasses from the shelf, got a can of 7up, and searched for the Canadian Club. "What makes you think it is going to be a girl?"

"Women know these things. I didn't go to college for nothing. I learned important stuff. Things they would never teach a boy."

"That makes sense. Men don't do those things and thus they belong in the sole and absolute jurisdiction of women with a capital W." He opened another cabinet. "Honey—think a minute. Where did you hide the Canadian Club?"

"I didn't hide it, silly. It's right in the cabinet next to the coat closet. Not in the coat closet. Move over to your right if they taught you your right from your left in that high-grade college you matriculated from."

Miles pulled the bottle out by the cap, swung it to the counter top, and poured two glasses. Eleanor watched the level. Her eyes went to his and she pulled the bottle toward her glass and tipped it again.

"That's too much," Miles said.

"Just right. Just this once won't kill it. Besides, remember what Nietzsche said: 'What doesn't kill you makes you stronger.'"

"Yeah, but we don't know what will kill him . . . her."

"There you go. You'll get the hang of it." She took a sip. "Too strong." She held the glass out and he poured more 7up into it. "We're celebrating two things. Your first day of school and our first pregnancy." She held both arms high in the air. "Both are landmarks in the lives of Eleanor and Miles Foster."

"Why does your name come first?"

"Because, silly, you don't separate the man's given name from his surname."

"Are you sure about that?"

"Absolutely. Now, let's sit down like people of leisure and enjoy this libation as it will probably be my last for the next eight months."

"Inside or outside?"

"Outside."

Miles set the chairs to watch the sun lift the shadows up the side of the hills across the valley. With the sun warm and comforting on their backs, the evening quiet settled through the juniper branches and into the short grass with barely a rustle. A quail sent its call through the air unanswered.

"We're lucky," Eleanor said. "Lucky to be here, in good health, in love, with work, and a family started. More than I thought possible at one time."

"Really?" Miles said.

She nodded. "Well sure. My dad always said life was tough and you had to claw your way through the muck and mire to get anything." She turned to him. "And here we are with everything first time away from home."

"Everything except chickens, thank heavens."

"Well—there is that."

ON SATURDAY MORNING, Miles was at the gas station getting kerosene for the emergency lanterns and also as a fire starter on a cold morning when the O'Neil family stopped for gas. Ready, Willing, and Able piled out and each did a separate task. Mr. O'Neil, locally known as Butch, got out and tested the tightness on the ropes holding down cages in the pickup bed. Miles had met him at the teacher greeting session and walked over to meet him.

"Good morning, Mr. O'Neil. Where you headed?"

Butch removed his hat and bobbed his head. "Good morning Mr. Foster. Heading to Prineville to do some shopping and sell our chickens."

Miles snapped his head to the cages. "How many have you got?"

"Got an even dozen." Del shifted into selling mode. "Good layin' hens too. And a rooster."

"What do you want for the hens?"

Butch looked off in the distance then down at his shoes and finally fixed his glance on Miles's forehead. "Two dollars a hen would do me." He stuck his hands in his overall pockets. "And five for the rooster."

"I don't want the rooster," Miles said.

"You do." Butch bobbed his head. "He keeps those hens in line. Keeps the eggs fertilized and if you want to raise chickens he does the job alright."

Miles took out his wallet. "I'll give you twenty dollars for the twelve hens. You keep the rooster."

Butch shook his head. "Can't do that. They're a group. They need to stay together. How about twenty-five for the lot of 'em?"

"I don't have twenty-five dollars . . . "

"I'll trust you for the five."

"I really don't want the rooster."

"He's part of the deal."

The boys had finished washing the windshield, airing the tires, and checking the oil, and stood listening to the negotiations. Mrs. O'Neil looked straight ahead out the now clean windshield, window rolled up.

Miles rubbed his chin. "Okay. Twenty now and five next month."

"That's fine with me. Where do you want 'em?"

"Could you swing up by the house and drop them off now?"

"Now's as good a time as any." Butch folded the twenty and put it in his overall breast pocket. A gust of wind coming from up valley tousled with his hair. He put his hat back on.

"I'll meet you up there," Miles said.

BUTCH BACKED UP to the chicken house and the three boys unloaded the chickens and put the cages back on the truck. Miles closed the door to let the chickens get acquainted with their new surroundings and the O'Neils were on their way to Prineville, twelve laying hens and one rooster lighter.

Eleanor came to the door. "What have you done?"

"We're in the chicken business," Miles said.

"I thought you didn't want chickens? Did you check them for mites?"

"No. Didn't think about that."

"Why do you think I cleaned the chicken house so good?"

"I thought *we* cleaned the chicken house."

"You got in on the tail end. Let's check them."

Eleanor cornered a hen, grabbed her and held both legs in one hand. Holding the chicken upside down until she was still, she took her other hand and pushed the feathers away from the skin.

"Clean as a baby's bottom. How about him?" she said pointing at the rooster.

"He's part of the family so I suppose he's clean too."

"Catch him and let's see."

The rooster was clean but spent several minutes objecting to his subrogation and after his examination, put his feathers in order.

"I'll clean the egg tray," Elé said. "We could have fresh eggs tomorrow."

"Fresh and fertile eggs."

"Yes. I'm so happy. They'll keep me company all day while you're gone and I'll name each one."

"Oh, Ele . . . don't do that," Miles said. "It'll be so hard to get rid of them."

"Who said we're getting rid of them? They're our family now. They get names and live with us and do their work and when they get sick or die we take care of them just like kin."

Miles rolled his eyes. "I don't see that being something we're gonna do."

"Sure we will. I love them already. Look at those darling faces, don't you just love them?"

"Frankly . . . no. They look like chickens, they act like chickens, and I'm going to treat them like chickens."

"See that red one with the comb that lays down the side of her head?" Ele stooped and picked the hen up and set it on her thighs, cooing to it and stroking its back feathers. "This one I'll name Brandy." The chicken's eyes closed and she settled down, her head drifting downward with each stroke of Ele's hands. "See how sensitive she is? She trusts me."

"I'd do that too if you put me on your legs and stroked me."

"Different thing. This is a wild animal. She's learning to love and trust humans and me in particular."

"I may have to bring the principal to you for taming. He seems set in his ways and intends to keep it that way."

"I'll check my schedule for any openings. I could maybe take him on Thursday at 3:30—I think I have an opening then."

Miles kissed her cheek while the chicken snoozed on her lap.

PRIOR TO THE FIRST peep of light when the sky was just warning of the coming dawn, the rooster crowed. It was one of those grating syncopated noises that rattles one out of a dead sleep. Miles looked at the clock.

"What time is it?" Ele asked.

"5:32."

"Are we going to have that every morning?"

"Hey—you wanted chickens. Now we've got chickens."

"I didn't ask for a rooster." She jammed the pillow over her head. Muffled through the pillow came her next complaint. "The baby will never put up with this."

The rooster didn't wait long before giving it another go. He crowed with meaningful pride; the last note, wavering, he held until it dropped out of hearing range.

"He intends to keep us awake," Miles said.

"Uh-huh. We'll have to go to bed at 7 o'clock to get enough sleep."

"Naw. Ten o'clock will do."

Miles threw the covers off and stood on the carpeted floor. He bent and touched his toes, then twisted from the hips a few times, ran in place for ten seconds, and headed for the bathroom. Ele threw on a robe, cooked oatmeal, and they sat at the kitchen table eating breakfast as the light grew over Rooster's Knob.

"Gosh," Ele said. "It's still early and I'm awake with only one coffee."

"Interesting. When was the last time you were up at this hour?"

"I think Easter Sunrise service ten years ago."

"Think I'll walk to school this morning. Do me good and I've got plenty of time."

"Pick up some milk when you come home. We don't have a cow yet."

"We need a cow?"

"Of course, silly. And a garden and a scarecrow and a couple of horses."

"Oh come on, Ele. We're city people, not farmers."

"We've got land. We've got chickens. We're going to have a child. Let's do the whole experience." She stood up. "Besides, what have I got to do all day but take care of stuff?"

Miles raised his eyebrows. "Okay. I got the chickens. You work on the cow part."

"So shall it be written. So shall it be done."

The wind crawling over the hills south of the house washed over his face when he stepped outside, carrying with it the early morning juniper scent as it washed down the hillside into the valley below. It was clean and cool. He breathed it in and held it, a smile coming to his face. What a life.

THE AUDITORIUM WAS STILL in the dark when Miles opened the door and turned on the lights. Nothing more empty than an auditorium without people. He made his way to the stage and opened the cabinets on the wall. They held broken music stands, chairs with one leg missing, and old can lights. He tried the other wall. That cabinet held the usable stands, chairs, and music in no particular order. He searched in every conceivable space. There were no uniforms.

The first football game was Friday afternoon. He wanted the pep band to be there, in uniform, and able to play at least three peppy pieces. They could repeat as often as needed, but who would take seriously a band dressed in Levi's, cowboy boots, and school dresses?

Roscoe, looking every bit the part of janitor in his gray shirt and pants, stuck his head in the doorway. "Oh, it's you, Miles."

"Morning, Roscoe. Where do they hide the band uniforms?"

"There aren't any."

"Have they ever had some?"

"Not that I know of."

"We'll have to fix that."

"They're expensive, I hear tell."

"Everything costs money, Roscoe. It's a matter of priorities."

"I got to go open the school. You need anything here?"

Miles shook his head. "No thanks. The rooster woke us up before dawn this morning so I thought I'd get an early start for the game Friday. "

"Yeah. Roosters will do that. My wife made me get rid of ours."

"We may end up in the same situation."

Miles followed Roscoe to the schoolhouse and up to his room. He put his feet up on the desk and started thinking.

In a moment he heard Roscoe knock on his door.

"What's up, Roscoe?"

"Well—thought you might like to see this. I'm been saving it for some reason and after you said something about band uniforms, I remembered where it was."

Miles looked at the flyer. There it was. Fifty-two used band uniforms at a high school in Indiana for sale for $1,500. There were eighteen members of the Tamarack High School Band. So—they would have thirty-four extras. No big deal.

"When did this come in, Roscoe?"

"Oh, bout a week ago. I've always had a soft spot for marching bands in uniforms." He scratched his cheek and reset his hat. "Could you figure out a way to get uniforms?"

"Roscoe, would you mind helping me in the auditorium for half an hour?"

"Be happy to. What we gonna do?"

"Clean out that cabinet to make room for band uniforms."

Roscoe pulled his head back, an astonished look on his face. "You getting the uniforms?"

"Not this moment. But I've got a feeling they're on their way."

MR. AND MRS. CALVIN Brooks arrived as usual at 8:45 a.m. with Mrs. Brooks behind the wheel. Miles met them in the parking lot as they got out of the car.

"Good morning, Miles," they said in unison, Calvin smiling.

"Morning, Mr. and Mrs. Brooks. Is there $1,500 in the budget for band uniforms?"

Mr. and Mrs. Brooks looked at each other. Calvin turned to Miles and shook his head. "There is no fund for that."

"Can you get the school board to provide it?"

"I don't think so. There are other priorities."

"There always are. But think of our band in uniforms at games, marching down Main Street before a game and at concerts. Think of the boost it will give the town and the students. "

"Miles—they haven't had a pep band or played a concert or marched downtown since I've been here."

"We will starting tomorrow. I'd like them to have uniforms."

Calvin turned his head on his shoulders, his double chins moving in unison. "I'll ask them at the next meeting and let you know."

"Thank you. Could I make a long distance call on the office phone?"

Calvin nodded half a dozen times. "I'll be up in a minute."

"I'll get Roscoe to open the office. Take your time." He turned and walked toward the schoolhouse.

Mrs. Brooks looked at her husband. "What's he up to now?"

"I have no idea. Here—you take the lunch."

She accepted the paper sack and he walked, arms swinging, head down, across the gravel, dressed in his gray suit just back from the cleaners, and ready to start the second week of his fourth year at Tamarack. With their double teachers' pensions they could retire soon if he could hold on to the principalship for two more years.

MILES CONSULTED THE CLOCK on the office wall. There was a time difference to Indiana so he felt comfortable and dialed the number. A pleasant voice answered. "Good morning, Preston High School. How may I direct your call?"

"This is Miles Foster, band director at Tamarack High School in Oregon calling about the band uniforms for sale."

"Hold please for the music department."

Wow—a music department.

"This is Mr. Rhinehold, director of music. You are calling about the band uniforms?"

"Yes. Do you still have them and will you hold them for me?"

"We have them but how long do you want us to hold them?"

"Ninety days would work."

"Can you put down a deposit?"

"Yes. Say 10 percent ... $150 ... "

"That would do. With the balance due in ninety days?"

"Yes."

"Fine. I'll put you on the phone with the school treasurer and you can work out the details with him. Is it cool where you are? Because these uniforms are made of heavy wool. They're quite warm."

"It will be getting cooler after I hang up."

"Hmmm. Thanks for calling and a good day to you, Mr. Foster."

"And to you, Mr. Rhinehold."

CALVIN BROOKS STEPPED INTO the office as the conversation ended.

"Mr. Brooks. I need $150 for a deposit on the uniforms."

"Miles—I said I would ask the board for the money."

"Certainly you have some discretionary funds that have $150 in it, don't you?"

"Yes, but—"

"—I just need a loan of the $150 for a month or so. We'll pay it back with what we earn."

"We—?"

"The band. Can't you just see that wonderful band marching down the street looking like a million dollars in their new uniforms . . . people clapping and yelling? It's a chance to really do something to boost your school and your town."

Calvin hesitated, looked out the window at the hillside starting to turn brown and trees with leaves turning to autumn colors, the limbs leaning toward the earth. "I can't do that, Miles. I don't have that authority. But I will ask."

"You have money for impromptu convocations, don't you? If somebody comes by with a swell program, can't you pay them $100 or $200 for their show?"

Calvin nodded.

"This is like that. Just loan it to the band. We'll pay it back in sixty days."

Calvin shook his head. "I can't do that. Don't you understand? I don't have the authority to buy band uniforms."

"You buy football and basketball uniforms—what's the difference?"

"Those are budgeted for in advance."

Miles took a deep breath, his eyes searching out an answer in the upper corners of the office. He nodded and continued nodding. "I see. Okay, we'll get it done another way."

TUESDAY, AFTER THREE CLASSES in the morning, and planning for the new typing class, Miles walked down the hill to pick up milk at the General Store, where he found Ralph pouring potatoes into a bin.

"Why, hello, Miles. Good to see you. Whatcha need today?"

"Milk." He pointed at the potatoes. "I wouldn't think you sell many of those in this town. Most people grow their own, don't they?"

Ralph smiled. "Townspeople mostly buy them. And the school runs out every so often. We sell a lot of potatoes." He walked over to the refrigerator unit. "What kind do you want?"

"Good old cow's milk with some cream and body to it."

"Yes, sir. That's the best kind. I'll put it on your account. Anything else?"

"Yeah. Lend the band $150 to buy some band uniforms. We'll pay you back in sixty days and pay interest too."

Ralph laughed. "Now that sounds like a good project. You mean you can get uniforms for $150?"

"That's the down payment. We pay the rest in ninety days."

"Wow . . . how are you going to do that?"

"Sell popcorn. We'll buy it from you. Maybe raffle off a gun. Have you got any guns for sale?"

"Sure. But that doesn't sound like something I should be doing." He patted Miles on the shoulder. "You'll figure out how to get it."

MILES WORKED HIS WAY up the side hill on a trail to his house, the groceries in a pack on his back. The occasional cars and trucks running on the main road through town sent their echoes bouncing back and forth between the two hillsides long ago divided by the periodic rampages of Tamarack Creek.

When he got home he put the milk on the table and hollered.

"I'm out here," Ele said. "Outside the laundry room."

He hugged her. Felt her soft hair and warm body against him.

"You feel cool," she said.

"There's a slight breeze coming up the hillside. It's in the shade so it's cool, but it smells so good."

"The whole countryside smells good, doesn't it?"

He nodded and held her out at arm's length. "Have you got $150 I can borrow?"

"What for?"

"Deposit on band uniforms."

"The school can't do that?"

He shook his head. "Can't or won't. I'm not sure which."

"I was saving that money to buy a cow."

"A cow? For cryin' out loud, Ele. I just put aside a lifetime avoidance of chickens and you want to add a cow to our household. Who's gonna take care of a cow?"

"Me." She pounded her chest. "Ele take care of cow."

"Yeah, and who will milk her, separate the cream, brush her, feed her when you're lyin' in the house with the baby?"

Ele stuck a finger in his chest. "You."

"A cow will cost a lot of money. And where will you put her?"

Ele pointed to the three-sided shed that at one time had been used to store baled hay, its open side toward the south in mistaken belief it would remain untouched by the occasional rain and snow. "Right there. You can tether her out during the day and put her in there at night."

Miles took her hand in his. "There you go again, using the pronoun 'you.' Honey, how would you like to make some interest on that money while you're looking for your cow and have the joy of seeing the Tamarack High School band in new uniforms?"

"I'll think about it."

"I need an answer today."

"Okay. I'll think about it fast."

He kissed her hand. "You're not as tough as people say."

"What people? And how tough?"

CHAPTER 5

COACH DONAVON RUSSELL had the team running in full uniform around the outside of the football field. Nine boys suited up. Tommy, the drummer, looked like a grade schooler and Harvey would have to be told what to do on each play. Tamarack High School was in a six-man football league, along with the other small mill towns in central Oregon. But the Tamarack Buffaloes were only going to field a team and a half this season.

As Miles watched the warm-up he smiled, remembering how he and Kerm had muffed through them in college. At the end of a mile the kids were shot. They played little pranks and tricks on each other, causing stumbling or dodging to avert collision.

Coach Russell blew his whistle, the universal signal to stop doing what you are doing and gather around me. The nine stood, hands on hips, panting like locomotives in a freight yard.

"Coach Foster will take the linemen for drills. Backfield with me."

Miles gathered the five boys around him. "Let's talk a minute about this game. First off, how many of you have played high school football before?"

All five raised their hands.

Miles nodded. "Good. Then you know the direction the game is going and what a lineman does. What's the goal of playing football?"

"To win," Nolan said.

"To win is nice, but there are other objectives. Like exercise, conditioning, sportsmanship, teamwork, good fellowship with your teammates and other athletes in the league. Tamarack is going to win some and lose some this year but I want you to be able to hold your heads high either way. You play hard and fair"—he looked in each face—"and you win or lose, but you always, always come off the field having done the best you could on that day."

He held up a football. "Who can tell me what this is?"

"A football," they yelled in unison.

"Okay. Let's play with it. Get in your position."

After forty minutes they were bushed. They all sat on scattered patches of grass that showed that the field was another victim of priorities in the school budget.

"Good workout guys. Jog into the gym easy like, shower and go home and rest. You've had a good day here at Tamarack High. Let's hear you bellow like a Tam Buffalo."

"Grrrrrrrrrrrrrrrummmmpphhhh."

"Sounds more like a lion than a buffalo. Get out of here."

AFTER HE MADE THE evening school bus run, he parked the bus in the schoolyard and walked home. Miles rang the doorbell on his house. Eleanor opened it and looked at him, a slight frown wrinkling her brow.

"Good evening, madam. I'm soliciting donations for Tamarack band uniforms. The biggest donor gets an evening out with me in Prineville, a dinner and movie and some cuddle later. Could I interest you in a book of tickets?"

"How much is a book?"

"One hundred and fifty dollars."

She put a finger to her chin, eyes on the ceiling, "I think I'll take a book."

"Wonderful. You win. Can you be ready by Saturday?"

"I think I can make that time frame. How intimate is it?"

"Just the two of us in Tamarack dress code."

"And that is . . . ?"

"Levi's, cowboy boots, snap button Western shirts."

"I'll be ready."

THE NEXT MORNING, MILES was waiting at the principal's office when Calvin topped the stairs and ambled in his familiar gait down the hall.

Calvin nodded. "You're here early." He fumbled with the key ring he carried in his coat pocket, found the key, and opened the door.

"Good morning Mr. Brooks. I need a school envelope and a stamp, please. I'm mailing the deposit for the band uniforms."

Calvin looked him directly in the eyes. "I have not gotten approval to buy the uniforms."

"I know that. But I got the deposit money and I know I can raise the balance before the ninety days is up."

"That is improper: purchasing something without my permission."

"I didn't think you were against it. Just that you didn't have the money for it. So if I get the money outside of the school budget, what could it hurt?"

"It hurts the process. There is a way of doing things in this district, which I am following. You seem to be ignoring it."

"Calvin . . . I'm not trying to ignore anything. I just want to get uniforms for the band so we can build a music organization here. We've got little kids coming up and if they see the band uniforms it will spark more interest."

Brooks brought his hand down through the air like a cleaver. "There is a board process and it has worked for years. I intend that it keep working. I will submit your request to the board. Now, is there anything else?"

"Are you telling me I can't buy them outside of the school budget?"

"Mr. Foster, we are through discussing this. Good day."

MILES'S FOREHEAD WAS ON fire. His breathing short. Over it, under it, around it. He looked at his watch. There was time to do this. He borrowed Coach Russell's car and parked in front of the General Store. Ralph came forward from the back room. "You're up early, Miles."

"Yeah, everyone tells me that. I need an envelope and stamp. Do you have such things?"

"Of course. We have one of everything."

"How much?"

"Twenty-five cents." He looked at Miles filling out the address. "Where's this going?"

"Indiana. I got $150 for the deposit on the band uniforms. Now I only need $1,350 more."

Ralph straightened up. "That's all the money in the world, isn't it?"

"Naw. I'll get it in ninety days. Somehow."

Ralph took a wallet out of his overalls pocket, spread it open, and laid five dollars on the counter. "There's your first donation."

"That's great, Ralph," Miles said smiling. "Can we put a jar up on your counter for donations?"

Ralph nodded. "You betcha. Got one right here in fact. I'll put the five in it to show it's started."

"What a way to start the day." Miles handed the envelope to Ralph. "Would you please give that to the mailman when he swings by."

"You betcha. Good luck on getting the rest of it."

WHEN MILES DELIVERED THE car keys back to Donavon, he saw a note taped to his room door:

Typing Class at 9:00 Tuesday in room 3-A.

"Who put this up?"

Donavon cracked a wry smile. "The new school administrative assistant."

"You mean Roscoe?"

Donavon nodded. "The very one."

Miles went to his room, got the Typing Teachers Manual and headed for room 3-A, which was through Marion Stillson's homeroom and along the back wall.

Inside the converted closet six small tables had been set up, each with a typewriter on it and a folding chair shoved under it. There was no place for him to sit or stand. He placed the manual on the windowsill and waited. The bell rang and six girls came in, pink faced and chatty from volleyball practice. They looked at the room. Miles smiled at them.

"Pick a seat and settle down. It's not like you've got a lot of choices." He grabbed the manual and stood in the front corner by the door. "We're going to learn this together. I took two years of typing in high school so I know how to do it. I don't know how to teach it, but this book"—he held up the manual—"tells me how. And if I can read instructions and you can understand them, we'll get you out at the end of the year doing a respectable job of typing. Now, the first thing it tells us to do is to insert paper in the machine. So take a piece of paper and insert it at the back of the roller and when it catches, roll it through and under the carriage until it shows one inch above the roller. Then let the bar down and move the carriage all the way to the right. Okay—let's all do that."

Everyone did it. *This is going to be easy.*

CHAPTER 6

FOURTH PERIOD BAND WAS a scurry. "Come on people. Get your instruments and look at the music I have set up on your stands. It is called rally music. The pieces are short and snappy."

"We know these," Tommy said.

"Oh yeah? Good. Show me. Let's try the first one. One, two, three, four . . . ."

It was close. Not great, not even good, but close. It would have to do for Friday's experiment.

"Okay, try #2. One, two, three, four . . . ."

Miles set the baton down and crossed his arms. "Here's the plan—if you're agreeable. Tomorrow we march from this castle on the hill, down the main street of Tamarack, horns blaring, drums rolling, cymbals crashing. Down to the service station and back. We play these four pieces, one after the other and then repeat.

"I sent in a deposit for band uniforms this morning. We need to raise $1,500 but we can do that."

Nolan raised his hand. "How do we know if they fit?"

"There are fifty-two uniforms. We'll make one to fit each of you." He took the flyer off the stand. "Here's a picture of them." He passed it the clarinet section. "This is going to be the snazziest band in the district. We're going to make the town so proud of the Tam Buffalo Band they'll bust their suspenders. Are you with me on this?"

"Yesssss."

He took up the baton. "Okay. We've got forty minutes to practice these four pieces so we don't leave our guts on Main Street tomorrow."

COACH DONAVON CANCELLED THURSDAY'S football practice. He didn't want anybody hurt before Friday's game. Miles closed out his last class and walked to the bus, always amazed at the miniature size of the children lined up to board.

Would his and Ele's child go to school here when she is this small? Probably.

He opened the bus door and the first in line mounted the stairs unaided. Little legs reaching for the step, little hands grabbing the handrails, pigtails flying so intent on the process of bus riding; finding their usual seats, bouncing on them until they settled down for the thirty minute drive to their distant homes.

There was no choice of roads for the school bus route: one road in and one road out of town. Miles stopped at every group of mailboxes, opened the bus door, and waited while third graders to ninth graders jumped down the three stairs and out onto the road.

He had opened the door and let Mandy, the last passenger, out, when he saw two hunters step onto the roadway ahead. They carried rifles in the crook of their arms. He thought he recognized the two biggest guys in school, and pulled up with the bus door still open.

"Where's the deer?"

Jay Caldwell, the red-haired one, pointed to a field ahead on the right. "We chased them out of the woods and we think they're over there."

Richard Kenkey nodded.

"Get aboard and we'll see if you're right," Miles said.

There was an ungraded dirt road leading off the highway alongside the field. Miles turned onto it. Dust cascaded from every flexing joint in the bus as each pothole took a turn at trying to break it down. Midway up the road, Miles braked to a stop, killed the engine, and the three of them sat in silence scanning the field. The hot engine pinged as it cooled. Rich slid down a window. He shook his head.

"I don't see anything."

"Neither do I," Jay said.

"Look up in the far corner," Miles said. "Is that a deer?"

It was silent as they each strained to see if anything was there or if it was a cow or a stump or an old bale of hay browned by the summer sun.

"Not enough light to make it out for sure," Jay said.

Jay nudged Miles in the back. "Could you drive on up there to the corner? Maybe we could see it better."

Whatever the object was, it did not move when Miles started the bus, nor when it reached the corner and shut down again.

"I can't tell," Jay said.

"Me neither," Rich said.

Miles turned to them. "Why don't you guys do what you came out here to do? Go hunt that thing and find out."

"It's nice and warm in here. It'll move in a minute and we can see what it is," Jay offered.

"It just moved," Rich said. "Lemme out."

Miles opened the bus door and Jay and Rich slunk down the stairs, gun barrels in the air. Jay went along the fence line, Rich over the fence and towards the object in the field. Rich raised his rifle and fired. Jay fired. Then they both fired again. Rich was running across the field and up toward the fence line.

The sun was behind the Ochoco Mountains; shadows were gone. Miles could just make out the two boys as they converged at the dark spot they had watched for so long. He saw them bend over and gave them a little time before he started the bus and drove up and turned on the section line road. It hadn't been graded since the Civil War and the ruts made by tractor wheels were much wider than the bus that traveled with one wheel in a rut and the other one chewing up frozen dirt.

The hunters were smiling, excited. Rich had the carcass of a small buck over his shoulders and Jay carried the liver in his hands. They approached the bus door.

"You're not putting that deer in here," Miles said.

Rich laughed. "You want it up on top?"

"The blood will run down the sides," Jay threw in. He nodded at the bus floor. "We'll clean it up when we get back to town."

Miles looked them in the eyes. "You promise?" He shook his head. "I don't want the superintendent to find out we went deer hunting with his school bus."

"No problem. We absolutely will do it."

They took off their Levi's and jackets and laid them in the aisle, put the carcass on top, the liver in the chest cavity, and sat on the bus seat in their underwear.

Miles started the bus, thinking of whether to go ahead or back up to the section corner. He decided to back up. All three occupants were looking out the rear window when there was a sudden lurch and the bus stopped.

"What was that?" Jay said.

Miles gunned the engine but the bus didn't move.

"Better check 'er out," Rich said. He climbed down the stairs in his underwear and looked underneath the bus.

"Transmission housing is high centered on the road." They looked at each other.

"Someone has to drive and someone has to dig," Miles said.

Jay took the jack handle and crawled under the front of the bus. He started chipping at the mound of frozen soil under the housing.

Rich got the jack out, grabbed the handle while Jay rested, and jacked the frontend up high enough to clear the frozen mud. Then Rich and Jay, who could have carried the bus on their shoulders, pushed it off the raised jack so that it cleared the road and Miles put the brakes on after a few yards. With big smiles the boys got back into the bus and huddled around the heater outlet.

"You guys looked funny out there in your underwear," Miles said.

"How about we go home, Mr. Foster," Jay said.

"Good idea."

WHEN MILES GOT IN the bus the next morning to run the regular route as a substitute for the morning driver, it was clean as a whistle. Even the dust had been removed from the seats and windowsills and dashboard. The rubber matting down the middle had been painted with tire black and looked new. The windows had been washed inside and out. He was wishing there was a radio in it to provide some music to the wonderful morning as the sun rose fresh and clear over Rooster's Knob and the cool, damp scent of juniper trees ran along the ground waiting for the sun to diffuse it. It was a morning to behold.

On his fourth pickup, after the children had settled in their seats and he was heading back to town, he heard a small voice call out.

"What is it, Mandy?"

"There's a deer tail hanging on the rear door handle."

Miles smiled. "Well for heaven's sake. How do you suppose it got there?"

THE ENTIRE BAND WAS standing in formation in the schoolyard. On the second floor of the school, windows were raised and students stuck their heads out and yelled.

"Is that the army?"

"Where are the guns?"

"Whoooo, wooo. Go get 'em."

Miles hollered above the catcalls. "Tommy, give us a beat that we can march to. Try and stay in step, you guys. This is our first big impression. When you're not playing look down the line and keep it straight. Ready, Tommy?"

The beat was snappy, crisp—it cut the air and put a rod in everyone's back. The Tamarack High School band moved out of the gravel schoolyard onto the road. Cars pulled to the side to let them pass. Windows came down and drivers smiled and waved. "Go get 'em Buffaloes."

At the bottom of the hill they turned left at the stop sign. Miles yelled in between drum beats, "Number one."

The trumpets struck the first note hard and finished the first measure, which invited the other instruments in. And then in grand harmony, with sound bouncing off the buildings on each side of Main Street, doors opened and folks came out. Ralph, at the General Store starting it, standing on the porch, arms crossed and a smile on his face that was visible across to the beauty salon where two women in the process of hair care along with two beauticians, poured out. Someone started clapping but it was unheard by the musicians. There was another beat: the sound of eighteen feet hitting the ground at the same time. They had never marched together but for a reason unknown to them, that moment they had an inner beat that was in sync with every person that marched that day. A mother came out of the antique store, holding her child, and pointed at the band. The child watched with two fingers stuffed in her mouth.

By the time they reached the service station they had finished the first two marches. The owner, Rod Baumgartner, and two customers came out and hung on a gas pump looking like they were watching someone rise from a grave. Rod smiled and slapped one of the customers on the shoulder.

The band turned around. Tommy hit the drum, feet pounded the road, and back it went, with more than thirty people standing on the sidewalks as the music echoed up and down the small canyon of Main Street.

He couldn't tell what it was, but to Miles it seemed that each instrument was in tune, on time, and a bit part of the whole that flowed over the road, the buildings, the people, and enveloped the community in a giant embrace. When they reached the right turn to go back to the school, the last of the notes drifted in the heated afternoon air. Some would later claim they could hear the trickle of Tamarack Creek flowing thirty feet away.

"Take us up the hill, Tommy," Miles said.

With a smile on his face, Tommy changed beat and the percussion unit—one snare drum, one bass drum, one pair of cymbals— drove the invigorated band up the hill and into the schoolyard where the entire student body, plus Calvin Brooks, stood applauding.

Miles blew his whistle, giving the signal for Tommy to end the beat. It didn't just die out. Tommy looked at the bass player and they came to a glorious close, with both drums and the cymbals hitting a last note together.

Miles walked over to Tommy. "You guys practiced that, huh?" Tommy smiled. "We did."

IN THE LOCKER ROOM before the first game Miles watched the band members, who also constituted 60 percent of the football team, put on their uniforms. Coach Russell waited until all were dressed and looked complete before he called them together. He looked like he knew what he wanted to say but was unsure of how to say it. Miles waited for him to start.

"Guys. This first game will show us what we've got for the year. We have seven games—after today, only six—to prove that we are the tri-county champions. You know your assignments; you are all healthy and strong. Go out there and show everyone that you are contenders." He paused, looking down at his shoes, a hand tugging on his chin. "Everyone knows of the tragedy that took three top players away from this town and from this squad, but you have a chance today to prove that you are beyond that. That you can overcome it. That the Tamarack Buffaloes are champions. What do you say?"

Jay Caldwell held up his hand. "Coach . . . I'd like to say a couple of words." He ran a finger under his nose, sniffed, then went on. "Everybody here knew those guys. We were friends . . . buddies. Rich and I would be with them instead of here today just by luck. We owe them to win this game and all the games this year. We could have done it with them and we can do it with them looking down." He sniffed once. "You guys winners?" he shouted. "Are the Tam Buffaloes winners?"

Nine students and two coaches erupted, arms raised, and they took off in small groups for the field three blocks down the road where the student body cheered them as they ran around the field once and took positions to do warm up exercises. Nolan, the team captain, led them.

After the coin toss, which they lost, the referee blew his whistle and the game began with the Tamarack Buffaloes receiving the ball. The game went back and forth with no timeouts and the Dufer Giants scored at the end of the first quarter.

Miles raised the baton and the six-member pep band struck up the school song. It sounded hollow and weak in the open air. Five instruments and a drum did not provide the emotion that the full band had done yesterday.

The cheerleaders jumped and clapped and so did the spectators—all sixteen of them. At half time, a bunch of the locals gathered around a pickup at the far end of the field and could be seen tilting their heads back and lifting their arms. They were a little louder the second half.

Tamarack scored early in the second half, tying the game. Coach Russell paced up and down the sidelines like a penned coyote, the playbook rolled up and held alongside his neck like it was pasted there.

The band gave it noise, the sun shone, and the breeze that always rose from the valley to the mountains in the late afternoon came burbling along the ground, stirring dust and broken bits of grass in little swirls. The game ended before sunset with the Tamarack Buffaloes winning their first game, fourteen to seven.

Nolan had a big smile on his face as he showered, joking with his teammates over plays and how Carla would treat him after the win. Coach Russell showered with them but it didn't dim their playfulness. He probably walked six miles along the sidelines, sweat over every play, and needed the steam and heat of a good shower. Besides, the house he had rented only had a tub. If he stayed another year he vowed to fix that deficiency.

Miles locked the music room, listening to the jabber from the showers. It was a good beginning. He would need to figure out some pieces for the pep band to play with six members. His linemen had done well and he went downstairs to congratulate them.

"Nice blocking and tackling, Jay. You too, Rich. Good to know you can remember those things," Miles said.

"Did you see me take out that center?" Jay said. "He must have weighed 250 pounds."

"Hit 'em low like we practiced. Isn't a man alive can stay on his feet if they aren't connected to the ground."

"Yeah—but his left leg weighed as much as Tommy."

"Tommy did his job. They thought he had the ball while Nolan ran for the touchdown."

"I almost got killed for it," Tommy said.

"Next time show them your empty hands," Nolan said.

"Good game, guys," Miles said. "I'm heading home. See you next week."

"Does the little Misses get a kiss after a big win like that?" someone yelled.

Another muffled voice responded. "Probably more than that."

"Okay guys, knock it off," Coach Russell said.

The shower room turned silent except for the hissing of showers and the sloppy sound of bare feet padding on wet concrete.

CHAPTER 7

MONDAY MORNING, MARION STILLSON brought in homemade cupcakes. At lunch break, Coach Russell, Miles, and Marion ate in the faculty lounge: the discussion started and ended with last Friday's football game.

Miles put his tray on top of the cabinet and turned to the other two teachers. "I've ordered band uniforms with a borrowed deposit. We need to raise $1,500 in the next ninety days. Any ideas?"

Marion sat up straight, her mouth agape. "Calvin let you order uniforms?"

"Just said he needed to get approval."

"That's a no."

Miles moved his head from left to right. "Not really. A no is when he says no."

"Not around here. Calvin will entertain anything subject to getting approval, which he never gets." She pointed at the typing room. "That bunch of old junk should have been replaced years ago. He always said he would see if he could get approval. That's why I haven't agreed to teach typing for the last three years."

Miles grinned. "So he stuck it on me."

"He saw you coming a mile away."

Donavon set his tray down, crossed his legs in front of him, his arms folded across his thick chest. "Why not sell popcorn at the games. I hear there's a big profit in every bag."

"You think the guys down by the pickup would like some popcorn with whatever they're drinking?"

Donavon smiled. "Might be. Our pep girls at college sold popcorn to raise money."

"I can see where pep girls in short skirts tripping up and down the aisles selling popcorn could hold some promise," Miles said.

"I think I saw a catalog for stuff like that come in before school started," Marion said. "Calvin may have it in his office. You want me to fetch it?"

"Sure. Good idea—both of you. Thanks."

FOURTH PERIOD STARTED A little late. Someone had locked the band cabinet and Tommy was dispatched to find Roscoe to unlock it. After the band was warmed up Miles put the question to them.

"We need to raise $1,500 for the band uniforms. Any and all ideas are in order."

"Raise a steer and sell it."

"Raffle off a car."

"Steal it from the bank."

"Ask the school board for it."

"Get parents to donate."

The fired in answers whirled around the room. "Let's vote on them," Miles said. "Who will buy the steer and raise it?" No hands went up. "Okay—who's got a car we can raffle?" No hands went up. It was silent until Roscoe cleared his throat.

"Could you hold a barbeque and dance? You've got a band that could play dance music and the parents would help with the barbeque." His head bobbed once. "The ranchers would come from all over. Might could pay for it all at once that-a-way."

Miles looked at him. "That's a good idea, Roscoe."

"Yup," Roscoe said. He turned and left the stage.

"This is not a democratic organization. No school is. But I'm willing to put it to a vote because if you vote to do this it will take every one of us to pull it off and if anyone lags on the job we'll tar and feather him."

Heads nodded.

"Those in favor of having a barbeque and dance raise their right hand." Seventeen hands went up. All but Dan Glover.

"What have you got against it, Dan?"

"My folks won't let me go to a dance. It's against our religion."

"I see," Miles said.

Tommy hit the drum one beat. "We'll disguise you so no one will recognize you."

Miles raised the baton. "Let's see if you can raise the roof on this building like you did downtown last Friday." He hesitated at the top of the stroke, just a second or two, but then slid the baton onto the stand in a motion as slow as a mallard gliding in to land on a pond. In a raspy voice, he said: "I want to thank you guys for the great marching on Friday. You made heads spin. People talked about it all weekend and are probably still taking bets on who that band was. You were great."

He blinked several times to clear his eyes and lifted the baton. "Colonel Bogey's March" erupted in the empty auditorium. He caught the eyes of students looking up from their music to follow his beat. The drums were crisp, the trumpets and clarinets, the baritone and flute, all blended into a miracle of sound so superb that it lifted them above their present talents. The march ended in a flurry, the tones vibrating down and back in the empty building.

Roscoe opened the door at the end of the auditorium. He raised his hands and clapped.

BILLY LET HIS EYES come off his desk and they locked with Miles. Miles beckoned for him to come up to the desk. Billy brought his long legs back under the desk, scooted his fanny back in the chair, propped both forearms on the desktop and lurched to the left and up. Then there was the adjusting of the shirt in the pants, raising of the pants up over the tops of his cowboy boots and he was ready to walk. Miles stood up and they went outside in the hall.

"Billy, you aren't enjoying school are you?"

He shook his head.

"Why do you come?"

"Folks make me."

Miles looked out the second floor windows at the end of the hall, a view that showed just a glimpse of the lumber mill at the edge of town, the employer of most of the working people in town. "What do you plan on doing after school is over?"

"Today?"

"No—when you graduate."

"Work in the mill."

Why would he need geography or history to stack lumber or pull on the green chain?

"What's the hardest part of school for you?"

"Reading. I can't read."

"What do you mean you can't read?"

"Can't read good."

"Anything?"

Billy moved his head, looked out the window, put his arms behind his back, and leaned against the wall. "I can read some."

"Wait here." Miles opened the classroom door and went to the library against the back wall of his homeroom. He pulled out *The Old Man and the Sea*, turned and went back into the hall, opening the book to page one and handing it to Billy. "Read that for me."

Billy pulled out his hands to take the book and brought it up to his face. His lips moved. "He was an old man who fished alone in a..."

"... skiff..." Miles said.

Billy looked up. "Skiff." Then back at the book. "And he had gone..."

"... eighty-four..."

"Eighty-four days now without taking a fish." Billy looked up.

Miles nodded. "Was that so hard?"

Billy shook his head.

"Have you ever had a reading test?"

Billy shook his head again.

"Come with me." Miles led down the stairs to Rodney Belker's grade school room. The class was working on something. He peeked through the window in the door and caught Rodney's eye. Rodney motioned him in.

"I need a fifth grade level literature book. Have you got an extra that I can borrow for a bit?"

"Sure."

Miles took the book, went back into the hall, opened it to the first chapter, handed it to Billy, and asked him to read it.

"When the boy found the horse he knew they would be friends forever. It was time for his father . . . "

Miles interrupted him. "Do you remember this book, Billy?"

Billy shook his head.

Miles took the book from him, closed it, and looked in his eyes. "When did you quit reading and doing the lessons?"

"About five years ago."

"And the teachers kept promoting you?"

Billy nodded.

Miles took a breath: one that pushed all of his fury out through his pores, his anger settling in the pit of his stomach. He put his arm around Billy's shoulders. "We're going to solve this, Billy. We're going to see that you get the best job at the mill because you're going to understand it. You willing to work on that?"

Billy nodded, his mouth a little open.

"Let's go back to class."

AT THE END of FIFTH period and forty minutes before the evening bus run, Miles drove down Highway 26 to the mill, a mass of steel sheeted wooden frame buildings rising out of the flat lands with smoke boiling out of a smoke stack. He parked in the lot and walked to the superintendent's shack, pulled the sheet iron door open, and looked right at Christmas Howell sitting at his desk.

Christmas lifted his head, his eyes visible under bushy eyebrows. "Do I need some more schoolin'?"

"Not unless you can play left end. We need another end."

"I was a halfback until my knee got busted up. 'Fraid I'd make a poor end."

"Christmas, I need your help."

"Ask away," he said leaning back in his chair.

"There is a student whose goal it is to work in this mill upon graduation. He can only read at fifth grade level. What kind of reading material do you have that would motivate him to read better?"

Christmas intertwined his hands behind his head and stared at the wall. "Well—there's the lumber grading rule book." He pulled a copy from his desk drawer. "Most of these jobs are taught orally— you know, one guy teaches the next one how to do it." He patted the book. "But this book takes some reading."

Miles scanned it. "Could you talk with him about the need to get a high school education, to read and learn math . . . "

" . . . Now math—that comes into play every day around here. Everything gets measured in inches or feet or height or weight. We're high on arithmetic. Yeah—a guy has got to know his numbers. Same with working on the machinery. Someone might tell him to get a 5/16th and he'd have to know what that was. Who is this kid?"

"I'd rather not say now. But if you would agree to talk with him for ten minutes—he doesn't say much so you'll have to do most of the talking . . . "

" . . . My wife tells me I'm good at that."

"When would be a good time to send him out?"

"I'm usually in the shack by 3:30 of an afternoon. I could take ten minutes anytime between then and four o'clock."

"What happens at four?"

"Whistle blows, my shift is done, and I need a cold beer shortly thereafter."

Miles nodded. "Thanks, Christmas. I'll see if I can get him to come out."

"Okay. By the way, that was a swell parade your outfit put on last week before the game—ran shivers up my old spine. Wanted to suit up for the game."

"We didn't need you for that one, but this week we will. Playing Spray and they whipped us good last year. What size pants do you wear?"

Christmas laughed. "I'd ask my wife to let out the waist on my old uniform but I doubt there's enough material to get it around me."

"I'll let you know if the boy will come out. Thanks."

"You bet, anytime." Christmas hitched up his pants. "Oh, Miles, you might want to consider something. We're operating on short supply of logs right now. This old mill might not be around if we don't get some government timber sales soon. Boy might not have a local mill to work at."

Miles paused. "That would hurt the town."

"Yes," Christmas said. "Yes it would."

"And the school."

Christmas was still nodding. "I 'spect it would." He pushed his lower lip up, turned his head to make sure where his chair was and backed down into it.

CHAPTER 8

MILES HAD NOT SEEN Earl Benson since their friendly conversation about teaching versus educating at the Sunday meet-and-greet
held in the school auditorium. Daily, Miles saw the influence Earl
had on his two children, Nolan and Rebecca, and how they continued the family tradition of hard work, humor, and confidence. After
delivering the last student on the bus route, Miles drove into the
vehicle parking lot of Earl's ranch house overlooking 10,000 acres of
small creek bottoms, grazing land and timber. He saw Earl through
the window get up from his living room chair and open the door.

"Well howdy, howdy, howdy," Earl said, offering his hand for a
shake. "I'm having a coffee. You want one?"

"I'll join you, thank you."

Earl poured coffee for Miles and himself.

Earl was taking the coffee pot back to the kitchen when he said,
"I've been thinking about truth, when we know it and how we prove
it." He set the pot on the burner, turned the gas down, and, with a
smile dancing over his lean tanned face, continued. "I think truth
is one of the hardest things to prove there is. You and I hold certain
ideas and we run our lives on what we think is true. But how do we
know and how do we question it if we don't know or want to?"

"What brings that up?"

The smile stayed on. "You're a teacher. You must be teaching
what you think is the truth and when you are educating"—his
smiled widened—"aren't you asking the kids to find the truth in
their studies?"

"I have a book," Miles said, "the title's *The First Casualty of War*, and the first casualty is truth. So probably a good deal of what we heard during World War II was not true."

Earl raised his hand. "I can believe that. But you and I—where would we go to learn the truth about anything? I mean, I can believe if I plant a seed a plant will grow, and if it does I believe it and it becomes truth and I tell other people and they accept it as truth. But sometimes people plant seeds and nothing grows; what then is the truth?"

"It becomes relative," Miles said. "You adjust the argument to say, most of the time if you plant this kind of seed you get this kind of plant."

"So that isn't an absolute truth."

"Right."

"Then we apply it to deeper truths."

"If four people see a car accident, each person will give a different version of it and the officer has to figure out the truth. You and I don't spend time doing that. We are not responsible for providing the truth for events unless we're asked."

"Juries are," Earl said. "And they don't agree unanimously. They are presented evidence that is supposed to be the truth and they vote ten to two that the guy is guilty, but the two don't see the same truth the other ten see. What I want to know is how can the average citizen—you and me—know the truth of anything?"

Miles sipped his coffee. "Are you saying there is no way to know the absolute truth to anything?"

Earl nodded. "I'm just saying we live in a world of universal laws but we operate daily without knowing the absolute truth about much of it."

"And if we did would it change how we lived our lives?" Miles said.

"I don't know. I'm just trying to get to what is absolute truth and I think it eludes most people with most things. Now, you take a particle of sodium and it is the same anywhere in the known universe."

"Earl—I know nothing about a particle of sodium. How does that come into this discussion."

He beamed, his smile exposing his strong teeth. "Oh, I thought you'd know about those things." He sipped his coffee.

"What I want to know is how to deal with Calvin Brooks. He puts the skids to me every time I ask for something. It's frustrating, and—"

"—What is the truth about Calvin Brooks?"

"Well—first time I asked him politely to change band period. Flat refusal. Second time I asked to buy band uniforms. Third—"

"—Maybe you're asking too much."

"I'm trying to make things better for the students and the town. There's always a better way to do things if you can find it."

"I agree." Earl looked over the top of his coffee cup. "More coffee?"

"Sure."

"But the truth is in his position in this." Earl poured to the top of the cup. "He's within two years of retirement. Doesn't want to rock the boat—"

"—I can't take two years of status quo."

"Or what?"

Miles looked around the room, his eyes roaming over the peace and tranquility of it. "I don't know."

"Calvin is in with the school board. He's been here four years and he does exactly what the board wants. These rural districts don't get fireballs for superintendents, they get those who comply. He wants teachers who will go along . . . not make waves . . . teach the curriculum and come back next year so he doesn't have to spend his summer time recruiting for vacancies in his teaching staff. You are stepping out of that mold, asking things, pushing. Where do you think the truth is in your relationship?"

"Probably dead in the water."

"He's got the power to end your teaching career here and now and he's an old fox. He's cunning. You gotta figure if he hasn't done it before he isn't likely to allow you to do it." Earl scratched the back of his neck. "He's also got Mabel Kreneke on his side and she is a formidable opponent."

"I'm not looking for opponents. The truth is, some kids in my classes are reading at fifth grade levels. They've been passed along to get along. They don't know the subject, they sit in class like obedient gnomes, and they'll graduate not knowing how to write a letter or pay their bills, let alone geography or history."

"What do you want to do?"

"I want to make school interesting, fun. I want them to enjoy learning things that apply to their lives and get a handle on it. Your kids and some of the others know where they're going but everyone can use some enthusiasm and pride and so can this town."

"I know the school board members. Maybe I can glean a thing or two from them and sow some seeds on your behalf." He took a sip of coffee. "Want me to try?"

Miles nodded. "That'd be great." He looked down at his coffee cup. "Another thing, I want to know how I can pay for the uniforms with a dance and a barbeque?"

"Yeah, the kids told me about that. That's crazy you know? You sure you want to buck the school board and Calvin on something like band uniforms?"

"Is that the way you see it?" Miles said.

"Yes sir, I do." He was nodding. "I think it is. But worth doing."

"I don't see it as bucking. I'm just solving a financing problem without their involvement."

"They won't see it that way. They'll say you broke the rules."

"But, Earl—the rules stink. What if a wealthy donor gave us the money for the uniforms, could we use it then?"

"Don't know. They might insist it go into the school general fund."

"Well—I've ordered the uniforms, sent the borrowed deposit, and the barbeque and dance could end up paying for it. I just need half a beef and a barbeque unit."

Earl popped his hands together and a smile stretched from ear to ear. "I've got everything you need. I'll donate half a beef and help you build the barbeque. You done any arc welding?"

Miles shook his head. "Never heard of it."

"You'll get plenty of practice doing this. We were gonna butcher a steer anyway, so I'll get that done while you're building the barbeque."

"Earl—I know nothing about that."

He smiled again. "I know. That's good. I'm working on unplowed ground. Come back Wednesday afternoon and we'll get started."

MILES DROVE TO TOWN ten miles under the speed limit trying to convince himself that this was a reasonable thing to do. Every other mile he switched opinions. He parked the bus at school and drove his car home. Ele was waiting supper on him.

"I've been to see Earl Benson. He think's I'm bucking the system on the uniforms."

"Well you are, aren't you?" Ele said.

"I don't look at it that way."

"Honey—when you do something the superintendent says to not do, what do you call that?"

"He didn't say don't do it. He said he'd ask the school board."

"And then you went out around him and ordered the uniforms."

Miles looked across the table, his eyes dancing from the chair to the picture hanging on the wall, and back. "I think they will all feel really good about it when they see the band dressed up and hear the compliments from people."

Ele turned from the stove. "And that may be, but it will have to set on top of the sourness they'll have from your refusal to go through them. This is our first school, Miles. Learn the system and then play with it. Don't start out alienating the superintendent and the school board on your first job. If they fire you you'll never get another job."

"We can raise chickens. Be a chicken farmer."

"No—now Miles, look at me. Stop bucking the system for a minute and listen to my plea. We've got a baby coming, we're new in the town, and it won't kill you to just do a good job and let the other stuff go."

"Well—I'm going ahead with the barbeque anyway. We've got to have the money from that. I don't see a problem with that, do you?"

"Not at the moment."

Miles lifted his legs onto an empty chair. "Earl wants me to build the barbeque. I've never arc welded anything; don't even know what it is. I can't glue two pieces of wood together and make them stick."

"You have an advanced degree from a college of respectable quality. You can figure it out. Afterwards, you can bring it home to barbeque the chickens I'll be raising."

"Ele, this thing will barbeque half a cow. You'd need eight chickens to stick on it."

"Then eight chickens it will be. Do you want hot sauce with your chili?"

"If I have a cold beer to put the fire out."

"Coming up. I'll just have a sip of your beer as I am off liquor you know, but sipping won't hurt either of us."

"I'll watch the size of your sip."

"You do that, cowboy."

THE NEXT MORNING AFTER Geography class, Miles motioned to Billy.

"Billy—wait just a minute." Miles closed the door and leaned against it. "Do you know Mr. Christmas Howell out at the mill?"

Billy shook his head and crossed his arms over his chest.

"He'd like to talk with you about a job after graduation. Can you get out there someday soon between 3:30 and 4 o'clock?"

He nodded.

"You've got transportation?"

He nodded again.

Miles nodded. *He's got me doing it.* "Okay. Let me know how it goes, will you?" Miles reached for the door handle. "Oh—could you help me build a barbeque unit out at Earl Benson's place? I don't know anything about that kind of stuff."

Billy smiled and nodded. "I know how to do that."

Miles opened the door and the next class jammed through the opening.

"You don't want us in class?" Carla said as she and Nolan passed him. "Keeping the door locked?"

"Billy and I are hatching a serious plot and we don't need upper-classmen spoiling it."

"You'll need help if it is a serious plot. You and Billy won't be enough."

"We'll let you know if we need help. In the meantime, have you got the tickets figured out for the barbeque dance?"

She pulled a sheet from her workbook. "Does this look okay?"

"I'll check it and give it back to you after class." He closed the door and counted. All juniors and seniors were there. World History class could start.

THURSDAY AFTER SCHOOL, MILES got Coach Donavon to drive the evening school bus route and he and Billy drove up to Earl Benson's ranch with their work clothes on. It was build a barbeque night. Earl got out the arc welding equipment and selected the various pieces of iron he thought they would need. He plugged in the welder and, with a steady hand on the electrode holder, welded two pieces of iron together.

He lifted the helmet off and handed the electrode holder to Miles. "Your turn. Now don't inhale a bunch of those fumes coming off there and keep your eyes covered at all times."

He watched Miles weld two pieces together. The popping red-hot molten metal careened off his arms and he flinched each time one burned through his shirt to sting his skin. The acrid smell of the electric weld stung his nose. He held his breath through the short weld. Finally, he lifted the welding helmet and straightened up.

"You've got it," Earl said. He patted Miles on the shoulder. "Good luck." With that he walked out the door, hopped on a tractor and drove towards the meadows.

Miles looked at Billy. "You know how to do this?"

Billy nodded.

"Well—get busy then. How do you figure we build a barbeque?"

Billy looked at him and smiled. "We just need something that turns, has four legs and one end has a crank on it."

"Okay. Let's see you put two of the legs together." He handed the helmet, gloves, and welder to Billy. "Blaze away, Billy."

Miles pulled out pieces of rebar and angle iron from Earl's recycle heap and stacked them in a row beside the welder, careful to keep his eyes away from the damaging light of the arc welder.

He began to see the shape Billy was making. It made sense to him. Billy took off the helmet and Miles clapped him on the back. "By golly, I think that will work." He tried to envision how they would keep half a steer on a rod that turned.

"Wire it on," Billy said and nodded several times.

"I don't feel comfortable with that."

"We could weld a couple of bars and bend them against the meat . . . "

"How would that work?"

Billy described how the two rods would be welded on one end, bent over the meat and hooked in on the other end.

"That works for me," Miles said.

It was dark by the time they finished. Earl had come to the ranch house by a different route leaving them to work it out by themselves. When they knocked on the door, Earl answered, his usual smile warming his greeting. "How'd it go?"

"Fine," Miles said. "After Billy did the welding."

"Good . . . good. Come in and have a drink."

"Don't suppose he's much into whiskey," Miles said clapping Billy on the shoulder.

"Billy can have a pop." He turned toward the kitchen. "Tell me how you built it?"

FRIDAY MORNING, MILES PUT the sophomores to work in groups figuring out how to survey a piece of land using the property lines on local ranches. It involved measuring and describing lots within the city, roadways, highway rights of way, and where the houses sat on the lots. Geography had a lot of parts to it. When the conversation level rose to the problem solving level, Miles slipped out the door and went to the principal's office.

"Mr. Brooks—could I see you a minute?"

Brooks looked over his reading glasses, nodded, and put aside what he was working on.

Miles started. "Have you received permission from the board to buy the band uniforms?"

Brooks shook his head.

"The band would like to have a fundraiser in the form of a dance and barbeque. Do we need permission from the board for that?"

"We've never had that question before."

"We're planning on barbequing half a steer and have the band play for the dance."

"And you'll charge for that?"

Miles nodded. "I think we can make enough to pay for the uniforms."

Brooks nodded to himself, thinking. And then he said: "Where are you going to hold it?"

"Community Hall . . ."

"I see. Please keep me informed."

"Yes. I'll do that." Miles backed up. "Thank you."

Brooks nodded.

When Miles pulled the door open to his room he almost ran into the backside of Mabel Kreneke. She was standing, arms folded in front of her, beside his desk. The room was silent.

"Good morning, Mr. Foster. Just what does surveying have to do with the state curriculum on geography?"

"Why, hello Mrs. Kreneke. Geography is the study of the earth and surveying is how to measure that earth." He edged around her. "Excuse me, please."

She was holding a folder and opened it, laying a sheet of paper with itemized points on his desk. "I think if you look at the suggested items of study put out by the State Department of Education for high schools in Oregon, you will not find surveying to be listed."

Miles nodded. "Is that so?" He scanned the list. "You're right— it isn't on here. I wonder how they missed it. I'll send them a letter tonight."

She lifted her head until she was looking into his eyes, lips set, her eyelids contracting. "It would be good if you would stick to the offered curriculum, Mr. Foster, and confine yourself to teaching what has been found to be relevant to students throughout the state. I trust I make myself clear."

"I understand. Thank you for your interest in geography."

"I made an extra copy which I am leaving for you," she said, using her index finger to push the sheet of paper in front of him on the desk. "Good day, Mr. Foster."

"Goodbye, Mrs. Kreneke."

She opened the door, stopped in the opening and looked back at the class who sat staring at her departure. The door closed and she was gone.

Willing O'Neil looked up. "Whew," he said.

CALVIN BROOKS UNFOLDED THE wrapper on his sandwich as he sat at his wife's desk in the elementary school building. It was noon and their usual lunchtime together. Before taking a bite, Calvin said, "That Miles Foster is giving me a lot to think about."

Without waiting for him to explain, Mrs. Brooks said, "What is it now?"

"He has ordered band uniforms without consulting me and now he wants to have a barbeque and dance to raise money to pay for them."

"Have you tried the school board?"

"No. I'm not going to suggest the uniforms are a reasonable expense when the district is getting fewer pupils every year. No telling how long it can even afford a music teacher."

Mrs. Brooks chewed on her sandwich, swallowed, and looked out the window. "Do you think we can finish here?"

"I don't know," he said. "We only need two more years. If we can keep enough kids coming in we should be able to retire from here."

"I hope so. I detest moving."

They both chewed in silence.

"Mr. Foster needs to understand the chain of command," she said. "Why don't you discipline him for doing it without your approval."

"Like what?" he asked.

"Don't let him buy the uniforms. Call the place he bought them and cancel the order." She lifted her coffee cup. "Tell him no."

"I don't have any idea where he bought them."

"Ask him. He can't refuse to tell you."

Calvin nodded.

"You took a big chance hiring him. He had no experience, didn't like coming out here in the first place, and now he has no respect for your authority. Why don't you call and cancel the uniforms?"

Calvin chewed and nodded.

THE REED SECTION, MADE up of all girls, was on a volleyball trip so Miles set up a new seating arrangement at band in fourth period.

"Tommy, you and the drums over here. Nolan, let's put the trumpets here, and the bass and baritone on this side. Now—this is our dance band. The stands before you hold our dance band music. See how simple it is to have a dance band? Open the music to page five. This is called 'Blue Moon' and is to encourage people to dance slow and close together. I want the sounds coming from the band to be mellow and sexy. Take it from the top and follow me. One, two, three, four . . . ."

First time through it sounded like a logging truck shifting gears going up a grade.

"Guys . . . that doesn't sound romantic. Try it again."

Second time was better.

"Take these dance books home with you and practice your parts in them. We don't have long to make a good sound. Now turn to page eight. This is a lively number called the 'Beer Barrel Polka.' It is designed to get people moving, hot, sweaty, and wanting to buy something cool and refreshing."

Tommy raised his hand. "When do they break to eat the barbeque?"

"When the steer is cooked and they're hungry."

"How long does it take for the steer to cook?"

"I have no idea." Miles raised the baton. "Here we go on the polka. Ready?"

THERE WAS A NOTE on Miles's desk when he came back from band asking him to come into Principal Brooks's office. He slipped over with five minutes remaining before start of fifth period.

"You wanted to see me?" he said.

"Yes," Calvin said, looking up. "Would you please give me the address and phone number of the place you are trying to buy band uniforms?"

"And why is that?"

"As a school matter, I want to call and confirm certain things."

"Like what?"

Calvin looked down at his desk, patted the papers in a neat pile. "You have ordered uniforms without the board's approval or mine and I need to cancel that order."

"I've already sent a deposit. We're raising money to pay for them. Everybody's excited. Why would you cancel it?"

Calvin took a deep breath. "When you took school administration in college, did they not instill in you the chain of command in a school district?"

"More or less," Miles said. "But what problem is there if the band earns the money to pay for the uniforms? It's not out of the district budget or your operating budget."

"You are undermining my authority. What if every teacher decided to order something for his classroom and didn't get my permission? What kind of a school could I run?"

"I don't see it as the same. The typing class can't make enough money to buy new typewriters. The athletic teams can't earn enough to buy equipment but the band can. They can do it with their own talent and their parents backing. They don't need the school to pay for them."

"I'd like the name, address, and telephone number of the person you ordered the uniforms from before you leave the building this afternoon, Mr. Foster. Do you understand me?"

"I understand you but I don't believe it."

Calvin looked across his desk, staring at the two unoccupied chairs and the clock that had hung there since 1938. He said nothing more.

Miles slammed the door, strode across the hall, and opened the door to his homeroom. Students were milling around until they saw the look on his face. They scurried into their seats like mice fleeing a cat.

"I want absolute silence in here for the next thirty minutes. If you haven't outlined John Galt's speech in *Atlas Shrugged*, please do so now. If you have done that, then read beyond it. We'll cover that portion next week."

The sound of pages turning and the occasional scratch of an eraser on paper was all anybody heard in Room 12.

It was an effort, but Miles got control of his breathing and began to count the seconds between the ragged exhales. He didn't trust himself to think, only count the breaths letting his conscious self be aware only of that task. The second he had that under control, he applied the overall balm he always used when he was mad beyond belief.

Nobody will die from it.

He repeated it several times. No uniforms, the loss of $150, no reason for a dance and barbeque—none of them alone or all of them together would cause anyone to die. So—it wasn't *that* serious. Once he had convinced himself of that he moved to the second position. How do I resolve this? The three options he had used so far in life were go under it, around it, or over it. Immediately two options filled his head like bursts of Fourth of July rockets. He nodded to himself.

There was a way out of everything.

It was a day that heralded winter. Cooler by ten degrees, Friday morning broke clear with winds from the southeast tumbling over the dry lands to fill up the canyons and forests near Tamarack with the sharp tinge of sagebrush and juniper. Yesterday the Tam girls had won the volleyball game and were higher than the flagpole when they got to class.

Rebecca Benson had drilled six spikes across the net and her smile was there when she got to school, and stayed all during first period. The news of Miles Foster's afternoon brush-up with Superintendent Brooks had traveled the student circuit. Apparently one of the freshman girls had come by the office and was standing outside the door during the conversation between Brooks and Foster and passed the contents on during the class break. Marion and Donavon drifted by just before the period started, inquiring in quiet tones if he was still working for the Tamarack School District.

"I think so," Miles said. "He can't break my contract over such a small item."

Marion tossed her head back. "He'll do anything to avoid problems with the board."

"Where would he find a teacher this time of year?"

"The board would give him leeway if it came to that."

Donavon clapped him on the shoulder and let a smile start across his face. "You'll make it. This school district is dying but you haven't killed anybody yet."

Miles nodded. "No. Not yet."

CHAPTER 9

THE FIVE-MINUTE BELL rang. "Marion," Miles said. "Let me ask you something. Have you ever directed a one-act play?"

"Sure."

"Would you have time in your English classes to have each class prepare a one act play for presentation in the spring?"

"I've only got three students in the freshman class." She thought a moment. "I could combine the freshmen and sophomores."

"That would work. I'll fill you in at lunch."

Miles was a minute late starting class.

Nolan pointed a finger at him. "Teacher's late. Same penalty as students."

"Guys—we have a lot of world history to cover. I don't think you want to take up your valuable time with my reading poetry."

"A rule is a rule. When school started you said we'd all have to live with the same rules."

"You're late. You read," Becky said.

"I was out late at Benson's building a barbeque for the fund-raiser . . . "

"A deal is a deal. No excuses. That's what you told us and we did it."

Miles reached for *Ballads of a Cheechako* by Robert Service. He sat on the edge of his desk and opened it.

"No sitting on the desk. Stand up front just like we have to do," Nolan said. There was a general chorus of yes'es.

Miles swallowed, looked out at the class who would graduate and leave Tamarack and maybe, if they had a good friend or family member buried in the graveyard down by the football field, come back once or twice during their lifetimes to see their alma mater. They would chuckle thinking about making their teacher stand in front of the room and read poetry of his choice for being late to class.

"'The Ballad of Blasphemous Bill,' by Robert Service.

I took a contract to bury the body of blasphemous Bill MacKie,
Whenever, wherever or whatsoever the manner of death he die.
Whether he die in the light o'day or under the peak-faced moon;
In cabin or dance-hall, camp or dive, mucklucks or patent shoon...."

After filling his lunch plate, Miles sat with Marion and Donavon and started dunking the butter-slathered biscuit in his coffee.

Donavon scrunched up his face. "How can you do that?"

"I like them this way. You ought to try it. It's really good."

Marion said. "What's the story on the one-act plays?"

"I'm trying to think of ways to pay for the band uniforms. Each English class could put on a one-act play. The choirs could sing and the band could play, and at the end we'd have a combined band/chorus finale."

Donavon swallowed his bite. "I thought Calvin cancelled the order."

Miles dipped his head. "Well—he did. But that doesn't mean they can't be bought. I just need the money."

"That's half a year's salary for me," Donavon said. "Where are you going to get the money?"

"I don't know yet. But ways are piling up. I think we could sell food at this thing—"

"What are you going to call it?" Marion said.

"I've been thinking about Cinerama?"

Donavon shook his head. "Sounds okay to me. But what do I know?" He slid his tray aside. "Could you sell popcorn at the games?"

"That's one worth pursuing," Miles said, jabbing his finger in Donavon's chest.

The five-minute bell rang and the lunchroom evacuated. Miles grabbed a hot biscuit on his way upstairs and had his mouth full when he met Calvin in the hall.

Calvin handed him a slip of paper. "I canceled the uniforms. They will not refund the deposit."

Miles took the paper, walked to his room and sat in his chair. He worked at calming down until he could swallow the biscuit. The class waited. He opened the folded paper and read:

> The order for 52 band uniforms (used) is cancelled as of today. Deposit of $150 is not refundable. Do not go outside of authorized channels in this manner again.
>
> Calvin Brooks, Principal/Superintendent
> Tamarack School District.

Carla stretched to look over his desk. "What does the note say, Teacher?"

Miles looked up and smiled. "It says there is more than one way to skin a cat."

THE FOOTBALL TEAM TOOK off in the bus to play an away game, leaving only fifteen students to putter around the halls. Miles had to drive the after school bus, which gave him time to ponder his course of action. He got home just at twilight. A gentle wind wafted down the valley, causing the sturdy juniper tops to shudder and the bronzed grasses, heavy with fall seed, to ebb and flow like waves on the sea.

Every chicken's head was trained on something outside the cage and down the side of the hill. Miles parked the car and walked over to the pen. A young coyote jumped up and turned tail at his appearance, stopping at the top of the next rise to peer back. Miles aimed an imaginary rifle . . . "Blam!" The coyote turned and trotted out of sight.

"That's all right, girls. Studley the rooster would have fought him off."

"He's nothing but a chicken-hearted chicken," Ele said, coming up behind him.

Miles turned. "A coyote . . . "

"I heard them clucking. Looked out the window and saw them in the pen ahead of sunset and knew something was wrong." She backed up a step and looked him in the face. "You look like something's wrong with you too."

"Calvin cancelled the uniforms."

"For crying out loud. How could he do that?"

"He demanded the phone number, called, and cancelled them."

"So what do you do now?"

"My normal way of action when hitting a brick wall. Go under, go over, or go around."

"I'm not liking the sound of this. Are you going over his head too often?"

He hugged her. "It'll be fine, Ele. Nobody's going to die from it."

"Good. I can't afford a new dress for the funeral." She latched the gate to the chicken house. "And my $150 loan for the deposit . . . "

"Ah, that. I may need a wee extension on that."

Ele shook her head. "My daddy told me not to lend to dead-beats."

"And he was right. I think they'll send the money back and I can work off the interest you're owed. What's for supper?"

MONDAY MORNING AT 8:30, Marion met Miles when he came up the stairs. "I found some one-act plays that will engage all the members of each class in some way. I only need Calvin's permission to insert the play rehearsals into the English schedule."

Miles shook his head. "He'll never give that."

"He might," she said. "He needs us for the Christmas pageant. Besides, it is good English practice for the students. We might leverage this."

"It's worth a try."

"Besides, I'm a woman and not a direct threat to his rule."

"And I am?"

"Absolutely. You're young, well-liked, educated—just the kind to replace him."

"Who would want to be in charge of this district when it dies?"

"Calvin sees it as his last posting. Another two years and he can retire—he needs those two years. You don't, so you're dangerous."

"Marion—do you really see this school dying?"

She nodded. "Yes. I think my kids may make it through, but there are fewer students every year. If the mill closes the school is doomed."

"The band uniforms won't have a long life here if you're right."

"Nope. I'll ask him about the plays today and let you know what he says."

"Thanks, Marion. Make it a good day."

MONDAY AND WEDNESDAY OF every week the boys had been meeting in the old furnace room, where coal had been stored in earlier days, to practice boys' chorus. Tuesday and Thursday the girls did the same and on Friday, they combined for mixed chorus.

When the boys arrived, Miles had his speech ready.

"In February it is cold and windy and dark. People want a little entertainment but the roads are slippery, deer are on the highway, snow drifts can cut you off, so what better than some good entertainment right here in Tamarack?"

The guys looked at each other.

"So here's the plan. Come the first week in February, Tamarack High is going to put on a Cinerama."

"What's a Cinerama?" Nolan asked.

"I thought you'd like to know that. I just made it up. But here's what I envision. We have an evening where each of the English classes puts on a one-act play. In between the plays the boys' and girls' choruses perform and, at the end, the mixed chorus and band get in on the act to bring down the curtain, with 200 people rising up clapping and roaring for an encore, throwing twenty dollar bills on the stage and dancing in the aisles."

Nolan raised his hand. "Mr. Foster, what have you been smoking?"

"Good stuff. Only available to outstanding typing teachers."

"I'll bet . . . ."

"So what do you say? Are you game to learn two or three songs for the Cinerama?"

They nodded and chorused in with "yes!"

"'Tom Dooley,'" someone yelled.

"What's that?"

"A great song. You haven't heard it?" Nolan started it, Tommy chimed in, and the whole room was booming out, "Hang down your head, Tom Dooley."

Miles folded his arms across his chest and took it in.

Participation. That's what it is. They're buying into it.

It was deep and resonant and the guys smiled as they sang it, looking at each other as if to say they knew the words better than the next guy. Like singing in the shower. It wouldn't be that way on the stage the night of the Cinerama. They would be starched, unsmiling, unsure of the tune, and afraid of the words. They needed something to take their attention away from the people who would be out front staring at them, looking up with eyes wide, lips open a little, ears tuned in, and maybe mouthing the words if they knew them.

When they finished Miles clapped. "Okay. Now let's turn it into a real ballad."

"What do you think that was?" Nolan said.

"That was a shower room rendition of a ballad. And maybe that's what we ought to do. Strip you guys down, put you in the shower, and have you sing it down there. We could put a microphone up to the stage speakers."

"You gonna put a camera down there too?" Ready O'Neil said.

"You got something you want to show off?" Nolan shot in.

"Okay, guys. I take it you are in for it then?" Miles said.

There was general agreement.

"Where do I hear this song sung right?"

"Bring a pocket full of nickels down to the café. They have it on the machine there."

"You picked one. Now I'll pick one. Open the music books to page 22, 'They Call the Wind Maria.' Have you heard this before?"

CHRISTMAS HOWELL TURNED TO the knock on his door. Nobody had ever knocked on the tin-clad superintendent's shack door at the sawmill before. "Come in."

Billy Canfield pulled the door partway open and peered inside.

"Come on in and close the door," Christmas hollered.

Billy stood before him.

"You must be Billy Canfield," Christmas said.

"Yes sir."

"Well—take a seat there and let's jaw a little. You want coffee?"

Billy shook his head.

"If you don't mind, I'll have a cup. Too early for whiskey. You want a Coke?" Billy shook his head.

"That bus-drivin' school teacher said you were lookin' to work here after graduation. Is that right?"

Billy nodded.

"Billy—you can talk in here. Ain't nobody goin' to take a bite out of you if you say somethin'. At this mill you gotta talk cause often times the other person can't see you. You catch my drift?"

Billy nodded, then added, "Yes, sir."

Christmas nodded. "Good." He chuckled. *Now he's got me doin' it.* He took a sip of the coffee, then stood up and threw it in the sink. "Terrible. Terrible. Must'a boiled it." He sat in his chair. "What'd you figure to do out here, Billy?"

"I dunno."

"Well—most of the guys start on the green chain and work their way up. Then they go to the pond or the sawmill or the planer. Some drive truck. What were you thinking?"

"Just wanted a job. Make some money."

"When do you graduate?"

"Next year."

"Your grades alright?"

"I flunked some."

Christmas leaned back in the chair, clasped his hands behind his head and looked at Billy Canfield. "The thing is Billy, a man has gotta have his education to progress in life. You can start on the green chain with just a set of strong arms and a strong back, but before you finish your first can of snuff you're gonna wish you had some education to move on up the ladder. You know what I mean?"

Billy nodded.

"Now, can you get those grades up to where you can pass the school and come out with a high school certificate?"

"Yes."

"Good. Let me show you around a little. You got time?"

"Yes."

Christmas slid his hands on the metal pipe bannisters and pulled himself up the steep stairway to the mill floor. *He's a nice enough kid if you can get him to talk. Seems scared to death of his shadow.*

Down at the Tamarack Café, Miles fed in another nickel. The Kingston Trio started "The Ballad of Tom Dooley" for the third time. He was almost through writing down the words. The tune was simple enough and the guys all had that down pat. It was the words that he needed to capture before the boys' chorus turned it into what they wanted it to say. *A guy who stabs his girlfriend on a mountain and now is going to hang for it—this is their idea of a good song?*

After the fourth playing he had the words written down. He would have to change the starting pitch to match their adolescent voices. It had a good ring to it and the boys loved it so they would put their hearts into it. If he could add "Shenandoah" to it, they could pull it off.

Have I bitten off more than I can chew? These students haven't performed for anyone for years. Three plays, the band, the chorus . . . can it work; will it work? Cripes . . . just settle back and do the job you were hired to do; quit adding stuff to it.

"You about through, Mr. Foster?" Nellie, the waitress, said. "Some of the other people would like to hear something besides that song."

"Sure," Miles said. He picked up the three nickels he had left, stuffed them in his pocket, then pulled them out and laid them on the counter. "They can play with these."

He slipped into his jacket and walked up the hill to the house, the chickens, the empty cowshed, and his pregnant wife, carrying ten pounds of doubt that was cramping his early morning enthusiasm, stepping on his mid-day sense of well-being. It was the night—always the night that stole his confidence. Came in the dark and robbed him of what at the beginning of the day was a swelling sense of can-do. How could a man go from one end to the other in a day? If it was good in the morning, why wasn't it good at midnight? Why did dark and night and shadows fight with the morning prayer?

CHAPTER 10

TUESDAY MORNING, ROSCOE STOOD inside the coal room, a grin as big as all outdoors lighting up the grimy corners of the room.

Miles chuckled. "What have you got this morning, Roscoe?"

"Well, sir, you won't believe this, but I found a popcorn machine and they don't want much for it either."

"Where'd you find it?"

"The Masons had it. Used to use it when they showed movies. They even have a sack of popcorn that's probably too old to pop."

Miles smiled. "How long does it take for popcorn to lose its pop?"

"Well, I dunno," Roscoe shook his head. "But I don't reckon it's got much left in it after ten years, do you?" He looked at the smirk on Miles's face. "You were kidding me?"

"Yeah, I was. How much they want for this ancient machine?"

"Twenty-five dollars is all."

Miles lifted his eyebrows. "I've borrowed $150 from my wife for the deposit. Calvin has shut me off...."

Roscoe reached out his left leg and crushed a beetle under his shoe. "I got an idea. We can sell firewood. We can get five dollars for a pickup load."

"Who's this *we* you're talking about?"

Roscoe waved his hand back and forth between them. "You and me."

"We only need a pickup and a chain saw and an axe and a wedge and gas and oil cans...."

"I've got those."

Miles clapped him on the shoulder. "Anytime then."

"Yup," Roscoe said. He turned and walked out, his overalls flapping at the back of his legs.

The girls arrived, on time and chatty. He was sure the boys would have spread the word about the Cinerama, so he was silent setting out the music books.

"What's this we hear about a Cinerama?" Shelly asked.

"Thought you'd never get around to it," Miles said. "Picture this. The auditorium is full, standing room only; the lights are dimmed. The curtain opens and the Tamarack High School girls' chorus bursts into the opening notes of 'You'll Never Walk Alone.' After the applause dies down, and Shelly gets through picking up the money thrown on the stage, the chorus strikes up 'Oh, What a Beautiful Mornin',' followed by 'Zip-a-dee-Doo-Dah.'"

"Then what happens?" Brenda asked.

Miles lifted his hands. "Then the lights go back up and everyone goes and buys a bag of popcorn and we're closer to having enough money to buy the band uniforms."

"How come we have to help the band earn money for the uniforms?"

"Did you do anything to help buy the football or basketball uniforms?"

"No."

"Don't you think it's about time you did something to help get the band uniforms then?"

"No." She bent over and came up laughing. "Okay, we can do this."

"Whew!" Miles wiped his brow. "I thought I might have to torture you into it."

"And just how did you plan on doing that, Mr. Foster?" Shelly threw in, an eyebrow up and a wee smile on her painted lips.

Miles thought fast. "Make you listen to the boys' chorus."

"Ahhhhhhhh. That was disappointing," she said.

"You were looking for something else, weren't you, Shelly?" Brenda said.

"Oh, shut up, Brenda."

Miles held up his hand. "Girls—we have work to do. This child-ish banter must be carried on outside the classroom."

"And that's where she wants it to go," Brenda finished.

Blood flushed Miles's face. He swallowed twice, looked as solemn as he could and raised his hand to start the choir. It was a ragged start, partly due to the conversation just ending and partly the fact that his hand was not as steady as it should have been.

DONAVON AND MARION WERE not in the lunchroom when Miles got there. He took a seat looking at the door and was spreading butter on the baking powder biscuits when Shelly's face appeared in the glass, smiling and bobbing back and forth. Then she laughed, waved, and was gone.

Shelly was one of the lookers. Most of the good-looking girls had gone with the good-looking boys, as the choices were few. Shelly had been going steady with one of the boys killed on the highway. His death had caused her to be moody for the first weeks of school but she was unattached right now and was playing provocative with Miles. He finished lunch, slid his tray onto the wash table, and com-plimented Alma on the biscuits. "Good as ever," he said.

"You want to take home a dozen?" she said.

Miles raised an eyebrow. "Can I do that?"

"You can if you want to. I've got lots left over."

"Sure," he said.

Alma put them in a sack and handed them to him. "There ya go."

"Thank you, Alma. Ele and I will enjoy these a lot." He turned to leave and walked past Calvin Brooks coming back from lunch with his wife. Calvin looked at the sack Miles carried.

"Biscuits," Miles said lifting the sack.

Calvin nodded, his face as stony as Mt. Rushmore, and contin-ued on. He discarded his lunch sack in the garbage can, turned and walked back to the elementary building and to his wife's room. He motioned to her through the glass to meet him at the door.

"What is it, Calvin?" she said.

"I just saw Mr. Foster taking food out of the cafeteria. A sack full of biscuits."

"How often do you suppose he does that?"

Calvin shook his head. "No idea. But I don't like teachers taking food from the school. Our budget is tight enough without feeding them on the side."

Winifred nodded her head and spoke in a low tone. "Mark that down so you'll remember it when contract time comes around."

"Yes. Yes. Just thought you ought to know." He turned and adjusting his tie, walked out the door across the gravel lot to the high school.

FOURTH PERIOD WAS BAND again even though Miles had seven times asked Mr. Brooks to move it to some other period. Mr. Brooks always said he was looking into changing it, but it never happened.

Miles hollered above the noise. "Get the food particles out of your mouth before you play your instrument. You know what food does to a trumpet or reed. Plugs it like a gopher in a drain pipe."

Instead of tuning up as they usually did the minute they put together their instruments, they waited. There was a questioning atmosphere hanging around the stage. Miles could feel it. He looked up. "What?" he said.

Tommy lit up. "What does the band do in the Cinerama?"

"You heard?"

"Well of course. It's all over school. You told the boys' chorus and girls' chorus and that's all of us. So what is the band going to do?"

"Glad you asked," Miles said. "What would you like to do?"

General discussion followed for twenty seconds, reaching the conclusion that they didn't know.

"The band will finish it off. Big brassy sounds, drums, trumpets . . . the whole enchilada."

"What's an enchilada?" Tommy asked.

"A Mexican dish, stupid," Nolan said.

"Okay. At the end of the three one-act plays and after the choirs have sung, we'll have the mixed chorus and then the band. And how about one big finale with both the band and chorus together. Something like the 'Battle Hymn of the Republic'?"

Tommy raised his hand. "How are we gonna do that when half the chorus is in the band and half the band is in the chorus?"

Everybody turned and looked at him where he stood, small behind the drums, shaded by the hanging stage curtains.

"We'll figure it out, Tommy." He nodded. "We'll figure it out."

FRIDAY, AFTER THE GAME, which the Tams lost, Coach Donavon disappeared. After Miles helped Roscoe clean up the locker room he looked for him. "Roscoe—have you seen Coach?"

Roscoe shook his head and continued to the laundry room with a basket of towels.

In the parking lot he caught Jay and Richard just as they were leaving. They stopped and rolled down the window. "Need a ride, Mr. Foster?"

"No. I'm looking for Coach."

"Gone to town," Jay said. "The big town."

Miles turned to hear him better. "What big town?"

"We're not sure. We think Hood River."

"He has a sweetie over there?"

Richard shook his head, raised his arm and made a motion that imitated someone drinking.

"You sure?"

"No. But you never see him after Friday end of school. And come Monday morning sometimes he's a little beat up."

Miles stood up straight, looked over the top of the car. "How you guys doin' since the accident? You doin' okay?"

Jay and Rich looked at each other, then out the windshield.

"You know," Rich said. "We think we're getting ahold of it a little better every week but after a game, it pulls us down. If our buddies had been with us this would have been a different day."

Jay stared out the windshield.

"Wish I could have known them," Miles said.

The two boys nodded. The silence stuck to them while each held their hand on the car, not wanting to let go for fear something would be lost.

In the moment when Miles could feel tears welling behind his eyes, he forced a smile, slapped the top of the car, and said, "Thanks, guys. Have a safe weekend."

"Last weekend of hunting season. Want to grab the school bus and come with us?"

"Think I'll pass on that. Roscoe has some exercise lined up for me with a chainsaw."

"Okay. See you Monday. We'll have deer liver for lunch." Since Miles was behind them when they turned out of the parking lot they did not burn rubber and throw gravel. He was grateful for that.

SATURDAY MORNING ROSCOE PICKED Miles up at his house in a black 1941 Ford pickup. Miles was dressed for work and placed his lunch behind the seat.

He turned to Roscoe. "How far to where we can cut wood?"

"'Bout seven miles. I got me some special places."

Miles could just hear him above the noise of the car. Roscoe seemed satisfied with no conversation until they got to a log lying alongside the road. It was a large sixteen-foot-long pine log with a brand driven into the end of it.

"Looks like it belongs to the mill."

Roscoe nodded. "Yup. It does."

"And we're gonna cut it up?"

"Yup."

"Isn't that stealing?"

"Nope. They won't send a retriever out here for one log." He took out the chainsaw and the axe and a wedge, filled the chainsaw tank, pulled the cord, and the noise tore Miles's eardrums apart. He jammed a finger in each ear and watched the grin on Roscoe's face widen as the saw cut a clean line to within an inch of the bottom. He repeated that twice more then shut the saw off. He took a peavey out and the two of them rolled the log so the uncut portion was on top. Roscoe handed the axe to Miles.

"Chop those bridges out, split the wheels, and throw them in the truck."

Miles thought he knew what was required and after a few whacks came to enjoy the process. Roscoe cut, Miles split. The whole log filled the pickup and Roscoe piled the equipment in a box on the running board, snapped the cabinet shut, and brushed the sawdust and dirt off his overalls. "There. That's five bucks worth."

"Yeah," Miles said. "Four more logs and we've got it. Less paying for your gas and oil and the use of your tools."

Roscoe shook his head. "The school pays me enough to live on. I can afford the gas and oil for band uniforms. I think they'll look sharp in those."

Miles brushed himself off and opened the truck door. "Who's paying five bucks for this load?"

"Coach. He's got a wood burner in that house he rents."

The overloaded pickup swayed on the road. It felt as if the frame was sitting on the axles with no springs. Roscoe kept the steering wheel moving from side to side as if it were normal, put it in first gear to climb the hill, and bounced a chunk of wood out turning the corner too fast. Miles got out while Roscoe backed up the driveway of the house Coach Donavon Russell was renting.

Miles pulled on his gloves and started stacking the wood in the backyard.

"For five dollars we don't stack 'em," Roscoe said.

They threw the quarter-rounds into a pile and sat in the pickup drinking water from a mason jar.

"Roscoe—you ever see Coach on weekends?"

Roscoe shook his head. "Leaves town."

"Where's he go?"

"Don't know. Never followed him." He looked Miles up and down. "You ready for another load?"

"Another load? Two today?"

"You want the popcorn popper, don't you?"

Miles wiped his brow with a sleeve. "Yes. I also want to die in bed, not bucking firewood."

They got two loads, had lunch, and Miles got back around 3 o'clock to help Ele can produce she had bought from the locals.

"You're filthy," she said. "Shower and then I'll inspect you and see if you can work in the kitchen."

"Why do I always have to be the one to pass muster? Get cleaned, get shaved, comb my hair, polish my shoes—"

"—You haven't polished your shoes since we got here."

"Okay, so I slipped that one in, but—"

"No buts about it, mister. You have your schoolroom, I have my kitchen, and house, and chicken house, and cow shed—"

"Oh oh, you slipped that one in on me. What's about the cow shed?"

Ele put the wooden spoon down and hugged Miles. "Oh, honey, you won't believe who's living in the cow shed. A real live cow. I'm calling her Spot. She's gorgeous and she gives five gallons of milk a day and some of that can be cream and we can make butter and—"

"—Wait a doggone minute—"

"—And the best part is she's free. Absolutely free."

Miles placed his hand over her mouth and smiled at her. When she stopped wiggling and mumbling, he peeled his hand back little by little. "Who gave you a free cow?"

"Well, she really isn't ours to keep but I was at the store this morning and a neighbor down the street said they were going to another logging job for the winter but would be back in the spring or summer and she was looking for someone to keep her cow, so I volunteered. We get to keep all the milk and cream and everything."

"What else does she produce besides milk?"

"Well . . . nothing really, but we can make cream, butter, cheese, all kinds of things and it will be fresh and wholesome and wonderful. You'll love it. I know you will."

"And who does the maintenance on this cow?"

"You do, of course. I handle the chickens and grow the baby."

"Ele, I'm swamped at school. Now we've got the Christmas program, the Cinerama, and driving the bus. I can't keep up with a cow."

"Can we keep her, Miles? Please?"

Miles frowned. "I don't know, Ele. I'll need to have a talk with this cow and see what her intentions are."

"As soon as I'm through here and you clean up, I'll introduce you. You're gonna love her. She's got big long eyelashes, very flirty."

AFTER MILES CLEANED UP, Ele led him to the cowshed, strewing dead leaves, dried rose pedals, and mowed grass in his path while humming some ancient tune honoring conquering heroes. At the barn, the cow turned her head and examined the newcomer with wide eyes.

Ele took his hand and placed it on the cow's hipbone. "Miles, this is Spot. Spot, this is my husband, Miles. You two are going to be good friends."

"When was she milked last?" Miles said.

"This morning."

"So you're going to milk her?"

"Of course not, silly. I told you I take care of the kitchen, the chickens, and the baby. She awaits your hands on her mammary glands."

Miles threw his head back and patted Spot, who swung her tail and smacked him across his cheek. "This is gonna be bad news. I can tell it."

"Don't be silly. She's used to being milked. They brought a bucket and a brush and everything. Go to it, Cowboy."

Miles sat on the one-legged stool, put the bucket under her udder, and took ahold of one of her teats. Spot looked back at him one more time and kicked her left foot out as a warning.

"Did you see that?"

"Of course, honey. She's just nervous, that's all. She missed you didn't she?"

He tried it again. She pulled her leg forward and knocked the bucket out of his hand.

"See . . . she doesn't like me. Keeping her is not going to work."

"Miles, people have been milking cows for thousands of years. You can learn this, I know you can."

"Roscoe would know this. I'll call him."

ROSCOE SLID OFF THE front seat of his pickup with a smile on his face. "Your cow givin' you trouble, Mr. Foster."

"She's not my cow and she doesn't like me milking her."

"You're a new milker so she's putting the evil eye on you to see how much she can get away with. Show me how you were hobbling her."

"I wasn't hobbling her. Don't know what that is."

Roscoe got a pair of hobbles out of his pickup and stood, arms crossed over his chest, his flat stomach pushed forward, and smiled as Miles put the hobbles on Spot. She kicked them off at once.

"Problem is you aren't putting 'em on right. Here, lemme show you." He hooked one on each leg with the chain crossing over the front of her legs. "Now try it."

Spot took a bite of hay and let Miles milk her.

He looked up. "Well, she knows she lost that battle."

"Cows are a lot like kids. Once you show them who's boss they tend to behave. You got it now?"

"Sure do. Thanks, Roscoe."

Ele stood up. "Roscoe—could you and your family use some milk? We're gonna have five gallons a day and I doubt we can get rid of that much until our family grows a lot more."

Roscoe nodded. "We might could use some. That's mighty nice of you, Mrs. Foster."

"As soon as my milker gets his work done we'll drop by with a bucket."

CHAPTER 11

A NOTE WAS TAPED to the door-glass when Miles arrived Monday morning asking him to come to the superintendent's office as soon as possible. Miles put his books on the desk and walked across the hall to view Calvin Brooks glaring at him and motioning him in.

"Good morning, Mr. Brooks," Miles said.

"Please sit down, Mr. Foster. I have some serious allegations to discuss with you."

Miles's stomach turned over as he took a seat.

Brooks turned, looked out the window as if wondering how to start this conversation, and when he turned back it was like a prosecuting attorney trying to get a confession. "I was stopped on the street this weekend by Christmas Howell, the mill superintendent." He stopped and wet his lips. "He informed me that Billy was coming out there on a regular basis and reading some lumber manual in his office. Furthermore that you set it up." His glare intensified. "Is that true?"

"Mostly. I am trying—"

"—Mr. Foster, has it occurred to you that this school building along with the teachers therein and the school district as a whole are who should be teaching Billy to read?"

Miles straightened up in the chair. "Billy and every other student is being taught and, I might add, educating themselves in the prescribed course of study, but what some of them are studying is not going to help them when they leave this school. Christmas

Howell is assisting after hours and on his and Billy's own time, not
the school's or mine."

"Handing the responsibility for reading to a mill superintendent and letting Billy read lumber grading manuals instead of geography and history is not what you are being paid to do. The state of
Oregon has mandated what Billy and all the other students are to
study and know by the time they leave this school."

"I know that, but Billy—"

"—This will cease immediately—today—and I want a letter
from you to me and the board explaining this and vowing never to
do it again. Do I make myself clear?"

Miles nodded. "You do. But you don't understand the circumstances."

"Mr. Foster . . . I have been teaching for over forty years. I have
seen every circumstance that can exist in a school and contracting
out reading to a mill superintendent is not acceptable. Please have
the letter on my desk before you leave today. That is all." He turned
toward his desk. "Just a minute—and please do not take biscuits
or any other food from the school cafeteria. Feeding you and your
family was not in your contract. Am I clear on that? I pride myself
on being clear."

Inside, Miles's heart was pounding. A thousand words flew
through his subconscious while his teeth, bit-by-bit, clamped down
on his tongue. "Yes, sir. Your decisions and instructions are irratio-
nal, short-sighted and not based on facts, but I understand and will
conduct myself accordingly."

The color rose in Calvin's neck, above his collar and into his
hairline. He stared out the window, his arms leaning on the desk.

AFTER THE FIRST TWENTY minutes of discussing the Black Plague
and how it affected Europe for a century afterward, the class was
divided into discussion groups, each taking a sector of the economy to
determine what it did to the social structure, the church, the business
sector, and the arts. Billy, who never contributed to any classroom discussion whether open or in groups, was beckoned to Miles's desk.

"Billy, I gotta figure out another way for you to learn to read. There is a state test that you need to pass before graduation and the lumber-grading manual isn't going to cut it. Help me here. What do we do?"

Billy looked down at his feet, looked around, shook his head. "I don't know."

"Do you have the manual with you?"

Billy nodded.

"Get it, will you?"

Billy pulled it from his back pocket and smiled. "I keep it with me and read it all the time."

"Sit down and read me a section from it, will you, please?"

Billy opened the book, swallowed. His eyes ran down a line or two before he started to speak. "All U.S. rule writing agencies that write grading rules for western spruce, lodgepole and pine—" He looked up. "Is that enough?"

Miles nodded. "Yup." They both sat silent for a moment. "You can take your seat, Billy. I have a letter to write."

Principal/Superintendent Calvin Brooks
The Tamarack School Board
The Oregon Department of Education, Supt. of Education

Dear Sirs,

This letter addresses the issue of one-size fits all in public education. The senior class at Tamarack High School has students who read at fifth grade level up to and including sophomore level in college. Providing a meaningful class for all of them in geography or history from the same instruction manuals is daunting for the teacher, frustrating for those at the lower end of the spectrum, and boring for those at the top.

A large percentage of these students are destined for, and desire to work in, fields that do not require high school graduation, such as farm and ranch work, mill work and logging business. However, even in those fields they will need to be able to read at some level. But when a student reaches high school and cannot read high school text books, the learning process stops, boredom sets in and teachers move them on with barely passing grades rather than reaching out to take the student from where he is to an acceptable reading level. This student may not reach the level required for graduation but he might learn enough to perform well in the job he seeks.

I am aware of the state requirements for graduation in the various subject matters I teach, but trying to get someone who reads at fifth grade level to read, understand, and participate in group discussions day after day is fruitless. I propose that certain students be given alternative classes that will prepare them for their life's work instead of throwing uncomprehending work at them for six hours a day.

To this end I would like to work with Billy Canfield, a senior at Tamarack High School, to advance his reading from fifth grade level to a level acceptable to work at manual labor jobs he aspires to before he leaves this school. This will require out of school work with non-teachers but I guarantee that he will graduate with marketable skills if allowed to do so.

May I hear from you at your earliest convenience?

Sincerely yours,

Miles Foster, Teacher
Tamarack High School
Tamarack, Oregon

Miles made three carbon copies. He mailed one to the school board, one to the Superintendent of Education in Salem, Oregon, and laid the original face up on Calvin's desk. He put the last copy in his briefcase.

Writing the letter had dissipated his anguish. He felt the good vibes about teaching drift back from the interior walls of his classroom as the chosen speaker for each discussion group stood and described the effects of the Black Plague on his segment of fourteenth-century life in Europe.

Billy was in the back row. His legs were stretched out in front of him, his rearend scooted forward in his chair. He was reading the lumber grading manual.

MARION CORNERED MILES AFTER lunch. "Calvin finally agreed. I can use one period a week for the play. He thinks he can get the board to buy that. After all, it is reading and it is literature."

"Good. I was nearly executed this morning over Billy's reading and biscuits."

"Wow. At least you know why you're dying."

"Marion—that's no help. I'm just as dead."

"What's with the biscuits?"

"I took a dozen left over biscuits home last week."

"We all do that."

"I don't anymore. Calvin says it's not in my contract to feed me and my family."

"Yeah, but there are days when there is left over food, especially on Fridays sometimes when half the school is gone to a game."

"If you take some, put it under your coat so Calvin doesn't see it?"

Marion cocked her head. A wry smile lit her face. "I told you. He doesn't like you. He's going to make life tough for you."

Miles took a deep breath and let it out. "Forget that. How are the plays coming along?"

"They are all casted and we have Nolan and Carla heading up the staging operations to get furniture and stuff we need for the set."

"Good. The choruses are smoothing out. Now if I can get the band to come together with the right chemistry to pull off 'Battle Hymn of the Republic,' I'll be happy." He looked over her head for a moment before continuing. "You know, my image of that piece is the Mormon Tabernacle Choir singing it with organs, bands, drums, everything behind it. In the empty gym our eighteen-piece band doesn't even sound like an echo of that."

She clapped him on the shoulder. "Quit trying to make chocolate pudding out of chicken poot. This is Tamarack, not Portland."

Miles shook his head. "You are oh so right."

"Have you seen Donavon today?"

"No. Why?"

"He looks like a truck ran him down and then backed over him."

"Wow. He's okay? Hope he's ready for the game Friday."

"He usually is. We'll see."

THE BUCKET OF WARM soapy water felt good as Miles scrubbed Spot's udder to clear it of manure, grass, smashed bugs, and other objectionable objects not wanted in the bucket of milk that was going to come from it. Spot munched hay, ignoring him while he put on the hobbles, set up the stool and proceeded to milk her.

Steam rose from the milk and Miles leaned his head against her flank, enjoying the warmth of her body.

"You're a good girl, Spot. I'm glad you came to live with us."

Ele stood at the corner of the shed. "I'd like to try making some cheese from this bucket. We've already got two gallons of milk in the refrigerator . . . it'll take us a week to drink those."

"Hey—you're the one who got the cow. Now deal with the over supply."

"I am. Roscoe will start milking once a day tomorrow."

"And I'll have cream in my coffee, on my cereal, whipped on chocolate cake."

"Yes, isn't it exciting. We're so productive. Eggs, milk, cream, chickens, cheese—what more could a first year teacher want?"

"How about an understanding superintendent, willing students, and a permissive school board for openers?"

"Why don't you talk to Earl Benson about those issues. He seems to have a good head on him and I like him."

"Good idea."

Earl Benson opened the door and greeted Miles with a smile. He nodded his head and said, "Come in, come in. I'm having a beer, can I get you one?"

Miles shook his head. "Hi Earl. Have you got a little time to talk?"

"Always. Talking is about as much fun as drinking beer, don't you think?"

"Never looked at it that way."

"Well—you can start now if you want. Talking gets ideas out where you can work on them...massage them around a little. And a beer helps. Know what I mean?"

Miles rubbed his face with his hands, looked at Earl. "You know what? I'll have that beer with you." *Why not? Earl didn't get wealthy being stupid. And if he likes to drink a beer while he ponders the problems of life maybe it would help me.*

Earl handed him a beer, stirred the fire with a poker he had made from a broken spring harrow tooth that most people would have thrown away, and took his favorite seat facing the fireplace at an angle. He tipped the beer and drank a third of it in one pull. Then he belched and said, "What you got to talk about?"

Miles looked around the room. The view out the windows led your eyes across the meadow and into the hills covered with pine trees and into the scattered clouds that drifted with the wind across the Ochocos. The house had furniture that cradled a tired person after a good day's work and a clock that ticked away a man's life second by second. Miles sipped the beer, the cool tang leaving him wondering why people drank the stuff.

"Why did you take up farming when you could have done almost anything?" Miles said.

Earl smiled, looked at his beer then at the ceiling. "Do you know that if you plant one kernel of wheat, in less than six months you can get 100 back? It's the greatest gamble in the world and you're up against Mother Nature." He nodded. "She knows a lot more about wheat than I do." He bit his lip and went on. "Just think—every year we plant something and every day it's a gamble. You never know until you have that crop in the elevator if you are going to survive or not. It's just the most exciting thing around . . . I think. Wouldn't you think so?"

"I never looked at it that way."

"You've got a contract. You stick it out nine months and the school board pays your salary. You know you're going to get paid. A farmer doesn't. That's exciting to me."

"You've done well with it."

Earl's teeth showed behind his grin. "I like to think I've won my share. But you didn't come out here to talk about farming. What's in your craw?"

Miles ran over the dust-up with the superintendent and the letter he had sent the board. Earl was silent, nodded his head a time or two before Miles finished, then took another long swallow of the beer, smacked his lips, and smiled.

"Your problem is that you're trying to educate the kids. The school system is set up to teach them. Now what you need to do is find a way to educate them while the school board thinks you're teaching them." He shook his beer at Miles. "Remember when I met you in the gym and asked if you were going to educate our kids? Remember that?"

"Yes."

"Well—now you're into the machinery of making a difference. It isn't as easy as they taught it in school, is it?"

"Nope. And Calvin Brooks, dear Mr. Brooks, is trying to slam the door shut on outside help."

"You've gotta work with Brooks. He runs that place and the board backs him up. And it won't get easier until you get skilled at educating the kids while at the same time, teaching them enough to pass the tests the school system has worked out for them. Now how do you think you can do that?"

Miles leaned back full into the chair, rested his head on the leather back, and thought about Earl and the joy and peace of being wealthy, having your children almost out of school, having a beer in front of a fireplace chatting, with your wife finishing supper in the kitchen. He turned to Earl.

"The students have to pass a state test on the subjects before graduation. The question is how do I bring Billy up to the test level? I might be able to educate him outside of school, but will he have learned enough of what the state requires to make it out of school or will he simply quit and be a statistical drop-out?"

"He's not going to pass it doing what he's been doing," Earl said. "Brooks and the school board are gonna require you to continue that process. You can't keep that up and win."

"Right."

"We agree he needs to be educated. Needs to know where to find information and how to digest it and use it in his life. Now—how to apply that to knowing enough to graduate from this school system we've set up in Oregon." Earl upended his beer and set the empty bottle on the floor. "How much will Billy help?"

"A lot. He is really delving into the lumber grading manual. I expect him to start grading the wood in the library table and the desks soon."

"Somehow you've gotta get him to want to know the test information." Earl thought a minute. "Are there other kids like him?"

"Yes. Three in high school."

"Can you get them to form a club and pump each other up?"

"Shoot—I don't know."

"Could you try?"

"Well, sure, I can try. What's your point?"

Earl raised his hand and stabbed the air with his forefinger. "The point is," his smile broadened, "there is something those three kids have in common that can motivate them to learn enough—just enough—to pass the state test and still be educated. Does that make sense to you?"

Miles turned the words over in his head. *A common bond, a common goal, a common what . . . ?* He drank the rest of the beer and pointed the neck of the bottle at Earl. "If there is, I'll find it, come hell or high water."

"Atta boy. And don't forget Brooks. He has to be neutralized. You can do it. Get the townspeople and ranchers on your side. Make

sure he knows you're running a parallel program, one for graduation and one for vocation." A big smile took over his face. "And for
cryin' out loud, quit tickin' him off." He pointed at the bottle in
Miles's hand. "Want another beer?"

"No, thanks. It will dull my thinking about this and I've got to
get home to milk the cow before she explodes."

"Never saw one explode yet. Oh, they'll beller a lot but not
explode." He scratched his balding head. "They get to be a nuisance,
don't they?"

Miles nodded. "Only had her a week, but we've already deter-
mined one cow is too much milk for two people."

"Takes an army," Earl said. "Thanks for coming out. I enjoyed
our little talk."

"Me too. I'll let you know what I come up with."

"You do that. Drive safely now. That's a steep hill going into town."

CHAPTER 12

AT BAND PRACTICE, NOLAN handed Miles a flyer announcing a jazz band contest at the district music festival scheduled for early spring. "How about we form a jazz band?"

"We could do that. Who did you have in mind?"

Nolan smiled.

Smiles a lot like Earl. Like father like son.

"I was thinking that was your job," he said, his smile broadening.

Miles looked at the flyer. It specified no more than seven instruments. "We could use the whole band and then thin it out when we go to the contest. Any ideas for music?"

"You bet."

"Bring it on and I'll see if we have enough in the music kitty to buy it." Miles asked for quiet on the stage. Tommy hit a beat.

"Nolan just handed me a flyer announcing a jazz band contest at the district music festival. How many interested in being in the jazz band?"

Every hand went up.

"Whoa . . . the limit is seven members. Anybody want out? No? Okay—here's what we'll do. We'll all practice the jazz music and thin the band down to seven if we get to go to the festival."

Carla raised her hand. "What do you mean *if* we get to go?"

"We may not have the money or an instructor."

There was complete silence. Tommy hit a beat, then said: "We'd all strike if that happened. Now that we've learned how to march, we could at least have a protest march."

"We'd do that too," Nolan said.

Miles held up his hand. "Okay. Let's get serious here. We've got music to get ready for the game Friday and the Cinerama and the Christmas program."

The game music went first. Notes were attacked at the same time by the right instruments; Tommy and the other drummers had the rhythm and volume just right.

What an improvement. Joyful sounds, and they are enjoying it. And I'm enjoying it. Wait until we get the uniforms and they look like a real band. We'll knock 'em dead.

"That's great, guys. Really good."

They ran through the Christmas music—two pieces. Miles separated them into two groups at opposite ends of the gym, those playing in the dance band for the barbeque and the others to practice their parts of the Cinerama music.

When fourth period was over, Miles watched the students exit the gym and then in a vacuumed rush, the quiet floated down on him. He walked over and sat on the bleachers and rested his head in his hands. It was like death: one minute there is noise, light, confusion, laughter, and the next minute it's quiet, light fades, and that thing called tranquility settles on all objects within, animate and inanimate. He felt himself breathe, played with it until he could feel the membranes of his lungs expand, the air cooling his nostrils. *What have I gotten into coming here? Had I been so desperate?* The five-minute bell rang. He stood, took a deep breath and headed across the parking lot to the stone school building.

HE WROTE THREE NOTES, sealed each in a plain envelope and asked Carla to deliver them to Billy Canfield, Don Schiebel, and Warren Kirby as she went about the last two periods. Carla handing out sealed envelopes would be a lot less conspicuous than a teacher's doing it.

Billy took his to the restroom. It asked him to come to the sports locker room tomorrow at 12:45 and bring pen and paper. Don folded the envelope and put it in the bib pocket of his overalls.

He'd read it later. Warren gave it to his sister to read to him. He could have read it but he had problems with cursive writing. He could read typed words pretty good. It was the cursive that ate him up.

How each would react to his note was left for Miles to guess. At home he put triumphant records on the turntable, started the record player and relaxed in his chair. Eyes closed, he let them play one by one, adding cement to the blocks of his thoughts, stiffening his resolve to educate the pupils entrusted to him for this year. How could he pass them, let them go out into the world and get chewed up by society? There was no oath to be taken by a teacher, except in his heart. There had been no discipline of the teachers who had passed them grade after grade. They were gone now. But the soup they left behind needed ingredients and salt and he intended to be that cook. It mattered that the student body had dwindled to forty from the more robust 100 of years past and would drop year by year until someone, probably Calvin himself, would turn the key in the main door, locking it forever. It mattered to this class and these individuals. They had to be taught enough to graduate but they had to be educated to make a way for themselves in the world they were maturing in.

"Are you through resting?" Ele asked.

Miles spoke without opening his eyelids. "I'm working."

"You could fool me." She spread her arms. "I'm working and supper is ready."

He let Dvorak's 7th Symphony finish before he turned the phonograph off, rose from his chair, and sat at the table.

"What's your problem?" Ele said.

"I'm not sure I've articulated it correctly until now. But it seems I have two goals to reach: one to get the slowest kids to learn enough to graduate and secondly to educate them to the ways of the world they are going to run into with poor school experience." He buttered the bread and took a bite. "Ummm, good butter. You're getting better at this butter business."

"Did I make it too salty?"

He shook his head. "It's great."

"Good Spot. She is the gift that just keeps on giving. When the baby comes I hope she's still producing."

"Should be. The baby's due—"

"—End of May."

"Hmmm, in time for graduation."

"I'd like to graduate from this morning sickness. It leaves me woozy and depressed. I've never been depressed before."

"Is that normal?"

"Doc says it is, but what does he know? He's a man and so far history has not recorded a man having any children. I'm thinking I'm being seen by a spectator, not a practitioner."

"Keep eating the butter. The kid will slide out."

"Aren't we humorous tonight."

Miles raised his eyes. "Are you going to be able to handle the depression?"

"I will if I get a little help from you."

He looked down at his plate and swallowed. He reached over and took her hand. "I need to be here—at home, more for you. We're both first timers, aren't we? You with the baby and me with teaching. Do you think we're separating while we're both learning what to do?"

Ele shook her head. "It's not that so much." She turned and looked out the window, her eyes glistening. "It's getting to know each other and me being alone all day. Yes—the animals help, but they can't talk. They don't know what being pregnant is and away from my family and there isn't another pregnant woman in this blessed town, just older women who have been through it. Yes—you'll live through it, they say."

"When do they say that?"

"You know. When I go down to get the mail or go to the store for something. I run into them. They're all smiles and nod their heads and tell me how beautiful I look, and want to know when the baby is due and have we decided on a name yet. All that stuff."

"Is that tough?"

"Not really." She smiled. "Then there's that crazy Bernie Hall."

"What's with him?"

"He thinks he's a king and I'm his queen. You should see him. Sometimes he bows so low I think he'll topple over."

"I thought he worked days at the mill. What's he doing in town when you go down there?"

"He's on swing shift for a month. He is cute. If you hadn't of taken advantage of me at Portland State, I could have gone for him."

"You wouldn't be out here if I hadn't met you in Portland."

"Well—there is that."

He massaged the back of her hand with his thumb. Then he lifted it to his lips and kissed it. "I'll try harder."

"Umm," she said.

AT 12:45 P. M. BILLY, Don, and Warren showed up in the locker room. Miles locked the door from the inside. The boys sat on the bench with open expressions. Miles had gone over this scene several times by himself, but now, facing it, the prospects for success seemed dim. He had to find out where they were before he could get to them, energize them. Everybody starts someplace. Where was that starting line with these kids? An old Chinese proverb came to him; he smiled.

"Gentlemen, a journey of 1,000 miles begins with a single step. We are going to take that first step today. Thank you for coming. Please take out your writing materials, put your name on the paper and tell me anything you remember about history of anything, here in Tamarack, in Oregon, in the U.S., or the world. Just mention the item, like the Flood of '49. On the bottom half of the paper write anything you remember about geography anywhere. Mountains, rivers, deserts, anything you recall. Do that for fifteen minutes, then get to your next class. Okay?"

They looked at him with blank faces. Billy's lower lip hung down.

"Look—you can talk with each other if you want to. The list doesn't have to be long. Write it now."

Miles went to the equipment cage and sat down out of sight. It was quiet in the locker room, the smell of sweaty clothing drifting out of the lockers, the acrid scent of chlorinated water dripping in the showers and the occasional shuffling and whispering breaking through from time to time.

At the five-minute bell he collected the pages from the boys and unlocked the door.

The three filed out of the locker room door, missing the band students arriving for fourth period.

Good thing. There could have been questions with those three in here.

He could hardly wait until he got home to look at the three pages folded in his pocket. He was tempted to read them before the bus took off, but didn't want anyone asking any questions.

At home he put "Hannaford Overture" on the phonograph, sat, and opened the three folded pages. Eleanor brought him a beer. He took out his pen and read the first one, then the second and third. He laid the papers in his lap, his eyes blinking and moisture damming up in the corners. He looked straight ahead as the tears escaped his eyes, ran down his cheeks, and dropped on his shirt.

Ele took the papers from his hands, looked at each of them, and handed them back, the music and the slow tears ending now and she understood.

"There's hardly anything on them."

Miles nodded.

They had come this far and worked this hard only to find some of the kids had stopped learning before they ever got there, had walked along a level road not challenged, not excited, not having found anything to motivate them to move beyond basic communication. They could dress themselves, show up for school, buy something at the store, work, talk on a telephone, but nobody asked them to do better than they did. They were prisoners of the system—the teaching system that assumed every kid learned at the same pace from the same material from different teachers. These kids weren't dumb—they had just been turned off.

"What are you going to do?" Ele asked.

Miles shook his head. "I don't know. I just don't know."

"Do you want another beer?"

"No thanks." He laid the papers on a side table, rubbed his face with his hands and let out his breath. He was silent a minute before he pounded the side table with his fist. "This is the end of teaching and the beginning of educating from top to bottom. I don't care what the curriculum dictates. These kids are going to pass the state test and they are going to seek education to do their part in this world. They can't take up food and water and space without producing."

"Go get 'em cowboy."

He grabbed her and pulled her onto his lap. "You're such a big help. Never a discouraging word." He nuzzled her neck.

"We cowgirls never give off a discouraging word," she said, arms around his neck. "But Miles . . . would you please consider getting approval from Calvin first, before implementing whatever it is you're planning?"

"Was that a question or a request?"

"A question, I guess." She hunched her shoulders against his chest. "I'm concerned for your job . . . our job and our home and life. If they fire you, what do we do then?"

He kissed her bare shoulder. "They're not going to fire me. Where would they find a replacement for such a fine fellow as myself?"

"Well—there's that."

ON FRIDAY, SCHOOL WAS let out, and all of the Tamarack teachers drove to John Day to participate in the annual teachers' orientation day, where they would get updates from the state Superintendent of Education and the president of the Oregon Education Association which, for all intents and purposes, was the teachers' union. Membership was not mandatory, but recommended for a teacher's career. It had been in existence since 1858 and very much liked 100 percent participation by school district employees.

Hedi Martin, current president of the OEA, approached Miles in the hall. She reached out an arm, at the end of which was a paper.

"Good morning, Mr. Foster. I see that you are the last remaining teacher from Tamarack to join the OEA. Please fill out this application and I'll process it while we're here today." She reached into her purse for a pen. "It will be so good to have 100 percent from Tamarack. We always have had." She offered him the pen.

"Good morning, Madam President. It's good to see the state staff in our district. I have chosen not to join the OEA."

She looked confused, flustered. "Have I done something to offend you?"

Miles shook his head. "Not at all, Mrs. Martin. But after reading the goals and aspirations of the OEA, I find they conflict with my philosophy about instructing students in towns like Tamarack."

She laid her hand on his forearm. "Miles—may I call you Miles?"

He nodded.

"Miles, the OEA has been in existence since 1858 and we have over 4,000 school district employees in our membership . . . ."

"—I'm aware of that. But we've got serious issues that are not being addressed. Where is the OEA and the state when students are being passed in grade without knowing the information? What is the position on superintendents who harass teachers trying to improve student situations? Why are letters sent to you not answered? In fact, all of these are being glossed over by the school board, the superintendent, and the OEA—"

"—There will always be those areas. When you join the OEA I'm sure we can find a forum for you to express your ideas. In the meantime, your membership will greatly strengthen the position of Tamarack in making its voice heard in OEA meetings."

"Thank you, Madam President, but no, thank you." He moved around her.

She spun. "Miles . . . it will mean a lot if your school has 100 percent enrollment."

He turned, smiled and shook his head. "What will it do for the students?"

She stopped, feet spread, her arms holding the membership folder across her chest. "This is not going to look good on your resume."

He shrugged his shoulders, a slight smile lighting his lips.

"I will have to inform Superintendent Brooks of your decision. He is expecting 100 percent from his teachers."

Miles turned into the men's room. When he reached the paper towel dispenser, he realized Madam President was right behind him. "I don't take lightly to your refusal to join. It is almost mandatory that teachers become members. Do you know that all the other teachers are fighting for your rights in the state and you are being a block in the pipeline of educational success in Oregon."

Miles held up one finger. "Do you realize your office has not replied to one of my requests? Has not sent anybody to review the circumstances in our school? Our students are not being poorly served—they are being neglected. And you ask me to join an organization like that?"

"I'll get right on that, just as soon as you fill out this application."

"I'll fill out the application when I learn that the organization is effective, working on its basic principles."

"You will find that I do not take no for a final answer."

"Madam President—do you know that you are in the men's room?"

"I want every teacher in this state to join so we can fight for you."

"You should do your battles in the hall, not in the men's bathroom. Now, if you'll excuse me I am going to do what I came in here to do."

She looked around, froze, turned, and scuttled to the door.

THE REST OF THE day was spent hearing speeches and checking out the displays and vendor booths offering textbooks and other school supplies. Miles noticed Hedi close to Calvin with him bending to hear her and while neither of them looked his way, he could tell from the ear-burn they were talking about him.

AT THE JOHN DAY music store, aptly named Wood, Brass and String, Miles thumbed through the jazz scores for something suitable. He picked "Sweet Georgia Brown." It would resonate with the audience as the Globe Trotters' theme song, had a small number of instruments, and looked easy to play. The new Tamarack Jazz Band could earn their chops on that. At the counter he took out his wallet and paid for it.

By the time Calvin gets around to deciding if we have any money in the budget for jazz music the contest will be over.

MILES GOT HOME LATE afternoon on Sunday, kissed Ele hello, and flopped on the seven-foot couch they had bargained from his cousin and her husband who couldn't get it through the six-foot door of their new house.

"Pooped?" Ele asked.

"Entirely. And a lot irritated, somewhat mad with a tinge of get even-ness riding in my powerful body."

"Ooooohhhhhuuuuu . . . that sounds like a miserable set of ingredients. What can the Queen offer to the King to relieve these ghastly symptoms?"

"What does the Queen have available?"

Ele put her index finger on her chin. "The Castle has beer in the fridge, fresh eggs and milk, soft music, a hot shower, and matrimonial entanglement."

"And those are all available in this single establishment?"

"They are." She shrugged. "They come with the highest recommendations."

"Does one need an appointment?"

"My calendar is clear at the moment."

"I'll take them all. Where do I start?"

MILES LOOKED AT THE clock on his kitchen wall and picked up the phone. On the fourth ring Mr. Canfield picked up with a hoarse "hello."

"Mr. Canfield," Miles began. "This is Miles Foster calling . . . Billy's teacher. I would like your permission to administer a test to your son. I need something to tell me where he is in his ability to do some special work in history and geography. Only you and your wife and Billy will know the results of the test—and me, of course."

"What kinda test is it, Mr. Foster?"

"It is called an IQ test but it really tests Billy's ability to grab the essence of what is in the state prescribed textbooks. He needs to learn enough to graduate and then be comfortable in the world around him."

"He doesn't need to graduate. I've only got an eighth grade education and me and the wife are doin' okay."

"I understand. But you see—the world has changed since you were in high school. Jobs require more education, more ability to grasp new concepts. You know he's reading the lumber grading manual—"

"—Yeah, saw him reading that thing. He thinks he wants to work at the mill instead of farm work. The wife and me don't mind that, we're only leasing the farm so there's nothing to pass on to him anyways."

"If he's up for it then, do I have your permission?" Miles took a breath and held it. He heard a hand go over the phone and a mumbled female voice then the hand was removed.

"We don't know about this test. We never was tested as such. Don't seem like something we should be allowing the school to do."

"It isn't the school, Mr. Canfield. It's me doing it." Miles switched hands on the phone and dried the other one on his pants leg. "I think you'll find out a lot about your son and we'll both be able to help him when he graduates."

"Like what are we gonna find out?"

Miles swallowed and bit his lip. "We'll find out where he is amongst his peers, what his life's work ought to be, what basic life's skills he's in command of . . . " Miles couldn't put a period on it. He held his breath. He could hear muffled talk back and forth between the Canfields, like Canfield had his hand over the receiver. He could only make out one statement: "What's he gonna learn from that?" Then Canfield came back on the line.

"Lemme talk to the Mrs. and I'll call you back in a few minutes?"

"Sure. Sure. I'll be right here. Thank you Mr. Canfield."

Miles spun around, picked up the phone book and threw it at the door.

"And just what's that all about?" Ele said

"They're going to think about it. Think about it! What's there to think about? Their kid has flunked all through school, been moved on, and isn't going to be ready to figure out anything. They've got to let me test him so I know where to go and what to do to educate him."

"Seems he already taught you a thing or two about welding," Ele said, picking up the phone book.

Miles chuckled. "Well—he did that."

"Maybe he knows a thing or two about cow milking and chickens too."

"Oh come on, Ele. Help me here."

"I'm saying there are many areas of understanding and expertise that are not tested on an IQ test, especially one that you're likely to find for high schoolers."

The phone rang and Miles and Ele looked at it. It rang again. Miles took a deep breath and lifted the receiver to his ear. "This is Miles."

"When's he gonna take this test? We need him home after school to do chores. Can't have him hanging around in town, you know."

"I'm pretty sure I can get it done during the school day."

"Yeah, okay," Mr. Canfield said. "The missus and me agree then, but only if Billy wants to."

"Thank you, Mr. Canfield. And thank your wife for me too."

"I'll do that."

The phone calls to the Schiebels and Kirbys went about the same.

First things first. Now—where to get the tests and how to pay for them.

CHAPTER 13

DURING SECOND PERIOD, THE mail truck pulled into the school parking lot. Miles had a dual hit of elation and fear that met in his middle when he saw the rear gate lift to expose boxes and boxes stacked together. He excused himself from class and went down the stairs two at a time, hollering at Roscoe as he passed him on the landing.

Miles waved at the driver. "Over there," he shouted, pointing to the gym.

The driver backed the truck up to the gym and climbed out of the cab with a smile on his face as he slipped on his U.S. Mail cap. "Gotta bunch of boxes for you from Indiana. They ain't heavy but there's a lot of 'em."

Miles opened the gym door, turned, and saw Superintendent Brooks looking out of the second story window. He stood framed in the glass like a painting on an ancient castle wall—still, unmoving.

"They go in here," Miles said, leading the way to the closets on the stage floor.

Roscoe grabbed a box. "They ain't heavy."

The three of them unloaded a dozen boxes.

"I'm to collect the balance for these . . . that's $1,550 including the shipping."

"It was only $1,400," Miles said.

"Well, let me see here." He handed the billing to Miles. On the billing it noted the sales price of $1,500 plus shipping of $50. Then in bold it said: $150 deposit refunded. Collect full $1,550 upon delivery."

Miles tugged his ear lobe. "How can that be? I didn't get the deposit back."

He looked up at the window where moments before Calvin Brooks had been standing. He was gone. Miles pulled out his checkbook, wrote the check and handed it to the driver.

The truck was gone before Calvin came over to the gym between classes. He came up the steps and stood on the stage with his arms crossed over his chest. Miles and Roscoe had just taken out a uniform to shake and place on a hanger when Calvin lifted his head, nostrils flared. "How did you acquire these uniforms, Mr. Foster?"

"Sir—I borrowed the money and we'll pay it back with the dance and barbeque. It's all set, Billy and I built a barbeque rack, Earl Benson donated half a beef, and we're gonna make enough to pay for them."

"How did you pay for them now?"

"I wrote a personal check."

"I see. Are there sufficient funds in your account to cover that?"

Miles shook his head. "No."

Calvin moved his head up and down in what might pass for a nod. "Then you have written a non-sufficient funds check?"

"I guess you could call it that."

"What else would you call it?"

"A note to pay?"

"I hardly think so."

Miles shoved the bill of lading in front of Calvin. "This invoice says the deposit of $150 was returned. I didn't get it. Who got it?"

Calvin stared at it. "I expressly told you not to buy the uniforms." He turned and walked off the stage, his footsteps echoing through the gym like rocks dropping in a well.

Miles and Roscoe stood and looked at each other. It was if a lightning bolt had split the roof and burned a hole in the stage floor.

"He can't just take my money," Miles said.

"Looks like he already has," Roscoe said.

"That's not right."

"It's not right maybe, but he runs this place. You might hafta live with that."

"Now I've got to raise the whole amount."

"Yup. Seems like a ton of money doesn't it?"

"It is. It is." Miles looked behind him and then sat in a chair.

Roscoe took out his pocketknife and opened the boxes. There were five uniforms in each box. The extra two boxes contained a surprise: majorette's uniforms, a baton, and a director's uniform with an envelope.

Dear Mr. Foster,

We had to get the uniforms out of our storage to make room for the new ones and, even though we have not received payment, I am shipping these to you on the condition that you pay when you receive them. Hoping that is okay with you. There was a note from my office telling me someone had called from your school about the uniform purchase, and they had refunded the deposit, but I mislaid it. If this is not suitable to you, please call me.

As an extra, I've added the majorette's uniforms, boots, and the director's uniform. Hope they fit. Since our boosters have provided me with a new baton I'm including the one I've had for ten years. It has served me well and it leaves here with our best wishes to you and your band.

Good luck.

Jason Wrigley
Bandmaster

Miles took the baton in his hand. It was strong and light and the cork grip felt good in his hand. He made a couple of beats with it and Roscoe lifted his arms pretending to play a trumpet. They erupted in laughter together.

The rest of that day, Miles avoided Calvin Brooks and kept the back of his mind full of visions of the band—his band—marching down Main Street in the new uniforms before the game, before the barbeque, before anything and everything. Waiting for band class to meet fourth period was causing his scalp to itch. He ran a fingernail down the part. He skipped lunch, went to the gym stage, and hung the rest of the uniforms on hangers. He put the caps in a row by size. When the five-minute bell rang he was ready and in they came.

He raised his arms. "Line up by height."

A brief shuffle as the students aligned themselves, Nolan first and Tommy last. "There are fifty-two uniforms in various sizes with the smaller ones on the left going up to the larger ones. Try on the coats first. If they fit, take the pants and go to your respective locker rooms and try them on. Get a uniform that fits you even if you have to trade pants and coats. Plenty of hats as well—get one that doesn't touch your ears. When you've got a uniform, please assemble on the stage in marching order. Dismissed."

In fifteen minutes they stood on the stage admiring each other's fit. Nolan had deliberately taken the smallest hat and perched it on his head like a golf ball on a tee. He had one hand behind his back and as soon as Miles started toward him, he grinned and put a fitting hat on.

They spent the rest of the period marching around the gym, eyeing each other, smiling and stroking the uniforms. They marched in smart lines, made sharp turns and came to a stop in front of the stage. Miles, standing above them, held out his arms. "Wonderful. Put a piece of tape in the coat, write your name on it, hang it with the pants and put the cap above it and get to fifth period. You look great and I'm so proud of you I'll bust if you don't go right now. Dismissed."

BILLY LOOKED UP FROM his book and started to raise his hand, then got out of his chair by the usual process and walked up to Miles's desk, laid the lumber grading manual down and pointed to a word.

"How do you pronounce that?" he said.

"No-tay-shun," Miles whispered. "It means making a note of it or giving it a mark or something that defines it. Here it means the stamp the grader puts on the lumber for moisture content."

Billy nodded, his mouth part way open. "Oh. Thanks."

"Billy—do you understand it?"

He nodded. "I think I do."

"Write it for me in a sentence and bring it up to me."

In ten minutes Billy slid out of his chair and came back to the front of the room, slid a piece of ruled tablet paper onto Miles's desk and stood bent at the knees with his arms crossed over his chest, his eyes on the paper.

The grader made a notation on his tablet of the 2x4's.

Miles looked at it and nodded as he read. "Okay, that's close enough. You see, Billy, you want to know these words. You want to own them so you can use them whenever you want to. They tell the world what Billy Canfield is thinking. To own them you have to be able to pronounce them and use them in language. Use 'notation' four times today and you'll own it. It'll be yours. Here—" he handed him a piece of chalk. "Write the assignment for tomorrow on the board."

Billy took the chalk, held it, looked at it. He had never written on a blackboard. He turned to face the blackboard, hesitated with head down and finally lifted his hand and wrote: Chapter 8, "Thunder Over the Ochoco," and handed back the chalk.

Miles looked him in the eye. "You just wrote a . . . ." He nodded toward Billy.

"Notation."

"Say it out."

Billy moved his left foot and stood leaning back. "I wrote a notation."

"Only three more to go," Miles smiled and dismissed the class.

When the room was empty. Miles took the chalk and wrote on the blackboard:

The greatest waste in the world is the difference
between what we are and what we could be.
—Ben Herbster
(Note to Janitor: Do Not Erase)

Ralph was in the back of his grocery store stacking sacks of flour when Miles walked through the door, ringing the bell that hung over the transom.

"Be with you in a minute," Ralph shouted from the back room.

"No rush, Ralph. Miles here."

"Fresh coffee's in the pot there by the cookies. Cream and sugar."

"Thanks." Miles smelled the coffee. "When did you make it?"

"This morning."

"It's five o'clock, Ralph."

"Aw, taste it—you'll like it. New blend in from Portland." He came out of the back room with flour residue on his apron, shoe tops, and lanky arms. "What do you need today?"

"Information."

"On what?"

"Who is the oldest pioneer around these parts?"

Ralph stuck his tongue between his teeth, licked the corner of his mouth and let his eyes roam the ceiling. "I'd guess it's gotta be J. D. Wharton."

"You suppose he'd come in and talk with the students?"

"About what?"

"History of this county. The old days, farming, ranching, the Indians, floods . . . the whole kit and caboodle."

"You can ask him. I bet he would. You might have trouble stopping him once he gets started," Ralph chuckled. "He does like to go on." He put a foot up on a barrel and brushed the flour off a shoe. "What'd you have in mind?"

"I haven't been able to make the state required history as fresh and entertaining as I'd like. I want to bring in some real life history that they can relate to. Get them excited about where they're living and the people that have been here before them. Put them in personal touch with the people and the land."

Ralph nodded. "I see. Well—you couldn't find anyone who can talk about it better than old J. D. "

"You have his phone and address?"

"He doesn't like to talk on a phone. His address is just general delivery, Tamarack. He doesn't write well."

"Thanks, Ralph. Always a well of information."

"You don't want to buy anything?"

"Not today. How about me selling you some milk and eggs. We're starting to store up next year's supply already."

"Got all that I need. But if you get some fertile eggs I could sell those."

"I'll talk to Ele about that. To her, it will probably be like selling the unborn child."

"Know what'cha mean. Take it easy now."

SATURDAY MORNING J. D. WHARTON was standing in line at the post office waiting for the mail to be distributed when Miles approached him.

"Mr. Wharton, I'm Miles Foster, teacher at the high school. Could I buy you a cup of coffee and pick your brain?"

"Ain't had nobody call me Mr. Wharton since I went to court ten years ago. Name's J. D. and I get my coffee free over at the grocery store."

A slight smile slipped across Miles's face. "I'm talking fresh coffee and I'm paying for it. I'll even throw in a cinnamon roll if you like them."

"By the time the coffee gets past my upper plate I can't taste it anyways, but I'll take you up on your offer just as soon as my mail gets here. What'd you want to talk about?"

"History. Can you talk about the history of this country for an hour?"

"I can talk about it for a day or a week if I can eat and drink in between."

"You're my kinda guy."

"What's this talkin' pay?"

"Pay?"

"Well, yah. You get paid don't you?"

"I'm on contract."

"You get paid for teaching history."

"Yes."

"Well—why not pay me for talking history?"

Miles chuckled. "I'll see if we have money in the budget for that."

"That's more like it. Where you fixin' to go for coffee and this cinnamon roll you're braggin' about?"

"The only restaurant in town."

"I'll meet you there in a few. Gotta get my mail and then I'll be over."

Miles sat in one of the three booths, its upholstery showing the scarring of people sliding across them with keys, sheath knives, and metal buttons. He told Pamela he was waiting for J. D. and they wanted two fresh coffees and two cinnamon rolls.

"As soon as I see his face in the door, I'll get the rolls," she said. She had graduated three years ago, married a local handyman and lived in one of the rental units across the canyon. "I hear you all got new band uniforms."

"They're used but new to us and in good shape."

"When you coming down through town again?"

"Friday before the game. We'll make sure to play a tune in front of the café for you."

"Great. I'd like that a lot." She looked up. "Oh, here comes J. D."

There had been some great strength in his legs and shoulders when he was formed. Over forty years farming and cattle work had broken him down, but the framework was still there even though it shuddered every time he plopped a foot down on the linoleum floor. He scooted into the booth and tossed his mail on the table. Pam had the two coffees, still steaming, on the table by the time J. D. got settled.

"Cinnamon rolls coming up. Morning J. D."

J. D. looked at her and adjusted his bifocals. "Pamela—when you gonna leave that failed plumber and run away with me?"

"Where we goin' J. D.?"

"My ranch."

"That's not far enough. He'd find us there."

"Oh—you mean he still wants you?"

"It's what he says."

"Well, nuts . . . I need a good woman and I thought you'd fill the bill."

"Why don't you hire one?"

"I don't want to pay for the work. I want a wife."

"You've never had one. What makes you think you want one now?"

"I was thinking the next eighty years would be different."

Pamela chuckled. A dinger went off. "Rolls are ready. Be right back."

J. D. turned to Miles. "Always like to kid her. Her daddy worked for me a spell back before the war. He was a nice guy—just couldn't keep his goals straight. Always lookin' over the fence at greener grass."

She slid the cinnamon rolls in front of them, their icing blending with the melting butter and sliding down the side of the bun, a sweet warm fragrance pushing off the plate. "There ya go."

"What'd ya want to talk about?" J. D. said as he chucked a corner of the roll past his mustache into his mouth.

"Education."

J. D. moved the food around in his mouth, looked out the window and took a swig of coffee to wash it down, sat back, and looked at Miles. "That's a big subject."

"It is indeed. The problem here is that I've got kids who are reading at fifth grade level and kids at sophomore in college level and all in between and a state mandated course of study that's supposed to fit them all into it."

J. D. was shaking his head. "It never has worked. Everyone thinks we've got an egalitarian population and they're trying to make them all fit in the same mold." He took a sip of coffee. "Look at me. I've only got an eighth grade education but I've studied my whole life. I know more history than the professors teaching it. I can figure the weight and measure of my trucks and hay bales in my head and that isn't from school learning, that's from practical learning. That's from reading and learning on my own."

Miles lifted his hand. "And that's what I want to get across to some of these kids. They're not dumb. They just don't like the official learning system, haven't benefited by it, but more importantly, they don't see that it will help them in life. I need someone like you to show them that everyday life requires history and math and English and even band and sports."

"Yeah—that's true." J.D. wiped the crumbs off the table with his napkin and held his coffee cup in the air. "Can a man get a refill around here?"

"Can if he is polite about it and leaves a big tip," Pam shot back.

J. D. nodded at Miles. "He's buying and tipping. I'm just supplying valuable information, but I'm needing the coffee."

She filled both cups and removed the empty plates.

Miles sipped the coffee, looked over the rim at a man who had helped build the county, whose brain and brawn had shaped so many of the things the people enjoyed now. "Would you come talk to my classes. Pick a day, a Monday, Wednesday, or Friday and stay the morning. We get all three history classes on those days."

"How far back do you want me to go?"

Miles bobbed his head, looked at the ceiling. "Civil War forward."

"In an hour?"

"You want longer? We can do longer—several days if needed."

J. D. thought on it, looked out the window at the creek churning down the rock-strewn bed heading on its way to a bigger creek and to the John Day River. "You know, there is this personal responsibility thing that this country seems to be missing now. I'd like to bring that in. Showing what each person is taking from the earth and his personal responsibility for putting back in."

Miles nodded. It was silent except for the incomprehensible banter between Pamela and the cook drifting out over the otherwise empty café. J. D.'s lips pursed and he shoved his lower lip up over the top one and crossed his arms on the table.

"Wished I was younger now," J. D. said. "I have a few things to say to the world but nobody's listening."

"We are," Miles said. "When can you come?"

"Give me some time to put my thinking in order. Say three weeks from now?"

"Great. Done." Miles reached out his hand. "Thanks, J. D."

"I'll be in touch." He turned as he got out of the booth. "Thanks for the coffee and roll. That sure beat the grocery store coffee."

Miles left a two-dollar tip.

CHAPTER 14

Winifred Brooks smoothed the tablecloth with her free hand and set the cup of tea in front of Calvin. He stared at it, watching the steam rise, the color changing as the loose tea diffused in the Elks Lodge mug he liked for the process. He glanced up at the window to assure himself that there was light left in the day, then cupped his hands around the mug. "Thank you, dear."

"You're welcome, Calvin. Would you like a cookie with it?"

He shook his head and let a sigh escape his lips. "In forty years I have not had such an obstreperous teacher."

"Who are you talking about, dear?"

He looked at her. "Why, Mr. Foster, of course."

"Are you sure you mean obstreperous and not disobedient?"

"One or the other—I'm not sure anymore."

She lifted her tea to her lips, blew on it and sipped the cooled top layer. She waited for him to go on, content in their late-afternoon-before-supper ritual that allowed both of them to dispose of the day's troubles before eating.

"You know," Calvin began. "I have a list of things that he has done that just aren't right and against the regulations."

"You could fire him if you got the school board to go along with you."

"Yes, but how to find a replacement this time of the year."

"Is he ruining things or just annoying you?"

Calvin shrugged. "They might turn out all right, but so many things that I can hardly keep track of them."

"Like what lately?"

"Oh, the taking food from the kitchen; buying the band uniforms without my approval; letting students read materials outside of the curriculum; scheduling a barbeque and dance without approval . . . " He sipped his tea. "He found out I didn't return his deposit on the uniforms."

"I thought you canceled the uniform purchase?"

"I called. I did cancel them but they sent them anyway and he paid for them with a check that does not have sufficient funds."

"And you kept his deposit?"

He nodded.

She paused. Her eyes went to the window then back to Calvin. "Good for you. That should show him who's boss. Sounds like he goes his own road. Like he's running things."

Calvin nodded. "I feel like I'm irrelevant to his processes. Like I'm here only to sanction what he does."

Winifred chuckled. "You're the principal and superintendent. You're not irrelevant. You run the school." She sipped her tea. "What did you do with the deposit money?"

"It was a cashier's check. I cashed it."

"Yes, but what did you do with it, dear?"

"Well . . . temporarily I put it in our bank account."

She pursed her lips. "I see." She raised her head and looked at him. "We'll need to be able to explain that."

"I know. He launches into things on his own. The students and parents like what he does and most of the things are done by the time I find out about them, and then what? I shut them down or try to cancel them? That puts me at odds with everybody."

"But you're right, Calvin. You're in the right."

He nodded. "Sometimes in the right is hard to defend when you're alone."

"Then make a full report to the school board and enlist their support. Tell them what he's doing and why you are opposed to it and discipline him."

"That's easier said than done, Winnie. But yes . . . yes, I'll do that."

She settled back in her chair. It isn't enough that she listen to him and encourage him and back him up when needed; he had to take the first big step.

THE NEXT MORNING IN Oregon History class, Miles handed out the test with multiple choice questions and, while the students were busy, he dug through the papers piled in the bottom drawer of his desk, knowing that the state curriculum and test information had to have been in the huge packet he received the first day of school. In a crisp tan envelope was Oregon Achievement/Performance Standards. He hadn't opened it, but now was a good time. These were the requirements for graduation and they were the same for Billy, Don, and Warren as they were for Jay and Carla and Shelly and Richard and the Benson kids, Nolan and Rebecca, who were reading college textbooks in the same subjects that Billy was trying to read at fifth grade level.

A flush of guilt coursed through him as he realized that he had not read the requirements, had not opened the packet.

But there was so much to do: starting school, getting a house, helping with the football team.

He turned to the final pages where graduation expectations in geography and Oregon history were written out in plain language and read them in silence. A chuckle escaped him several times when he did not recognize the answer supplied. When finished, he rolled it up and propped his chin on it.

As if I could absorb it like this. Well—a ship sometimes gets off course so we correct the heading: we plan for the state test and get them educated at the same time.

Roscoe opened the door and reached in a large tan envelope. "Just came for you . . . thought you'd like to have it sooner rather than later."

Miles took the package. "Thanks, Roscoe. What's for lunch?"

"Chicken soup and baking powder biscuits." A smile crept over his face. "And I brought some of that raw honey I got from that old hollow log."

"Save me some."

"Yup."

The large envelope contained the IQ tests he had ordered for fifteen to eighteen year olds. He looked at the questions. He had never administered an IQ test, so he settled on taking them home even though he and Ele had a rule about bringing his work home. She, having lived with a father who brought his work home every evening and worked past the time she and her brother had gone to bed, did not want to live with that distraction in her household. Work and raising a family, milking a cow, feeding chickens and gathering eggs, was enough. Family needed to be like family: together, loving, interested, discussing their day, and enjoying one another. He'd just have to ask Ele for an exception, just this once. Although he believed in it, had agreed to it, this cause was too strong to let go another day.

The bell rang for noon lunch break and Miles stopped Billy as he walked by his desk.

"Billy, you've got cattle on your farm haven't you?"

Billy nodded.

"You have a squeeze chute?"

Bill nodded again.

"When you put a young bull in there, what do you do to him?"

"Inoculate him."

"You do more?"

The nod. "We castrate him."

"That all?"

"Brand and de-horn him."

Miles leaned back on his desk, his arms crossed in front of his chest. "We're putting you in a squeeze chute, Billy."

Billy's eyes widened.

"But we're only going to do two things—with your approval. Between now and the end of this school year you have two jobs that are very important. You are going to learn enough to pass the state test in Oregon history and geography and then, if you really want a lumber grading job, you are going to research, study, and plan to educate yourself to jump into that job when you graduate."

A grin formed on Billy's face.

"That sound all right to you?"

Billy nodded. "Yes sir."

Miles slapped him on the shoulder. "Good. Go get chow and save some of those biscuits for me."

After lunch, Miles cornered Don and Warren and gave them the same speech. Don wanted to work on the family ranch while Warren was already planning on the GMC pickup and sound system he was going to buy for it with his logging money as soon as he could get out of school.

"How much do you think you can make logging?" Miles asked.

"Twelve to fifteen thousand a year."

"That's more than I make," Miles said. "Three times as much."

"Yeah," Warren said, his face in a large grin.

"Does that seem right to you?"

Warren shrugged his shoulders. "I dunno."

"Well, think about it. I spent four years in college and get paid $4,200 a year to come over here and teach guys like you who leave high school and make $15,000."

"You get summers off."

Miles nodded. "Yes—I do."

"And you get to use the school bus for hunting."

"Who told you that?"

"I don't remember."

"Keep it to yourself, okay?"

Warren nodded. "I ain't never told nobody."

"That's a good start. You okay with the two goals then?"

"Yeah, I guess so."

"That's a firm commitment if I ever heard one."

CALVIN BROOKS, AT THE request of Miles Foster and Coach Donavon, and against his better judgment, decreed that lunch hour on Friday would extend for one-and-a-half hours to allow the band to march downtown prior to that afternoon's football game between the Tamarack Buffaloes and the Mt. Vernon Bears. It was a circus in the locker rooms as the band members got into their uniforms. They appeared on stage looking like they were in costumes, not uniforms.

"Hey, gang," Miles shouted. "Get tight. Button up those loose buttons, leave the top flap open, get your instruments, and look like a marching band."

They formed up on the parking lot. Roscoe slipped out of his pickup with camera in hand. They were in line and looked his way, and that photo would be on the second page of the annual.

Tommy hit a beat and the band moved in step en masse out of the parking lot, down the hill, and onto Main Street. Doors opened and the townspeople poured out onto the sidewalk on both sides as the band strode down the middle of the street to clapping and shouts. Pamela stood on the sidewalk outside the café clapping and smiling like she was still a cheerleader and not a mother, wife, and waitress in Tamarack.

The bass drum exploded, the pulsations reverberating from the buildings, the people smiling—it was their band—their sounds—and they took it in like sunshine. The percussion stiffened their backbones. The skin on the drum vibrated, it tickled something in each of them that had lain dormant for years. Took them back. Back to high school days—the men pulling on pads and helmets, the smell of steam and sweat—the girls cheering. Blood rushing through their bodies. The dance, the cokes, the band, the sneaked kisses in the dark. Young again. Oh God, to be young again.

They stopped in front of the café. Miles raised his baton. "Colonel Bogey's March" burst out of the trumpets. The drumheads vibrated. A WWII veteran, Rod Baumgartner closed his eyes, his lips whistling the melody. Pamela joined him. When the baritones and trombones chimed in, everybody started swaying. The sound they produced in that small canyon on that day would be remembered for years.

When the clapping died down, they hit the opening notes of "Stout Hearted Men." They marched to the end of the street, waved at Rod Baumgartner, executed a reverse march, coming back through the ranks with the brass hitting every note as the music pushed against the breeze blowing down the canyon from upstream. Pamela jumped and started marching in place, singing the words. Others followed until the whole boardwalk was puffing dust from the cracks as loafers and work boots pounded the thirty-year-old planking. At the General Store they stopped. Coach Donavon walked to the front of the crowd on the steps, his lower lip between his teeth. "There is a game with the Mt. Vernon Bears at 3 o'clock. The band . . . this band . . . will be there minus some of the football players. You'd like to hear them again, wouldn't you?"

The crowd exploded with clapping.

"There will be popcorn and snacks for sale to help pay for the new band uniforms."

The drum majorette whistled and brought her mace down with a sharp snap, starting the school pep song. The band, file by file, turned the corner and went up the hill, Tommy's drumbeat growing faint.

On the boardwalk, blood drained back down, the children started moving. Somewhere a car horn beeped, breaking the sudden quiet.

Afternoon classes were let out at 3 o'clock to go to the game. Buses were not to leave until after the game. It was game day and the Tamarack Buffaloes were in the arena.

Before the game started, the traveling pastor removed his hat and asked for a silent prayer in remembrance of the three young men killed just weeks ago. There was a rustle of hats being lifted. A silence settled over the field with only the wind ruffling the jackets and skirts as it danced over the dirt and grass.

How much to attribute to the band's march through town and how much to hand to the great weather that Friday was a point of discussion, but thirty-six people showed up, stood along the side lines, cheered, bought popcorn and overpriced candy bars, and took photos of the team and the pep band—short its football players and cheerleaders—and boosted the Buffaloes to a lopsided victory of 41 to 12.

MILES ARRANGED FOR BILLY, Don, and Warren to take the IQ tests on a Saturday between 10 a.m. and noon at the school. Roscoe would open it up and then leave so no cars would be in the parking lot. Miles would administer the tests in the typing room where there were no windows, and he would lock the door leading through the English department.

Ele helped him understand how the tests were to be administered. When he brought the work home, she balked at first. Her work at Portland State College had included giving entry tests and IQ tests, so she knew the drill. But she hadn't counted on Miles breaking their home rules so early.

She licked her fingers and turned the pages. "I haven't seen this one before, but it is similar to what we administered."

"Good," he said. "Now . . . brief me on the procedures."

"Sit closer, and don't ask a question without raising your hand."

"Yes, Momma."

"And don't call me Momma. I'm your wife until the baby is born."

"And after that?"

"Who knows? If I decide to have her in the manger there may be bigger things in our future."

Miles rolled his eyes. "I have a superintendent trying to run my school life and now I might have a savior born in our cow barn?"

"Play your cards right and we may give you a free pass to heaven."

"I'll need one after this session. Okay, hit me with the fundamentals."

TAKING THE TEST, THE students would never know if they made a mistake. With #2 pencils poised and heads down, they started shading in the circles that they thought were the correct answers to the questions.

They took a break at 11:00, then back at it at 11:10, and at noon Miles called a halt.

"Thanks, guys," he said as he picked up the papers. "This will help a lot."

After lunch he and Ele graded the tests.

"Well, they're not idiots. And they're not stupid either," Miles said.

"They are also not up to average intelligence."

"Who knows what average is out here?"

"American average."

"Plenty good enough for ranching, farming, logging or mill work—"

"—Or working for someone else who will direct them."

"You don't think they can direct themselves?"

She bobbed her head back and forth. "Maybe, if they can get their minds around it."

"Think I'll call their parents and give them the good news."

"Which is?"

"Their sons can make it—if they try harder."

"That should let them sleep well."

"Oh, shut up. They could probably graduate from Portland State."

"Not when I was there. You had to be able to tie both shoes."

He threw a pillow at her.

She screamed, "Spousal abuse. And I'm pregnant. Help! Help!"

"Go commiserate with Spot . . . she might be pregnant too."

"She's a cow."

"She's a girl. What difference does it make?"

CHAPTER 15

IT WAS STILL DARK when Miles awakened to Ele's moaning. Her arms lay across her forehead and she was moving her legs in slow motion like riding a bicycle. He reached over and shook her. She startled, then turned to look at him, eyes wide.

"Honey, I think you're having a bad dream," Miles said.

Ele held her stare, her face unchanged.

"You okay?"

She blinked twice. "Something's wrong. Get me to the doctor."

"Now?"

"My legs hurt like crazy."

Miles pulled the blanket off her legs and gasped. They were swollen like an elephant all the way to her knees, with beet red skin. Miles was taken back. He massaged them and noticed the tips of his fingers indented her flesh.

"Does that help?" Miles asked.

Ele shook her head. "No. I'm dying . . . I know it."

"You're not dying. You're a strong, young woman."

"Miles . . . get a bucket or pot . . . I'm gonna throw up."

"Let me help you to the bathroom."

"No, I'm gonna throw up now."

Miles ran into the utility room, grabbed a bucket and was almost to the doorway into the bedroom when she lost control. He stopped, went back, and got water in the bucket and some rags.

"I'm so sorry," she muttered, wiping her chin.

"No problem, honey. You couldn't help it."

"The baby made me do it."

"I know. "

"Please take me to the doctor?"

Miles nodded. He helped her dress. She was limp, her arms cool and moist as he guided her into the car.

"Can you drive any faster?" she asked.

"I can but there are a lot of deer in the fields. I don't want one to slip onto the highway and into the windshield."

"I don't care. Go faster, Miles," she said in a whisper before her head lolled to the side and her eyes closed.

FORTY-FIVE MINUTES LATER, they checked in at Prineville Memorial Hospital. The nurses took Ele on a gurney into the prep room, an IV already streaming into her arm delivering vital fluids drip by drip. Twenty minutes later a doctor arrived, hair mussed as he slipped a white gown over his pajama tops. When he emerged he walked toward Miles, removing his gloves. "Mr. Foster?"

"Yes, I'm Miles Foster."

"I've examined your wife. She has toxemia of pregnancy. Thankfully, it's in the early stages, but it can be quite serious if not recognized promptly and treated. With proper management she'll recover with no harm to herself or the baby, but she must rest and keep her legs elevated until the swelling lessens and her blood pressure comes down.

"Her blood pressure?"

"Very elevated. One of the first things we see in developing toxemia."

Miles paused, letting it sink in.

"What do we do?"

"She could develop kidney problems and even go into seizures if the condition worsens, so you don't want to neglect these symptoms. In addition to the bed rest with elevated legs at home, you must keep her away from salt and keep her well hydrated. Do you have a good water source at your home?"

"Yes, of course."

The doctor smiled and tilted his head. "Not always the case around here."

"How much should she drink?"

"Make sure she drinks at least eight glasses of water a day. And no alcohol."

"She hasn't been drinking any alcohol."

"Good . . . good. Well—" he reached out his hand. "I want to keep her here in the hospital overnight so I can reassess in the morning. If the blood pressure is improved and the leg swelling down, you can take her home."

Miles nodded. "Whatever you say, Doc."

The doctor turned as he walked away. "Oh, and I'll want to see her in a week. Please call my office and schedule an appointment. And should your wife begin to feel ill again, or you notice her legs swelling up, call immediately."

"We'll do that. Thanks, and sorry for disturbing your sleep."

The doctor smiled. "We learned this in residency. We did so much with so little sleep that we can now do anything with no sleep at all."

Miles snorted. "Good night, Doc."

THE HOSPITAL DID NOT release Eleanor Foster until the next evening. It took all day for the swelling to go down, followed by her blood pressure. Miles helped Ele to the car and they began the drive back to Tamarack. With Ele asleep and no other cars on the road, Miles looked at the stars through the windshield, and imagined how anybody could begin to count them. The half moon showing white now and sliding along the horizon seemed impossible to reach with a rocket from earth. Yet the government was going about doing just that. How high school science and physics would advance if that worked. He slumped behind the wheel.

So many changes taking place, and look at the moon. Does its light wash everything, everywhere? Will it wash relationships? Will it cover over writing a check I don't have money to pay? And what about me, school, wife, and upcoming family? Everything happening too fast nowadays. Every day something new. Something challenging me to get better, faster. Have I got it in me to give these kids what they need? There's the load. Why do I always challenge people? Challenge Brooks and buy uniforms? Now I have to pay for them. Involve other people, buy a popcorn machine, ask for short-term loans. Oh yeah—the chickens and the cow. Added to everything else, we've got animals expecting something from me every day.

ALL SUNDAY AFTERNOON, WHILE Eleanor slept, he went through the college level history and geography books he had ordered from the Oregon State Library. While Billy, Don, and Warren hacked away at fifth grade books, so Nolan Benson and his sister Rebecca, along with Carla, Shelly, and Brenda, were bored stiff with the high school materials. They needed stretching. Mind stretching. He also wanted some fieldwork for them so they could see how geography and history slid together to make and modify civilization. Some good projects to carry them through the year and earn their trust in higher education. He would be ready Monday morning to change the course of study described by the State Department of Education, and with God's help and the students' study they would meet the standards for graduation.

EARL BENSON SHOVED OPEN the door to Miles's classroom. "Where do you want it?"

"Hi, Earl. Want what?"

"The barbeque."

"It's done?"

"I welded a couple of pieces on but Billy had it almost done."

"Can you drop it off at the community center?"

"I can do that." Earl looked around, saw his kids Nolan and Rebecca in their seats, and smiled at them. "They learning anything?"

"I'm educating them."

He smiled and nodded. "Good . . . good. I'll drop it off at the community center." He turned to leave. "You're gonna need a pit, you know?"

"Why don't you dig that while you're there?"

Earl chuckled. "I might do that. I just might."

"Do you have a shovel?"

Earl shook his head. "No—and I'm not gonna get one." He let the door close as he slipped into the hallway.

At noon, Miles walked over to the community center and sitting over a well-dug pit was the finished barbeque unit. He smiled and shook his head. The ranchers around here were so resourceful that they could make anything out of stuff stored in their garages and shops.

THE MORNING SESSION WITH the college textbooks had gone well with the Tamarack Five, as he had started to refer to them in private. Wouldn't do to say it in front of others, but those five had the stars in alignment. Past tests in their student files had revealed their high IQs and comprehension skills. His job was to inspire them to put those to work in an enjoyable, taxing, rewarding way.

At noon, Coach Donavon had trouble keeping his chin out of his lunch and a bruise over his left eye told everyone the weekend had not gone well with him. Miles looked at him and decided to discuss last Friday's football game to keep him awake.

"The team played like a well-oiled machine Friday."

Donavon turned his head. "Thanks. It was a good score."

"Highest this year, isn't it?"

He nodded, lifted the soup to his lip that seemed swollen.

"And a good turnout. I counted almost fifty people there."

No response.

"What did you think, Marion?" Miles said.

"I didn't stay for it. We had a heifer calving and I had to get home."

"You mean a cow took precedence over our Buffaloes?"

"A thousand-dollar cow always takes precedence."

"Money, money, money—that's all you ranchers think about."

"It's the difference between having money for gas to drive to town or not," she said.

"Oh, lighten up, Marion. I'm just kidding." Miles said while stacking his tray.

"I know that, but you kid close to the line sometimes. Kinda prickles." She picked up her plate and cup and walked to the garbage can, threw her napkin away, set her tray down, and walked out of the cafeteria.

"Hmmm," Miles said. "Kinda ticked her off."

Donavon looked at him, then back at his soup. "Her time of the month."

Miles raised his eyebrows.

Shelly swung through the doors and sat next to Miles. "Anybody sitting here?"

"The occupant just left," Miles said.

"Could I get some private time with you on this new assignment? It looks a little beyond me. I could sure use your help."

"I'm always available during study hall if you want to come in."

Shelly put her folded hands on the table. "I was thinking private time." A slight smile crept around her lips.

"Like when?"

"Morning before school starts or after school."

Is this a come on or is she just being an eager student?

"Those are tough times for me, driving the school bus . . . "

"How about when you bring the bus back to the school?"

He nodded. "Well—I could do that."

"Great. Today okay?"

"I suppose."

"Great. See you then." She stood, spread her hands over her skirt, and walked out, leaving a sweet scent in the air.

Donavon looked up at him, his eyes dull, bloodshot, his forehead creased. "I'd be careful of that."

"She's a student needing help."

"Humph. She's a hot teenager with raging hormones and you in her sights."

Miles smirked, drew his head back. "You think so?"

"Absolutely. I've seen it before, had it before. Cheerleaders."

Miles squirmed in his seat. "And you," he said, pointing to the bruise on Donavon's face.

"I ducked but hit the bar. It was actually better to get knocked out by the bar than the logger I was arguing with. He might have killed me."

"You come in on Mondays looking pretty rough sometimes. Is that a fun way to spend your weekends?"

"I don't know. I usually don't remember it on Monday."

"I'll come with you next time. We'll gang up on him."

Donavon shook his head. "You don't want to go where I go. You don't want to do what I do. Stay here and hold down the fort so I've got someplace to come back to."

Miles nodded. "Okay. Sorry for prodding."

"What are friends for?"

THE DANCE BAND RAN through its selections while those who weren't in the dance band danced. It was a hot time on stage. Miles felt the twelve numbers they had chosen would suffice for a couple of hours of dancing and, with the hour barbeque break for carving and eating, the locals could get a rousing three hours of entertainment and food.

"What do we wear?" Tommy asked from the back row.

"What you'd normally wear to a dance," Miles replied.

"I don't dance."

"Knock it off. You know what I mean. Dress better than coming to school."

"I don't have anything better than this."

"Stand up."

Tommy stood. Long sleeve snap-button shirt and Levi's: standard wearing apparel for a male student at Tamarack High School.

"Would you wear that to a high school dance?"

"Yes," Nolan shouted.

"Then it'll work here. Besides, you'll be in the back where it's dark." He got ready to dismiss them, and thought better of it. "We need a crew to set up the band at the community hall and we need a crew to tend the fire during the day and a crew to carve the bar-beque, put it on plates, and someone to help with the condiments."

There were some sideward glances and chuckles.

Miles caught it, raised his hand and said, "I said *condiments.* Those are food additives like barbeque sauce, hot sauce, mayonnaise ... not what *you're* thinking."

That released the full laughter, and Miles chuckled with it.

Always good to be on the side that's having fun.

MILES BACKED THE SCHOOL bus into the spot beside the cyclone fence, shut off the motor but remained in the driver's seat. He took a deep breath, eased it out, and let his chest collapse against his belt. As he sat looking across the parking lot, the door to the gym opened and Shelly stood there.

Right ... I promised to meet with her today. Get going, buddy.

Shelly smiled as he approached, even held the door open for him.

"Where did you have in mind to study this problem?" he asked.

"I've got a table and chairs set up on the stage."

They climbed the four stairs to the stage and sat where the chairs were arranged next to each other on one side. Shelly's books were on the table. Miles grabbed the back of one of the chairs and moved it to the end and sat in it, put his forearms on the table, looked at her, and smiled. "What do we need to work on?"

She moved her chair closer, sat down, and smiled at him. "I'm having trouble understanding the wind patterns you assigned to me." She scooted her chair closer and opened the book to a marker. Her foot touched the top of his foot and stayed there.

Probably inadvertent.

"What does the book say about winds in and around the Clarno formation?"

"It doesn't much mention winds. Only the formation of the surface ... " Her voice trailed off and her foot slid up and down his leg.

He blinked and then swallowed. "Do you remember what we studied about how winds are formed, and how predominant wind patterns develop the erosion and type of plants and animals that can live there?"

Her foot moved to his thigh.

My gawd... her shoe is off.

"Yes," she said. "But I was hoping it would get more... intimate than that."

He felt the blood rushing to his groin as her bare foot got there. He pushed back his chair. "Shelly, this is not right. Stop this charade."

She stared at the bulge in his pants. "You want to, don't you?"

"That has nothing to do with it."

"It has everything to do with it. We want each other, and we've earned it. I'm sure your pregnant wife isn't giving you as much as you want. I've just had my period, so I'm safe. Come on."

Miles stood up and moved the chair between them. "You're a beautiful girl, Shelly and any man would be delighted to take you up on that, but it is poison for a teacher and student. You know it and I know it. It just can't happen."

"I'm not a virgin, if that's what you're thinking."

Miles shook his head, his breathing echoing in his ears. He held up both hands and closed his eyes. "It cannot be done. It just can't."

"Two people can make it happen." She lifted her skirt until her panties showed.

He turned, took the stairs two at a time, and was out the gym door into the parking lot. The sun was setting. The clean evening breeze whispered down from the mountains, across the winter-fallowed fields, down the gullies Tamarack Creek had cut in the topsoil, to dust his senses with the sharp scent of pitch, juniper, and sagebrush. He breathed it in, felt his passion relax, and walked to his car.

Coach Donavon was right. The danger is not just from the administration.

CHAPTER 16

FRIDAY NIGHT EVERYTHING WAS ready. Saturday morning Earl Benson brought in the half beef and the pit crew speared it on the iron rod that was to rotate over the fire, burning since dawn and now knocked down to roasting embers. The dance committee scattered soap flakes on the floor to make it slippery and decorated with crepe paper and old highway and business signs that had accumulated out back at the gas station. Nolan showed up with a handful of small bills for change and, standing in front of the community center, Miles crossed his arms and smiled.

Tommy came over to stand beside him. "Does it look okay, boss?"

Miles nodded. "It really looks fine, Tommy. Those old signs dress it up a lot, don't they? Now let's pray it draws a crowd."

"Everybody will be here."

"All fifty?"

Tommy laughed. "Maybe more. It's the talk all over the countryside."

A sign in the window of every business in town announced the barbeque and dance from 7 p.m. to 10 p.m. Some had heard that J. D. Wharton planned on coming. The mill had put up several signs advertising it and made sure the pay checks were distributed Friday after work and even had a cashier outside the pay office to cash checks for anyone wanting that service.

Miles touched his face, felt the moist skin, and took a deep breath. At lunchtime he went home, assured everything was under control, and ate with Ele. She was on the couch reading when he came in. He walked over and kissed her. "Having a good day?"

"Not particularly," she said. "Chickens didn't lay enough eggs to make custard and have our normal Sunday breakfast. The little buggers . . . where do they get off?"

"Aw, don't be too hard on them. They work seven days a week, you know. Not like teachers."

"Well, they better get to work or they'll be the main course."

Miles straightened his arms, palms out toward her. "No . . . not the ultimate sacrifice."

"We don't allow no slackers around here. This is a working ranch."

"Yeah, well, you play rancher. I'm going to take a shower and rest a bit before I go back to be a barbeque chef, band director, and janitor after it's over."

"Think you'll pay me back for the uniform loan?"

Miles nodded. "Absolutely. Even J. D. Wharton is coming. That ought to bring out the old maids in the village."

"You think he remembers how to dance?"

"We'll find out. He might just drink his way through it." Miles lifted off his shirt. "You feel well enough to come down?"

"I think I can make it for a while. If I get pooped, I'll get someone to bring me home."

"Yeah . . . like Bernie Hall."

"He won't mess with me while I'm pregnant."

Miles cocked his head. "I don't know. He sees mating going on all the time on his farm and he just naturally keeps it in the forefront of his mind."

"I'll get one of the ladies to take a break and drive me home." She looked around for him but he was gone.

True, she thought. *Bernie Hall's hugs last longer than anyone else's and he patted me on the fanny, laughing after a hug at the post office. He's the third man in my life who has made my blood rush. I can still feel his beard against my neck and the high school girly feeling I had to suppress when I walked away. I knew he was watching me.*

NOLAN AND BRENDA HAD the beef turning on a schedule of one revolution a minute. The meat was dark, the fat crispy. Coals flared and sizzled as the fat dripped on them and exploded the scent of cooking meat in the cool air. Every ten turns, Nolan took a wooden handled mop and spread barbeque sauce on it, the heat making him squint. Up close, it was burning hot; five feet away, you could see his breath.

Tommy stepped out on the porch. "Everyone's here and all set up. When do you want to start with the music?"

Miles chuckled. "Well, not until people are here."

"It'll be dark soon."

"Yeah—so?"

"Just noticing."

Miles nodded. "Okay, Tommy. You could get out the paper plates and knives and forks."

"Carla already did that."

"Then I guess we're set until the first folks get here and the scraunchin', raunchin', apple jackin', and honey dippin' gets started."

Shelly stood behind him. "Which part of that is mine?" she said.

Miles spun around. "Didn't see you come up."

She looked at him with a slight smile, waiting for an answer. "Well?"

He shook his head. "I can't imagine."

"I can."

"Shelly—"

Tommy nodded toward the road. "Mr. Wharton."

Miles turned.

J. D. Wharton listed to the right and then left as he came up the slight rise. The community center was 100 feet from the intersection, and he stopped three times. Miles, Nolan, and Tommy waited for him to start again. They could hear his breathing. He pulled out a handkerchief, mopped his forehead. Miles went out to greet him.

"J. D. —you are our first customer. Welcome to the barbeque and dance."

"I'm not sure I've got much dance left in me after that uphill walk."

"Let Shelly take your arm and guide you to your place of honor."

Shelly smiled and entwined her arm inside the crook of his elbow. "Mr. Wharton, good to see you here. May I direct you to your seat of honor?"

J. D. straightened up, his back stiffened, and a smile eased across his face. "Miss Shelly, it is my pleasure to have such a lovely young lady on my arm."

Shelly threw a glance at Miles that he didn't know how to interpret. But he could have sworn J. D. lost thirty years of age going into the community center with Shelly on his arm.

Mabel Kreneke was dropped off in front of the center by her son-in-law. After straightening her skirt, she glanced around and walked at a rapid pace to the front of the porch. "Good evening, Mr. Foster," she said.

Miles nodded. "Good evening, Ms. Kreneke. It's really good to see you here."

"Couldn't let the band down, you know. If I'm not poisoned by the barbeque and potato salad, I may get a few dances in. I hear J. D. is coming."

"He's already here—inside."

"Good. Good. We can have a chat then." She looked down at where her feet were going to go, and then, lifting her skirt, marched up the stairs and into the center looking every inch a queen preparing to meet her subjects.

Tommy tapped Miles on the shoulder. "Think she's gonna make a play for Mr. Wharton?"

Miles snorted. "He might make a play for *her*—who knows?"

Tommy shook his head. "I guess there's someone for everyone."

"You dating anyone, Tommy?"

"No."

"How about for the prom?"

"I doubt it. Who'd want to go with me?"

"I don't know, but we could start a list."

Tommy chuckled. "Yeah—like who do we put on it?"

"You keep a piece of paper and a pencil handy and we'll make a list as we go along."

"Yeah—that won't take long. We've got what—fourteen girls in school?"

"Don't forget Dayville, Mt. Vernon, John Day, Prineville . . . ."

"Fat chance they'd come over here to a prom."

"You can go get them. Show them an evening."

"You think so?"

"Absolutely." Miles turned to Nolan. "Have you tried the outside meat yet?"

"Yeah . . . it's getting past rare. We're gonna let the fire die down a little more and slow the rotations. Some of it's starting to fall off."

"Beans and potato salad ready?"

"On the table inside."

Miles felt a tug on his sleeve and turned.

"Mr. Foster," Roscoe said. "Some people are drinking out behind the hall."

"School kids or adults?"

Roscoe shook his head. "Don't know."

I'll bet it's the same guys who tip a beer at the football games.

"Thanks, Roscoe. I'll look into it."

Cars arrived in groups, honking and occupants talking in the parking lot. The center parking lot filled up; pickups lined up and down both sides of the street. Car doors slammed, people shouted greetings, and all moved toward the smell of barbequed meat and the light poking into the fall evening through the open front door.

Miles could see Carla seated inside collecting money as the people came in. He figured if fifty people showed up and paid, they could pay back the money he had borrowed for the down payment, and the bum check he had written as well as the cost of the event. So far they weren't close. He stepped back from the barbeque pit and walked around to the rear of the hall. He could just make out three figures standing near the back wall.

"How's it goin', guys?" he said.

"Things are just fine, teacher man, just fine."

"Are you coming to the barbeque and dance?"

"Be there shortly."

"Is that you, Neely?"

"Yes indeed."

"Try and keep the drinking down 'til it's over, will you?"

"Just sippin' a beer before we go in."

What to say? A new guy to three guys who grew up here, live here, know every stick and stone in this valley.

"I'd appreciate it if you were able to walk in upright."

Neely chuckled. "Take a lot more than a beer to knock my legs out."

"I know. Enjoy."

"Don't worry, teacher—we'll be there upright and pay for the privilege."

"ONE TWO ONE TWO . . . hit it," Miles said, his baton cutting the air like a cavalry saber. The band struck up the Tamarack High School fight song. Everybody but J. D. and Mabel stood up and sang. They continued on in their conversation, oblivious to others or the noise.

Shelly dimmed the lights and the band started with some slow numbers to get people off their chairs and onto the dance floor. Neely and his two pals came through to use the restroom and then hung out in one of the darker corners.

"How many paid?" Miles asked Carla.

"I'll count. They came in so fast I haven't had time to count."

"We need fifty."

"I don't think we got that many. I'll let you know in a few minutes."

Miles felt a touch on his arm. "How about a dance?" Shelly said.

"I haven't danced with my wife yet."

She smiled. "Later then."

He nodded.

I'm getting this nodding stuff down pat. I see why Billy nods all the time. Saves a lot of thinking about what to say. Could I dance once with her? No— it's a stupid idea. Stay away from that hot number. That would start Donavon yakking if he hears about it. He's probably in Prineville erasing this last week's memory, although someone said he went to Hood River. Hmmm.

The band did as well without him, so he asked Ele to dance. She looked ravishing in her gown despite the maternity bulge. They danced two numbers before Miles headed out to the barbeque pit to survey the main course.

Earl Benson and Roscoe were standing spraddle-legged, one on each side of the fire, carving off large pieces of meat to bring into the Center.

"Man, this is hot work," Earl said, his teeth reflecting the coals' shimmer.

"Thanks for helping, you guys."

"We get the best parts this way," Roscoe threw in.

The band stopped at 8:00, and food and drink took over. Neely's group had disappeared and along with them about ten men, as well.

"Where is everybody?" Miles asked.

Nolan cocked his head toward the back of the center. "Tipping a few."

"Oh." Miles filled a plate for Ele and headed back inside. He stopped by the table to check with Carla on sales and when he looked up he saw Bernie Hall sitting beside Ele with his hand on her thigh. They were laughing. When they saw him coming toward them, Bernie patted her leg twice then clasped his hands together.

Both had big smiles on their faces when he approached.

"Didn't know you were here, Bernie. Would have brought you a plate, too."

"That's alright, Miles. I was just flirting with your wife here. I can get a plate in a minute." He didn't get up and offer his chair to Miles.

Miles stood in front of them. "What do you want to drink with it?" His mouth was dry. He started to hand the paper plate to Ele and it collapsed in the middle.

She reached for the falling plate. "Oh!" she screamed. Beef and beans and barbeque sauce spread out in the air and landed on her legs. Bernie jumped.

"My dress is ruined," Ele said.

Miles scooped the food off her dress with his hand, onto the folded plate. "I'll get a rag." He straightened up and Bernie was there with a damp rag in his hand. He went down on one knee and wiped her legs. Ele looked up at Miles.

"I need to go home now," she said.

"I'll take you," Bernie said, without looking up at Miles.

Miles took the folded plate and threw it in the trash. As he turned around, Bernie was leading Ele from the dance floor, the barbeque sauce a brown splotch on her gown. He stood, his feat anchored to the floor.

Ele looked back over her shoulder. "It's okay, honey. Bernie will take me home. You stay and finish up the evening, and I'll see you when you get done."

Miles nodded. He watched her walk out the front door. He glanced at Shelly, who was watching them leave.

ROSCOE PULLED A FORTY-GALLON garbage can along the slippery floor, encouraging everyone to toss the plates and plastic utensils in. About the time he was finished gathering stuff, Neely's group re-entered the center along with the missing ten guys. Laughter and funny dancing and falls on the soapy floor took over the Tamarack Community Center while the band played on.

The band had run through its twelve dance numbers several times and had mixed up the songs, adjusted the usual methods of playing because lips were getting sore, fingers tired, and the drummer was going deaf. At the end of each set of numbers, a rancher would run up and put a twenty-dollar bill on the drum head and ask for more.

The lights dimmed when the band started playing "Moon River." Miles looked at the light switch on the far wall and saw Shelly standing there looking ravishing in the shadows. She came toward him, a half-smile softening her face.

"I believe this is our dance, Mr. Foster."

Miles looked around. Nobody was looking. Those dancing were totally consumed by the act of dancing; the lights were low, so low he couldn't make out people at the back of the center. She put her right arm on his shoulder and reached for his hand with the other. "Our first dance?"

He cupped his hand around her waist, took her hand, and they moved into the flow of dancers. She guided them to the back of the center, where she turned his back to the dancers and pressed against him with all her teenage passion. The heat and aroma of her perfume made him close his eyes for a moment. He responded. He pulled her arm in and kissed the back of her hand, pulled her tight with his right arm and thrust his hips against her.

Someone tapped him on the shoulder. "Mr. Foster, Earl Benson wants us to play another twenty minutes. Says he'll pay fifty dollars if we do."

Miles separated from Shelly, letting go of her hand. "T-Tommy," he stuttered. "Can the band do it?"

"I think so. Do we need the fifty to pay for everything?"

"Let me ask Carla. She has the tally." He turned to Shelly. "Excuse me for a moment, please." He bit his lip and looked into her eyes. The look in her eyes could have started wars, sunk ships, downed airplanes.

As Miles approached Carla, he saw Ele standing in the entrance. The overhead light filtered down across her face and the fresh dress. Her eyes were fierce, mouth partway open. She looked stunned. She turned and walked out, slamming the front door behind her.

"Ele, wait," he said. She was gone, but the slim door still trembled.

He passed the ticket table when Carla said, "Mr. Foster, we made it. We've got sixteen hundred forty dollars."

Miles sat down on a chair. He felt a hand on his shoulder and looked around.

"Can we finish our dance?" Shelly said.

Miles shook his head and took a deep breath. "Not now."

She looked at him, lowered her chin, and walked out the door down the steps and disappeared into the night.

AT 11:25 P. M., THEY ushered the last people out of the center. They vowed to return Sunday morning and clean the place up, repair the grounds where the barbeque pit had been, and count the money one more time to make sure.

Ele was propped up in bed with the light on when Miles came home. His breath came in shudders as he walked through the dark house to the bedroom where the one reading light cast a ghoulish pallor to her face, washed clean of makeup. She had had more than an hour to develop her speech. He stopped in the doorway and looked at her.

She swallowed, her arms lying by her legs. They looked at each other.

"That was pretty fancy dancing," she said.

He shook his head. "Honey . . . it was a momentary thing. It kinda got away from me. I'm sorry you saw it."

"Sorry I saw it? What about sorry it was so intimate?"

He winced. "I wouldn't call that intimate."

"Okay. You classify it for both of us." She pursed her lips, crossed her arms, and waited.

"Shelly is going through a lot of emotional problems because she lost her boyfriend in the—"

"Oh, let's not blame it all on Shelly. It takes two to dance like that—two very interested and possibly involved people."

Miles shook his head. "Not involved. It just happened. That's the first time, and it will be the last time."

There was a moment when only their breathing could be heard. Ele lifted her head and bit her cheek. "I'd like that to be so."

"It will be. I promise." Suddenly, a vision of Bernie Hall leading Ele out of the dance hall burst in front of him. "I suppose Bernie just dropped you off in the driveway?"

"He walked me to the front door."

"And kissed you?"

"And *tried* to kiss me."

"And you fought him off."

"Pretty much."

"How much is pretty much?"

"He kissed my cheek."

"Oh."

When Miles climbed into bed, Ele turned away.

"You smell like smoke and beer. I don't think I can handle that right now. My stomach's too queasy."

He kissed her on the back of her neck and pulled himself to the far side of the bed and closed his eyes. Shelly's face popped up like a jack-in-the-box, the half-smile turning her lips up at the corner and her eyes open, inviting. He mentally began taking one thing off her at a time. It was a slow process and he was asleep before it was done.

CHAPTER 17

SUPERINTENDENT CALVIN BROOKS, WITH the approval of his wife Winifred Brooks, nominated Mrs. Grant to conduct the annual Christmas Pageant. Mrs. Grant, who herded the third grade students like a mother hen, was marvelous at getting the grade school children to memorize all four verses of "O, Come All Ye Faithful." Two weeks before the pageant, Miles was asked to meet with her to discuss the high school's participation.

"I have taken the liberty of printing off the words to the song we will all sing at the conclusion of the program, 'O, Come All Ye Faithful.' I'm sure your students know the tune." She handed him the papers. "In addition, I'd like your boys' chorus to sing, 'We Three Kings' and the girls to sing 'O Holy Night.' Mr. Brooks has given us permission to use our regular classes to learn the words to the songs."

Miles took the papers, looked at them, and then at Mrs. Grant. "I think we can do most of this . . ."

"I'm sure you'll get it all in, Mr. Foster."

"Only two weeks before the pageant. We'll try getting them memorized, along with their regular classes . . ."

"You can suspend regular classes to learn these," she said, nodding her head in an up and down movement like a bobber on a windblown lake.

"We have some students who are not . . . shall we say, up to snuff in the courses and need all the class time they can get to meet the state graduation requirements."

She placed the papers she was holding in her lap, narrowed her eyes and let a skip of time occur before she began in a quiet and stern voice. "Mr. Foster . . . I do not intend to get into a discussion about this with you. Mr. Brooks has appointed me to conduct the Christmas Pageant, and I would like your full cooperation. Is that clear?"

"I understand what you are saying. Just not sure we can pull it all off."

"Our first joint rehearsal is next Friday during Geography class."

"The whole hour?"

"Yes, Mr. Foster. The full hour."

MILES PASSED OUT THE words to the songs in Geography class. The students joked about it.

"Knock it off. Here we have your assignment for the next two weeks. Learn the words to 'O, Come All Ye Faithful.'"

"All of them?" Nolan asked.

"Yes—all of them," Miles said.

"Boys learn, 'We Three Kings' and girls learn, 'O Holy Night.' Got it?"

"Yes, boss," Nolan quipped. He looked at the paper. "Boss— there's five verses to 'O, Come All Ye Faithful.'"

"Isn't that interesting?" Miles said.

Nolan acted like he had been hit in the head with hammer.

"Okay—boys on left side, girls on right side. Sing in low tones or whispers. Try and connect the words with the tune and for now you don't need to work on harmony, just get the melody and the words in your shrunken heads."

"Da boss makes fun of us," Nolan said.

Miles sat at his desk, trying to figure out how to cover the required lessons, assignments, homework, and reports in the time remaining after cutting out Christmas and Easter vacations, and getting them to the state test in the spring with everything they needed to know. There was no way he could get it all in if they spent the next two weeks on songs. There had to be a shortcut.

AT THE END OF the first week, the boys knew most of the words to their song; the girls knew all the words to theirs, and most of them knew half of the words to "Faithful."

"What's up with you guys?" Miles asked. "It isn't that hard to learn a few words."

Shelly raised her hand. "It's so much all at once. Can we cut back on 'Faithful' . . . only sing the first and last verse and hum the others?"

Miles thought about that a minute. "That could work. I'll see. Now pass your essays forward, and don't forget to practice over the weekend. You've all got a debate next week for Public Speaking class, so work on that and I'll see you bright and shiny here Monday morning."

"Yeah," Nolan threw in. "God willing and the Creek don't rise."

Miles chuckled. "The Creek Indians have been gone from here for hundreds of years."

"Never were here," Nolan countered. "They lived in the Georgia area." He nodded, a smile covering his face. "Learned that in American History."

"Well, give that man a cigar."

"Thank you. Thank you." He bowed low, a smile creeping onto his face.

MRS. GRANT, ALONG WITH Mr. and Mrs. Calvin Brooks, sat in the superintendent's office after school closed on Friday. It was between football and basketball seasons, so there was no game scheduled. Winifred Brooks brought her tea set into the office along with a tin box of Scottish shortbread cookies she got for Calvin from time to time when their budget and his cholesterol were in good shape. The meeting was to discuss progress on the Christmas Pageant.

Calvin took a bite, closed his eyes and chewed. Then, raising his teacup, he took in a sip of Earl Grey Tea and washed it down. He opened his eyes and smiled at Winifred. "Thank you, dear. This is very thoughtful of you. You know how I love these cookies."

Winifred smiled. "Just remember, Calvin. Two of those have two hundred and forty-four calories and sixteen grams of fat."

"I don't care. I don't care a whit. Having these takes me back to my youth."

"Well, it won't take your heart or your waistline back to your youth."

"Winifred . . . sometimes I need to step over and enjoy some of the fruits of life. Running a school for nine months and chasing around finding teachers for the other three is hard work. I enjoy this break."

"My husband's weakness is for a beer on Friday nights," Mrs. Grant put in. "He just loves Old Milwaukee. He'd drink a six pack if I'd let him." She reached over and patted Winifred on the knee. "We need to keep our men in good shape, don't we?"

Winifred lifted her eyebrows. "Indeed, we do—and alive."

They all chuckled.

Calvin had polished off his allotted two cookies and wiped his lips with a paper napkin, reset his glasses, and turned to Mrs. Grant. "Now, Mrs. Grant, how is the pageant coming?"

"We've only been working on it a week, as you know, and I believe we will be ready in good time. Mr. Foster is a bit put out given the assignment of the high school chorus's responsibilities, but I believe he will come around. We have our first joint session next week."

"Well, if he gives you any problem, send him to me."

"It was just a matter of his squeezing this into his regular classes."

"I see. Well—we want a good Christmas Pageant. The town expects it every year." He brushed a few crumbs off his shirt. "Let's plan to meet next Friday prior to the pageant then. Meeting adjourned." He stood up, a broad smile on his face, and shook hands with Mrs. Grant.

"Are you going to Prineville tomorrow?" Mrs. Grant asked.

"Yes," Calvin said.

"Would you mind picking me up a book at the library?"

"Not at all. We can do that, can't we, Winifred?"

"Yes—of course."

"Good. I'll call you the title and author from the house. Good night."

"Good night, Mrs. Grant."

SATURDAY AFTERNOON AT 4:30 p. m., the telephone rang in the Foster house. Miles picked it up. "Hello."

"Mr. Foster, this is Mrs. Grant. I have some terrible news. Mr. and Mrs. Brooks have been in an accident and are in the hospital in Prineville. My husband has been drinking and I don't drive and I thought you would be the best one to take over and see how we can help."

"My gosh . . . what happened?!"

"I believe their car hit a deer. I'm just too frazzled at the moment to be of any good assistance to them. Could you run over there and see what has happened?"

"Yes . . . I'll do that. Ele and I have been to the hospital with the pregnancy so we know our way around there."

"I would be ever so grateful if you would do that. It would mean so much to us all. Thank you." She hung up.

Ele stood in the doorway. "What did you agree to *now*?"

"Want to take a drive to Prineville? The Brooks have been in a car accident and are in the hospital. I'm gonna go check on them."

"Oh, no. How badly are they hurt?"

"Mrs. Grant didn't know. You coming or not?"

Ele shook her head. "You go. I just don't feel up to it right now."

Miles grabbed the car keys and his wallet.

"You haven't had supper or anything . . . "

"I'll grab a bite in Prineville." He bent over and kissed her.

"Drive carefully. You've got a family, twelve chickens, and a cow to support."

"Always do."

Miles started the car, glanced at the gas gauge, saw that it was only a quarter-full, and drove to the gas station. Shelly Baines was there, gassing up the family car.

"Where you going this time of day?" Shelly said.

Miles told her about the accident. "I'm going over to check on them."

"Hold up a minute and I'll go with you."

Miles's heart stuttered. "You can't go. Your folks don't know about this." His breathing stopped and he ran the gas over. He jumped back and put the nozzle in the pump, paid, and by the time he got to the car, Shelly was in the passenger seat.

Miles pointed at Shelly. "You stay on your seat; do you understand?"

She nodded but there was a mischievous glint in her eyes.

THE NURSE LOOKED UP as he rushed to the counter. "Mr. and Mrs. Calvin Brooks—what room are they in?"

"And who are you?"

"Miles Foster. I'm a teacher at the school in Tamarack. How are they?"

"I just came on duty. Let me check with the doctor."

Shelly came up and took hold of Miles's hand. He squeezed it and then let go.

The nurse looked up. "Are you family?"

Miles shook his head. "No—I teach at the school where he is superintendent. I've driven over here to see how they are and to get word back to the faculty and students."

"And the lady?"

"She's one of our students."

The nurse looked back and forth at Miles and Shelly. There was a dubious look in her eyes as the tip of her tongue went to the corner of her mouth. "Just a minute."

Miles let out his breath. Shelly touched his shoulder. She started to speak but Miles turned away. "Shelly . . . " he said.

"Okay." She moved to one side.

The nurse was talking in a low tone and then turned her back on them and spoke the other way. When she turned back, her face was stern. "You can see them for five minutes. Visiting hours are over and they need rest. I need your word on this."

"I just want to see them and get any instructions. May I borrow a pen and some paper?"

CALVIN BROOKS HAD HIS eyes closed, but he didn't look bad. Winifred had a bandage across her forehead and one eye was blackened. Calvin opened his eyes, frowned, then closed them—but the frown stayed. "Mr. Foster, you are the one person I cannot abide seeing today."

"Sorry, Mr. Brooks. I was the only one who could come. If you are going to be laid up here for a while, is there anything you want me to do at school? Or anything I can do for you here?"

Mrs. Brooks opened her one good eye and looked at him without moving her head, then closed it. Neither moved at all.

"If you could get someone to take over my Civics class . . . *you,* probably. And any important mail . . . if you could bring it."

"Absolutely. I'll do that," Miles said.

"We also need some authority there. I appoint you to vice principal in my absence."

"Why me?"

"You're here."

"Okay. Anything else? Do you need anything from your house?"

"Don't know."

"I'm sure Mr. and Mrs. Grant will come over as soon as they can."

"Tell them not to hurry. I think we'll be here a spell."

"Need anything done at your house?"

"Quit trying to be so helpful." He turned his head away. "Everything will be alright."

Miles straightened up. Shelly came over to the bedside. Calvin winced, turning his head back to look at them. "What's she doing here?" he asked.

"Shelly rode over with me to see you."

He turned away again. "Leave us now, please."

Miles nodded. "Okay. Rest and get well." He turned and walked out the door and down the hall, Shelly hurrying behind him out to the parking lot.

Shelly said, "He doesn't take to you much, does he?"

"He's hurting. Nobody's going to get a good reception in that room."

They stopped at The Logger Restaurant, ordered to go, and headed back to Tamarack. Miles placed his food on the small bench between them.

"Shelly, did you know the kids that were killed before school started?"

"Of course. Everybody knew them."

"Would you say their deaths had anything to do with the atmosphere in school or town? Do you think it affected Mr. and Mrs. Brooks in any way?"

Shelly chewed and swallowed. "Yes. But I don't know how exactly. It was a shock to all of us. I was dating Darrell."

"Did you go to the funeral?"

She nodded.

It was quiet as they drove the darkened highway back to Tamarack. Along the roadside, they could see pairs of eyes pick up and stare at them, deer feeding alongside and in the ditch. Fish and Game had said 240,000 deer were killed on Oregon highways the previous year. Miles could see why. They were lured out of the woods to the alfalfa fields always planted in the flat areas near creeks where the highway was built.

Is that chumming?

"Tell me about Darrell," he said.

Shelly turned her head and looked out the side window for a long while. She started to talk from there. "Darrell was a sweet boy—with a streak of crazy in him. He loved his parents—and me. He went to church over in Dayville with his parents but every so often he would get ahold of some beer and that's when the crazy part came out. I don't know who got the beer that night but he would have drunk his part of it. That's for sure."

"He was a good athlete."

Shelly nodded. "Good one. Played right-end and was a star. Also in basketball."

"What a loss."

"It really was. *Is . . .* " she said.

"How'd the town take the funeral?"

Shelly turned in the seat to look at Miles. "It was kinda funny. Just old people had died around town to anyone's memory. Having three young men killed in one night put sort of a blanket over the whole community. I mean, you'd go into the General Store and see one of the family members—there must be fifteen or twenty related to them—and you could see the hollow eyes, the slow response to laughter or merriment by anyone nearby. It was creepy."

"You miss Darrell?"

She nodded. She pursed her lips and looked out the passenger side window.

Miles couldn't tell if she was crying or not.

"What happened to the driver of the car that hit them?"

Shelly shook her head. "The sheriff came over from Fossil and had the car towed away. The front end was caved in and the windshield was broken. I don't know what happened to the driver. He wasn't drunk or anything. At night everybody comes down that road in the middle 'cause they can see oncoming headlights if anyone's coming. According to Jay and Rich, they were all walking down the middle of the road."

Silence slipped inside the car from the quiet night, melting the sounds and word choices and stilling their tongues. They sipped their drinks through straws as they drove along, and watched the moon rise over the Painted Hills.

Miles slowed as they entered town, and stopped the car beside Shelly's in the gas station parking lot. "Thanks for going over, Shelly."

"Thanks for the dinner."

"You're welcome. See you Monday."

She leaned over and kissed him on the cheek. "Drive safely."

"It's only four blocks."

"I know, but most accidents happen within twenty miles of home."

"I'll try to remember that. Good night."

MONDAY MORNING IN THE faculty closet, Donavon was a raft of smiles and no bruises. "Saw you drop Shelly off at the gas station Saturday night. Did you take my hint about cheerleaders?"

"No. She was gassing her car when I pulled in headed to Prineville to see Brooks in the hospital. She hopped in."

"Yup. They'll do that sometimes."

"Oh, knock it off, Donavon."

Donavon raised his head, looked down his nose at Miles and stuck his tongue in his cheek. "I'm just saying . . . "

Marion Stillson walked in, cuddling her morning coffee mug in both hands.

"Brooks appointed me vice principal from his hospital bed. I don't know what that means, but if any of you have anything that you'd normally take to Calvin, give me a shout and we'll work it out together."

"How about discipline?" Marion asked.

"I guess."

She smiled.

"Something coming down the road I should know about?"

She shook her head. "Rumors is all."

"I'll be teaching his Civics class instead of my study hall. I'd appreciate it if each of you would poke your head in there once or twice during the hour and quell any open warfare."

"You got it," Donavon said as he rose. He winked at Miles, then turned and left the room.

"So what's the secret between you two?" Marion asked.

"No secret," Miles said.

"Why the winking?"

"Donavon likes to think he knows something he won't tell, so he seals it with a wink. I gotta find Roscoe and let him know about Brooks."

"You've told the grade school teachers?"

Miles nodded. "First thing this morning." He stood. "Remember—check on my inmates."

Marion nodded as she lifted the coffee mug to her lips.

That mug must weigh two pounds.

BEFORE 11:00 A.M., THE substitute seventh grade teacher stepped into Miles's classroom. She had an unusual look on her face, flushed with splotches of white and without a hint of humor.

"Mr. Foster, I want to send two students up to you for fighting."

"You want me to fight them?"

"No. *They* were fighting."

"In class?"

She nodded.

Does everyone in this whole town nod for conversation?

"Send them up to the principal's office. I'll be right there."

Miles sat in the high-backed chair that had formed itself to Calvin Brooks's frame, scooted around on it several times, leaned back, and waited.

In walked Jack Pitts and Judy Stanley, abashed, holding their arms behind their backs. He left them standing, crossed his arms over his chest, and stared at them. They looked at the floor.

"Want to tell me about it?" Miles said.

They looked at each other and shook their heads.

"You did physically fight in the classroom?"

They both nodded.

He stumbled through his mind. The offense pushed him to run over options. He thought of Judy's dad, Deb Stanley, knew he would be draconian. Jack's parents he did not know. Suddenly, how anyone else would react to it didn't seem relevant.

He stood up, unbuckled his belt, pulled it out of the belt loops and folded it double. "Bend over and grab your ankles."

Jack complied at once. Judy looked at him like he was crazy. Miles nodded at her to bend over. He walked behind them and waited.

Waiting is the worst part. I've been there.

He saw the blood drain to their heads, Jack gritted his teeth. Judy's hands wrapped around the top of her socks.

He waited, the belt resting in his hand.

I'm not going to start my vice principalship out with a belting.

Miles swung the belt through the air in a circle above them. Jack jumped and Miles could hear Judy sniffling and see her nose dripping on the floor. "Stay down," he said. He waited a long moment. "You may assume an upright position now."

He put his belt back on and resumed his seat in the principal's chair. "Is this something you are going to repeat?"

They both shook their heads.

"You are to report to Roscoe for janitorial work for an hour after school each day this week. Think about it before you start swinging at someone next time." He stood up and looked down at them. "Return to your class, please."

They turned and disappeared.

"I HEAR JUDY STANLEY'S dad is gunnin' for you," Donavon said after school.

"Do tell," Miles said. "And what would have him so upset?"

"Almost whipping his little girl."

"I didn't whip her. I made her *think* she was going to get one."

"That's a whipping in his eyes."

"A whipping is when you tie someone to the mast and give him fifty lashes with the cat of nine tails."

"You'll see there may be a different definition in Tamarack."

"I'm in good shape. I can handle myself."

"Deb's a logger, about six feet three and weights around two hundred and thirty pounds, I'd say."

"Yeah, but he smokes. I can outrun him."

"Not in his pickup."

"Oh, knock it off, Donavon. He's not going to try anything."

"I'm just sayin' . . . ."

AFTER SCHOOL, MILES WENT to the grocery store to pick up the material Ele had ordered to make the baby clothes. He was at the back counter with Ralph when the bell that hung over the front door clanged and Deb Stanley's frame filled the space where the door had opened. He moved down the aisle toward the counter, his caulk boots crunching as they dug in to the wooden floor. Miles turned to see the grim look on his face; but it was always grim unless he was talking.

Deb stuck out his hand. "Miles—I thank you for teaching my daughter she can't do that fightin' in school house."

Miles swallowed but the saliva kept piling up. "No hard feelings, Deb?"

Deb shook his head. "None." He nodded. "Good for her. I gave her a spanking when she came home. She might not sit too well in school next few days."

Miles wiped his mouth with the back of his hand. "Thank you, Deb. I appreciate your support."

"You got it. Good day to you." He nodded to Ralph. "See ya."

His back looked as broad as a yardstick walking back down the aisle and out the door. The bell was still ringing when Miles turned to Ralph. Ralph's eyes were bright, both hands flat on the counter.

"Wow," Ralph said with a chuckle, a smile lighting his face. "I think we lived through that."

Miles swallowed. "We did. We did. He can be awfully nice when he wants to be."

"Yes, indeed. Well—did you get everything you want?"

"Not everything I want, Ralph, but everything I *need*."

Ralph smiled. "Good. Let me add it up."

CHAPTER 18

DISCIPLINE CEASED TO BE a problem after Jack and Judy explained their trip to the principal's office. The boys patted their belts and smiled when they ran into Miles in school. The girls averted their eyes, except for Shelly, who tucked her chin down and looked at him from the tops of her eyes.

What does that mean?

Billy and Christmas Howell worked out a test for Billy to perform before Christmas vacation. The test was to determine if Billy was learning anything useful and if this alternative education could serve to meet the state's requirements. Before going home on Wednesday, Christmas and Miles had a meeting.

"Well, whaddaya think?" Christmas said.

Miles nodded. "I'm thinking it could work." He thought some more, then said, "Would you hire him?"

Christmas shook his head. "Not yet."

"But he's progressing?"

"Yes, he is. I think he'll be ready by graduation."

Miles grimaced. "Would you be willing to give him an employment agreement, subject to graduation and meeting certain standards, now . . . kinda as a Christmas present?"

"Or a present from Christmas?" he said, grinning.

"I'll bet you get a lot of that around this time of year."

"Oh, yes. But I live with it. It's better than any other holiday."

"Yeah. I can't see you being called Fourth of July . . . "

" . . . Or Easter."

" . . . Or Memorial."

"How about Armistice?"

They chuckled. "Ever figure out why your parents named you that?"

"They figured they got pregnant that day, is what they told me."

"That's as good a reason as any, I suppose."

"It is. It is for a fact."

"Where were we . . . ?"

"Me givin' Billy a conditional hiring agreement." He shook his head. "I just can't do it, Miles. Not in good conscience." He rubbed his chin. "And you know, the mill being short of logs could mean a closure before Billy even gets ready for hire."

"I understand. Well—we'll have him take the test and see what the results are."

"Okay. I'll write it up and get it ready for you. You want him to take it at school or at the mill?"

"School."

"Got it. Okay." Christmas stood up and extended his hand. "I sure hope this works out for you and for Billy. We could get a lot of these kids headed into work situations with a head start."

Miles shook the heavy, calloused hand. "Thanks for your help. I'm praying Billy makes the grade because he's sure not making it in history and diagramming sentences."

"Didn't do too well in those matters myself. But I learned how to turn a log into boards after a few rough years, and Billy will, too."

IN TYPING CLASS, THE students kept their heads down, did their work, turned in their papers, and left with little conversation between them or with Miles. The half-yearly tests would come before Christmas vacation, but their papers showed they had all progressed well beyond that level. He sat leafing through the papers, checking for errors the students might have missed. He found only one. A surge of pride flooded his brain and he smiled, leaned back in the chair, and closed his eyes.

He thought back to the day he had signed on to teach at Tamarack. He'd had no idea what he would encounter. His student teaching class had been rather loose and, other than helping a social studies teacher in one of the local Portland high schools, he had never given much thought as to the actual type of students he might encounter out in the world. The wide range of talents and personalities and the degree of dedication were a revelation to him. He'd seen it in other groups of people he had worked with, but not a whole town. The huge spread of intelligence and skills, from fifth grade to college sophomore level, in the same class floored him. Yet when it was over and they were out in their worlds, each would perform at or above his level and knit the part of the world they inhabited together with smiles, humor, work, personality, friendship and, hopefully, love. They would marry, have children, send them to school, and the whole process would begin again.

"Whaddaya doin', Teach?" Nolan said.

Miles jerked his head up. "Didn't hear you come in, Nolan." He lifted the papers in his hands off his lap as if he was weighing them. "Just thinking about how typing tests predict the future."

"You into some kind of hokey-pokus?"

"Don't think so. But I do believe each person's test can show a teacher what that student is going to do in life."

"What's it say for me?"

Miles shuffled the papers. "Let's see—slovenly, disorganized, unmindful of rules and regulations, despair, heavy use of alcohol, and general disregard for any sort of authority . . . ."

"By golly, it hit it right on the head."

They laughed together, the student knowing it wasn't true and the teacher knowing the one standing before him had the best chance of them all of being exactly the opposite. There was a commitment deep down in both student and teacher to be the best that they could be.

"So why are you swinging into the Typing room?" Miles said.

"I'm going to Prineville in an hour—be back tonight. Anything you want me to take to Mr. Brooks or tell him?"

"Great. Thanks, Nolan. I'll have an envelope for you. Stop by my room before you go."

Nolan saluted. "Aye, aye, sir."

"Appreciate," Miles said.

FRIDAY, AT 12:00 noon, the marching band members donned their uniforms and hit the street with drums pounding. When they turned on Main Street, the trumpets played a bugle call and then the band stopped halfway between the café and the General Store. People, shading their eyes against the sun, came out on the sidewalk to watch.

Miles lifted the megaphone. "The first basketball game is a home game tomorrow afternoon against our rivals, Dayville. Come cheer the Tamarack Buffaloes on to victory and buy popcorn. Helps pay for programs." He turned to Tommy and brought the baton down to start the music.

The snare drums erupted and all nine members snapped to attention as the band marched down the road, executed a "To the rear, march!" command and proceeded back up the street, stopped in front of the post office, and played three pieces, including the Tam Buffaloes' fight song. At the end of that, Ralph stepped out of the store holding up the jar.

"We've got a donations jar right here," he said.

People stepped over on the sidewalk, took out their wallets or purses, and stuffed money into the jar. Tommy had a smile on his face you could see a mile away, but he didn't miss a beat.

Up the hill they went, and the last drum beat called a halt in front of the gym.

"Phew," Tommy said.

"Amen," Miles said. "That was beautiful, guys. Just beautiful. Remember, the money in that jar goes to the band fund. It is *not* for personal use."

"Awwww," they cried.

"Tommy, please make an accounting. That was very unusual. Very unusual."

The band changed clothes and Tommy handed an envelope to Miles.

"A hundred thirty dollars," he said.

"Yikes. Have you ever seen that happen before?"

"This is my first year here."

"Oh, right. Great support from town."

"We wearing our uniforms for the game?"

"Sure. Why not?"

"I think it'd be good."

Miles nodded. "Let's do it. See to it, will you, Tommy?"

Tommy smiled. "You bet."

MILES WAS THE LAST one into the teachers' closet for lunch.

"Heard you killed them down on Main Street," Donavon said.

"We made a few converts," Miles said.

"You should come march in front of some of the ranchers' houses in the evening," Marion said. "There are five or six that would really enjoy it."

"What is that—about a twenty-mile trek?"

Marion squinted. "More like twenty-five. Might take all night."

"Would you put us up for the night?" Miles looked up, a bit of a smile on his face.

"A couple could stay in the house. The rest would have to be in the barn."

"Sounds cozy."

"Not advocating; just suggesting."

"Gotcha."

Marion swallowed her bite. "Any word on Brooks?"

"Nolan's going in after school. He'll bring back a full report."

Marion and Donavon exchanged glances.

Donavon looked up from his lunch. "You and Shelly aren't going to do the checking?"

"Knock it off, Donavon. That was a freak accident."

Marion gazed in her soup, stirred it with a spoon.

Miles looked at each of them. "Is there something you want to tell me?"

"No," Marion said, continuing to stir her soup.

Donavon shook his head. They looked at each other again and the room fell silent.

Roscoe pushed open the door. "Sorry to disturb you, but I think you ought to come see this."

Miles stood up and followed him out the door.

Roscoe pointed at a gathering of children and Miles walked over. The third grade boys were pitching rocks and sticks at a small badger that was surrounded by children and a cyclone fence. His back against the fence, he made vicious sounds and threatening moves toward them. At each lunge the girls shrieked and backed up, and the boys found new missiles to hurl. Miles looked around for Mrs. Grant, normally with her brood. Not finding her on the grounds, he waded in.

He grabbed the arm of the closest boy ready to launch a rock. "Hold it."

The kid looked up at him and let go of the rock.

"Knock it off—all of you. You have the animal terrified and all it can do is hiss and lunge. Back away. You boys put the stones down." He walked back ten steps. "Come back to here and watch it."

The girls ran back and the boys sauntered, casting their eyes over their shoulders to see what the badger was doing. The badger soon realized the threat was over and started looking for a way out of the fenced-in yard.

"Watch him. See what he's doing," Miles said.

"How do you know it's a boy?" one of the girls asked.

"He's too ugly to be a girl."

The kids laughed. The boys stood with hands in their pockets and the girls with hands to their mouths, watching the badger out of his element.

"Is he trying to get away from us?"

"He's not where he is supposed to be. Somehow, he got in the playground. What would you do if you were somewhere you weren't supposed to be?"

A chorus let out: "Get out . . . "

"He's probably this year's baby, and he's looking for a place to build a den for the winter."

"His parents kicked him out?"

Miles nodded. "Probably." He turned to Roscoe for confirmation. Roscoe shrugged.

"Aren't you glad you didn't hurt him?"

There were mumbled "Yes"-es and the collective nodding of heads.

By that time, the high school students were gathered around joking, jabbing each other, and cracking up over private jokes being told behind hands at their mouths.

Mrs. Grant bored a path through high schoolers and third graders and popped up where Miles stood amongst her brood. "I'll take charge now, Mr. Foster. This is my class."

"Yes Mrs. Grant, it is. And they need some training in treatment of wild animals."

"That is not in our curriculum."

"Well, it should be. Talk with them about stoning an innocent animal that wanders into the playground. You could use this incident to instill some humanity in them."

"I don't know that doing that would prevent them from shooting an innocent deer from the school bus when they are in high school; do you, Mr. Foster?" Her eyes squinted as she lowered her head an inch for emphasis. She spread her arms like a mother hen and shooed the third graders toward the grade school building.

Miles turned to Roscoe and shrugged. "Lot of good that did."

"I don't know," Roscoe said. "Might have made a difference."

"Not in my life."

"You never know. You just never know," he said, shaking his head.

NOLAN OPENED THE DOOR and stuck his head in. "I'm headed out."

Miles stood up and handed him an envelope. "Please give this to Mr. Brooks, if he seems able to open it."

"And if he doesn't?"

Miles turned his head and looked out the window a moment before turning back. "Aw—give it to him anyway."

"Anything else?"

Miles shook his head. "Oh—give him our best wishes for a speedy recovery."

"Yah. Will do." He closed the door.

Was it important to send that note telling of the actions he had taken in the absence of the superintendent? I doubt it. He'd know if he were here, so why not let him know when he's laid up in the hospital? No big things. A discipline problem, and a badger, and a brush-up with Mrs. Grant. Not earth-shattering.

"WHERE ARE YOU, HONEY?" Miles said, entering the back door of the house.

"In the kitchen. Don't come in for a minute."

"What do you want me to do hanging out in the utility room?"

"Go feed the chickens. I'll be ready in five minutes."

Miles went out to the chicken house and lifted the lid on the barrel of feed. Every chicken's head immediately turned toward him and, muttering through their beaks, they trotted in. He scattered five cups of cracked corn on the ground, filled up the water bottles, and, when they all had found their way inside the fence, closed and locked the gate.

"Good night, ladies. We'd like to see some nice big brown eggs in the morning, so do your best to not disappoint us." He stroked the rooster who stood five inches above the hens. "Keep control of your harem, Robbie. And get a little production out of them."

He changed his clothes, milked the cow and came back to the rear door, entering the laundry room, and set the bucket of milk down. "Are your five minutes up yet?"

"Almost."

He looked at his watch. "Honey, it's been twenty minutes since I went out to feed the chickens."

"So kill me. I can't tell time when I'm doing this."

He poured the milk into the separator, cranked the handle, and watched the milk flow into one bucket, the cream into another.

How does it know how to do that?

"Okay," Ele shouted. "You can come in now."

He removed his outside shoes, took three steps, launched off his back foot and skated on the linoleum floor in his stockinged feet, coming to a stop beside Ele.

"Ta-da . . ." he proclaimed.

Stepping back she revealed a three-layer chocolate cake with an iced message on top. It read: *Principal Miles Foster.*

"Wow," he said.

"Congratulations!"

"It's only temporary."

"I know, but it's a title, and you were the one out of all the teachers to be chosen. So, in your honor, I baked a cake to celebrate."

"I didn't know we had enough stuff to make a cake with."

"I used a window screen for a sifter. You can tell me if it worked."

He hugged her. "You're wonderful."

"Don't squeeze. You and me and baby make three."

"Oh, right."

She untied the apron and set the cake in the middle of the table. "Supper is ready. Chicken soup, fresh vegetables from our garden, and sourdough rolls."

Miles squinted his face. "Any of our chickens?"

"No. This one came from the market. But if they don't get their egg production back up, some of them may end up in the pot."

"When it comes time for that, please don't tell me the name of the cooked one."

"That chicken will remain anonymous."

"Let me wash my hands and I'm ready to eat and relax."

"Been a hard day?"

He nodded and pursed his lips. "You could say that. Mrs. Grant and me again."

Ele shook her head, lit the candles on the table, and sat down.

CHAPTER 19

J. D. WHARTON, RANCHER AND historian, showed up to teach local history as he had agreed with Miles in the restaurant. His Levi's were pressed and he wore a sport coat with leather elbow patches. A folder was tucked under his arm and a smile warmed his face, all pink from a shave. He took a chair next to Miles's desk, set the folder down, and put his hands on his knees.

Miles took attendance before introducing Mr. Wharton. He had arranged to have the Geography class come in to the Oregon History class to hear him.

"Ladies and gentlemen," Miles began. "The man who is going to present intimate history and geography of this area was born just after the Civil War. He moved west and settled here, and has seen and heard everything from a band of Indians chasing buffalo to a train whistle and an eighteen-wheeler chugging up Highway 26. He's watched rivers overflow, ravines fill up, game come and go, and trees grow to commercial size during his lifetime. I'd like you to listen respectfully to what J. D. Wharton has to tell you about the last eighty years in this valley."

J. D. sat for a moment, then stood up. Miles noticed for the second time that J. D. was a big man.

It took a big man to tame this country, Miles thought.

"You know," J. D. began. "It wasn't so long ago I sat in one of those chairs and had a teacher standing up here trying to teach me stuff. I was a hard learner. Rather been out in the fields and mountains, hunting, trapping, or fishing. But you know what? When I

found out I didn't know everything—which was about age thirty—
I started to learn what I should've learned in school. That was when
I started a pipeline from the state library to my house. Questions.
Questions always arose that I couldn't answer.

"Why did half the crop wash out of my lower field? Why did
the timber take over the South slope so fast? What'd the Indians do
for food when the fish didn't run up the John Day River?

"Ya see . . . all these things were available to me in high school.
In Geography and History classes, but I didn't like them shoved
down my throat. Miles here, he asked me to come discuss with you
how this country was formed, how the waters run, and what the
mountains do to the weather. We'll touch on the native peoples that
were here and why we chased them out, and the early people that
built this country, started ranches and farms, built roadways and
dams, made electricity, drilled wells, and built this town."

J. D. took up an hour and a half and, by the end of it, hands
were raised with questions for the remaining half-hour. When the
last question had been answered, Nolan started clapping. Everyone
joined in. J. D. had a smile on his face you could have seen from town.

"Sometime again?" Miles said.

J. D. Wharton nodded. "You betcha. I enjoyed it."

They shook hands. J. D. picked up his folder, which he hadn't
opened, and walked out the door, down the stairs and to his pickup.

"Hope you all took notes. Tomorrow's class will be a test on what
you learned today from one of the county's grandest old citizens. You
may discuss it amongst yourselves but know that I was making notes
for test questions as he talked. Good information, huh?"

At four o'clock that afternoon Miles sat in the office at the mill
looking at the test Christmas Howell had devised for Billy. The questions were in simple language, but he couldn't answer any of them.
They pertained to trees and wood and water content and teeth for
the huge circular saw and frozen wood and growth rings and knots
and fungus and everything else that confronted a mill manager.

"Do you think Billy can answer these?" Miles asked.

Christmas shook his head. "I hope not. If he can, he'll have *my* job. But I wanted to know how far he got into the whole process. We started with lumber grading in the fall. I was hoping by the end of the first semester he'd be farther along than that."

"What do you think?"

"I just don't know. You know, Billy doesn't talk much."

"Tell me about it. It was weeks before I got more than a nod out of him." Miles put the test on the desk and rubbed his hands together. "Well—we'll know after tomorrow."

"What are you gonna do if this doesn't work?"

Miles shook his head. "Don't know. I'm counting on this and J. D. Wharton's work to get some real life experience into the subjects, to make them meaningful to the students, get them interested, and keep them interested."

"They most likely get some of it from their parents—"

"—Yes, but what teenager listens to his parents?"

"You got a point there."

"I'll send the completed test out to you tomorrow after Billy completes it. Let me know what it looks like."

"You got it."

AT FOURTH PERIOD TUESDAY, Miles assembled the high school mixed chorus to run through the songs for the Christmas program. The boys' and girls' choirs had both sung their songs, all memorized and in tune. Then he joined them together for their grand finale, with the whole school singing "O, Come All Ye Faithful"—all five verses.

Carla held up her hand. "Mr. Foster, I found a version that has eight verses."

"Well, don't tell Mrs. Grant. She's only printed out five."

"I thought we were going to memorize first and last and hum the others? That's what I did."

Miles looked at their faces. "How many of you did that?"

They all raised their hands. He took a deep breath and let it out with a snort. "Okay. Let's sing the first and last verses and hum the others. Got that?"

"We're going to hum the three middle verses?"

"Not now. We will at the concert, but not now."

"What if we forget?"

"I'll break your leg." He lifted his baton. "One, two, three, four … "

The song was passable. Mixed with the un-tuned chorus of grade school children, individual voices and tonal quality would be missed anyway except by their parents who would be following their children's lip movements.

When practice was over, he turned to leave and saw Mrs. Grant walking up from the back of the gym.

"Mr. Foster, may I have a word with you."

It wasn't a question: it was a demand.

"Yes, Mrs. Grant."

"My instructions were for the high school to join the grade school children in singing all five verses."

Miles nodded. "Yes. I am aware of that. But you see—"

"—Mr. Foster," she said as she raised her head to look at him through her bifocals. "I was put in charge of the Christmas Program, as I have been for the past five years, and the instructions were made clear. If you don't follow my instructions I will be forced to turn this matter over to Mr. Brooks."

"Look, we simply don't have time to memorize all five verses and get our other schoolwork done. Some of the children you sent up from grade school are not at the top of their skills and we—"

"—Are you saying we are failing the students?"

"I'm saying that the students I have in high school now are the same students you had in third grade during your last five years here. When they come to me, they are about to go out into the world and if they can't read and write and speak proper English because they spent hours learning five verses of a Christmas carol that nobody in the world knows except your third grade, then I have failed them as a teacher and counselor and friend. Furthermore—"

Mrs. Grant turned and left by the side door. He was standing alone in the gym on the stage with nothing but emptiness around him and shallow sunlight stabbing through the high windows across the top of the west wall. He felt heavy. He took a deep breath and walked down the four stairs to the gym floor and out the door. In the parking lot, a rush of cold air poured around the building, touching him with the edge until he got the full current of it close to the flagpole. The crystal clear penetrating smell of sagebrush beat through his loose clothes until he slid through the door and into the warmed hall, where lunch aromas circled.

MRS. GRANT WAITED UNTIL the end of the school day before taking the matter up with Calvin Brooks. He was stunted and slowed by the accident, and had only been back to work for two days. He was in the process of clearing off his desk to go home when she knocked and he motioned her to come in.

"Mr. Brooks, I have the most dreadful thing to say." Without waiting for his response, she said, "Mr. Foster is not following my instructions for the Christmas program. He is not having his choir learn the music as I requested."

"Is that so? I wonder what his reason is?"

She tilted her head. "He says they need the time for regular classes rather than learning the necessary verses."

"You have mentioned this to him before?"

"Oh, yes, several times. I expected him to comply. It is much easier for high school students to learn it than our third graders."

"Hmmm. Yes. Well—let me have a talk with him. I'll see what I can do."

"Do? You're the principal and superintendent, you can make him do it."

"Mrs. Grant—there is a limit to what I can enforce teachers to do in the confines of their classroom. I have to count on them to do what is required. I'll have a talk with him—"

"—As soon as possible?"

He nodded. "As soon as possible."

"Thank you. I hope you can get him to see how critical this is. Good day, Mr. Brooks."

"Good day, Mrs. Grant."

Calvin put the papers from the top of his desk into a drawer and locked it, pulled on the handle twice, put the key in his vest pocket, and stood up. The accident injury caused him to wince. He took a breath, straightened up and, with a hand on the desk to steady him, walked around it, took his coat off the rack and closed the door behind him, locked it, and tested it twice. He hoped the pain would go away soon. Winter did not favor cracked ribs and torn muscles.

THE WHISTLE WENT OFF at noon and as the school emptied for lunch, Billy sat down in Miles Foster's room to take a test.

"Billy—you want some coffee or a soda?" Miles said.

Billy shook his head.

"Okay. Here it is. Just circle the 'T' for True or the 'F' for False on each of these. I can't help you during the test, so don't ask for it. We clear on that?"

Billy nodded.

"You're supposed to do this in an hour, so get started. If you need to go to the bathroom or get a drink during the test, we'll stop the clock. Okay, Billy—go to it."

Billy's lips moved as he read the first question. He smiled and circled the capital T.

Miles got a cup of coffee from the kitchen, dumped some powdered cream and sugar in it, grabbed a lunch tray, and went back to his room. His neck bothered him and he closed his eyes and twisted his head in circles, first one way, then the other. When he looked up he saw Billy circling an answer and smiled. At one o'clock, he got Donavon to take his fifth-period study hall, and he drove out to the mill to deliver Billy's test to Christmas for grading.

THAT AFTERNOON AT THE end of study hall period, Mr. Brooks stuck his head in and nodded to Miles. "Could I see you in my office for a moment?"

"Sure."

In the principal's office, Calvin Brooks stood looking out the window toward town. He did not turn around when Miles entered.

"Mr. Foster, is it true that your students are not learning all the verses to some songs for the Christmas program?"

"Yes."

"Would you like to explain that?"

"I have, to Mrs. Grant and the students. If she had done her work with her third-grade students, then the students in high school who can't read, write, or speak correct English could spare the time now to learn a bunch of verses that nobody knows or ever heard of."

It was silent, and neither man moved. The old-fashioned steam radiator clicked several times, punctuating the silence.

"That will be all, Mr. Foster."

Miles spun and jerked the door open, letting it slide shut. He glanced over his shoulder to see Mr. Brooks still standing at the window, his right hand stroking the side of his face.

THIS TIME CALVIN BROOKS did not wait for period change, nor did he just stick his head into Miles's room. He opened the door full wide and walked straight to the front of his desk and looked down at Miles seated in his chair.

"I just received a phone call from Mr. Howell at the mill regarding a test Billy took here today. He would like you to call him back."

Miles straightened up, took a breath, and nodded. "Okay, thank you. I'll do that."

"Could you tell me why Mr. Howell would be interested in a test Billy took here and what authority he has for that information?"

"Could we step into the hall, please?"

Calvin nodded.

When the door closed, Miles said, "Billy is taking a lumber grading course as extracurricular activity. He wants to do that work when he graduates. Christmas made up the exam and I administered it over the noon hour. I ran it out to the mill for Christmas to grade it." He shook his head. "It is not officially school business."

Calvin straightened up. "I see." He turned and walked toward his room.

CALVIN AND WINIFRED SAT beside the fireplace, each with a lap robe over their legs and a glass of wine in their hand. They stared into the fire, as it crackled and popped against the screen.

"I would let him go in an instant if I could find his replacement. Finding someone to teach history and geography wouldn't be hard, but music would."

"Why don't you call Portland State and see if they have any graduates looking for employment? I think you could get someone, based on an emergency order, for the last half of the year that wasn't certified to teach those subjects."

"I might. We'd have to cancel the Cinerama he has put so much time and effort into. The students might take it poorly. They've worked hard on the plays and music."

"Marion can handle the plays. Maybe someone in the community with some music skills could take over the band and chorus."

"Hmm. That's a possibility, I suppose." He took a sip of wine. "You know, Winnie, I'm not up to the job of replacing him just now. The accident and the coming school board meetings . . . I don't want to have to spend time searching for his replacement."

"Well," she said. "Then we'll just have to get him to understand that you run this school."

"I've tried that. I don't know what else to do at this point."

"Censor him. Report him to the Department of Education in Salem."

"What are they going to do? This school only has a couple more years to run before they close it. The enrollment now doesn't justify the money spent on it." He tugged the robe up higher. "If we can make it through the next two years, we will have retirement without moving again. I don't want to move until we retire. Get all our stuff in one place and live the rest of our lives in peace."

"But you can't just let it go. I think he wants your job. And think of what the other teachers will think of you if you allow him to make his own rules on everything. First the band uniforms, then bringing in that horrid old man Wharton."

"He was showered and shaved and cleanly dressed—"

"—He tracked cow manure halfway down the first-floor hall."

"Well, Roscoe can handle that."

"Yes, he can. But you need to look at these things for what they are: a breakdown of your authority, and an indication to the rest of the staff that you won't do anything about it."

Calvin sipped the wine and continued looking into the fire. He had never won an argument with his wife and he didn't feel up to working at winning this one. Maybe he would report Miles Foster. That wouldn't take much effort or time.

"This is good wine, Winnie."

"This is a bottle that Mr. Foster gave us in the basket he brought to the hospital."

"Hmm. Very thoughtful of him."

"Don't let the alcohol sway your thoughts, Calvin. Stay firm on this."

CHAPTER 20

Mrs. Mildred Olson, from the Oregon Department of Education, climbed the stairs to the principal's office. She found Principal Calvin Brooks was not in his office, but teaching a Civics class. She sat down to wait and, as usual, perused the walls and trappings of the office. She got out of her chair to read some of the certificates framed on the back wall. She sat down, smoothed her dress, and crossed her legs.

Mr. Brooks arrived after the bell rang and smiled as he shook her hand. "Very good of you to come all this way."

"Not such a thing. I am doing my annual trip to the Central and Eastern school districts and made a special point to meet with you regarding the letter you sent in reference to Mr. Miles Foster. Would you be so kind as to expound on your letter?"

After Calvin explained in detail, the two sat in silence for a moment.

Mildred Olson looked out the window, collecting her thoughts. When she turned to him, she touched the eraser end of a pencil to her lower lip, something that distracted Calvin a lot. "I see the break from the normal curriculum and understand your frustration with that. There is a movement within the educational community to bring in outside sources and, while it may not be academic, it does provide a touchstone for local communities with their history and local setting. Even large cities like Portland started with a few people; log roads up over the hills, daily shipping on the Willamette River and all that is a part of their history. And—"

"—Mrs. Olson, pardon me for interrupting, but the point here is that he has gone over my head and instituted these changes without my approval or even consideration."

"Yes . . . well . . . *that* certainly cannot be condoned." She crossed her legs again and straightened her dress. "You have spoken to him about these items?"

Calvin nodded, his hands clasped in front of him.

"Do you believe his students will not be able to pass the state tests because of this variance in the planned program?"

"I am leery of it, yes."

"Hmmm. The tests will be distributed in March, with the results tallied in April. That is a little late for the seniors. What particularly has you incensed about the substitute items that Mr. Foster is interjecting into the curriculum?"

"One of the senior boys is studying a lumber mill manual instead of the prescribed reading material. The entire senior History and Geography class is listening to a local pioneer about weather and local history instead of the class title, which is 'Oregon History and Oregon Geography.'"

"Does he have test results from these students?"

Calvin shook his head. "I don't know."

"You've heard the old saw about giving a person enough rope to hang himself?"

"Yes."

"Let's do that—with your approval, of course. Let him proceed in this course and spring a surprise test on those classes after Christmas vacation. If they pass it, you have no worries. If they fail, you have time to give him his comeuppance and return to the regular curriculum. Does that meet with your approval?"

Calvin thought a minute, nodded. "Yes—that will be fine."

"Good. I'll send you the state test forms for those classes that cover what they should have learned by that time. You administer them and we'll see where this has led."

Calvin rose. "I'll see you out, Mrs. Olson."

"Please don't. I'd like to prowl the halls a bit to get the feel of a country school again. I went to school in Camas and seldom get to spend time in a small school like this. "

MILES DIDN'T EAT LUNCH in the faculty closet. Instead he grabbed a sandwich and an apple in the cafeteria, along with two cinnamon rolls, and drove out to the mill.

"Hi, Christmas." He held up the cinnamon rolls. "Look what I brought ya."

Christmas patted his belly. "Good fodder. Thank you."

They sat at the desk and spread out their lunch.

"I suppose you want to save the test results for last?" Miles said.

"Not necessarily. I'm willing to do it anytime. You got a preference?"

Miles stopped and stared out the only window, cut through the metal siding. "If Billy did well, I'd like to know now. If he did poorly, I'd rather wait until after we've eaten."

"So you'll know by whether I give you the results now or eat first; is that it?"

"Yeah, I guess. That's a lousy answer, isn't it?"

Christmas nodded.

"Oh, nuts. Do what you want to do." Miles took a bite of his sandwich.

Christmas unwrapped his own sandwich, peeled a banana, and set them down on a paper towel he used as a placemat. He tugged at each end of the paper towel until they were straight and rearranged the sandwich and banana equidistant between each side and the top and bottom, and set his coffee cup dead center.

A smile crept across Miles's face. "He passed it, didn't he?"

Christmas looked up, his grin covering every wrinkle and crease he'd built up over the last fifty years. "Yup."

Miles jumped up. "Hot dog! Hallelujah!" He danced around the end of the desk and hugged Christmas across the shoulders. "Man oh man oh man! That is something. Did he just clear the bar?"

"He cleared it a foot."

"So you'd hire him now . . . give him some sort of intent to employ him when he finishes school?"

"Yes. Providing we're open."

"Christmas—that's just great. That the best news I've heard since my wife told me we're going to have a baby."

"Two kinda different things . . . "

"Sure, but . . . hey, it's a grand feeling either way."

Miles took another bite of the sandwich and Christmas started with a cinnamon roll. "Don't want it to dry out," he said.

ROSCOE STOPPED MILES ON his way to the auditorium. "Can I see you a minute?"

"Sure."

"I noticed a state car here this morning. The occupant, a . . ." he pulled a card out of his breast pocket, "is a Mrs. Olson from the Oregon Department of Education. She was walking around the school, looking at things. Asked me about you and your students."

"What did you tell her?"

"Said you were a good man, that the kids liked you and you were doing a lot for the school and the town."

"Wow . . . all that?"

"Well, I had to say good stuff. She couldn't leave here thinking anything else. She came from the principal's office, so I knew she got the other side there most likely."

"Next thing you know, they'll accuse me of animal cruelty for milking the cow."

"She didn't ask about that." Roscoe tugged off his hat, ran his hand through his thick hair and repositioned the cap just so. "By the way, I've got a pickup load of good firewood if you're needing some."

"How much?"

"For you, nothing."

"How about some eggs in trade?"

"By golly, that would be good. Done deal. I'll bring it up Friday before the basketball game, if that's okay with you."

"I'll let Ele know. She handles the farm business. I'm in charge of the heating."

Roscoe smiled. "Sounds like a fair deal to me."

"It's worked so far."

Miles continued on into the auditorium. Shelly was standing in the hallway, wearing a tight skirt and peasant blouse. "What were you two plotting?" she said.

"Hi, Shelly. Roscoe was bargaining firewood for eggs."

"Is that why he gave you the Education Department woman's card?"

Miles canted his head, a frown formed on his brow. "What would you know about that?"

"I overheard her asking Roscoe about you in the hall."

"You spying for a living now?"

"No, silly, I was coming out of the girls' room and I have sharp ears."

"That's not all you have that's sharp."

"Ummm. Thank you."

"I meant your skills and IQ."

"I can take it any way I want."

"If you don't mind being mistaken." He turned sideways and moved past her, taking the stairs two at a time. "Come on, we've got practicing to do."

"I'd love to."

He kept walking.

The choir had the notes right, they had memorized the words, but somehow it didn't create the coordinated beautiful lulling feeling that Christmas carols used to engender in him. There was something missing. After twenty minutes of practice in timing, and at various volumes, he put a stop to it and stood looking at the students.

"What's wrong with this?"

Shelly stuck up her hand. "It's so grade school-ish."

"The Mormon Tabernacle Choir sings them."

"Yes, but they have an organ and a band behind them," Randall said.

"We've got a band," Tommy said. "But we're all singing."

"Maybe that's it. Band members, please get your instruments and let's try it together," Miles said.

The last ten minutes, the combined band and choir ran through the Christmas program music. There was life and song and volume to it, and Miles could feel the tingle start like it did when he was a child and came down on Christmas morning with carols playing on the record player. He could even smell the cinnamon rolls, sausage, and coffee that his dad prepared for the family. That's what was missing—the band and the food. Peace and goodwill to all men.

MILES HOLLERED AT ELE while removing his shoes in the utility room. "Roscoe is coming by with a load of firewood. I told him we'd trade him some eggs for it."

"You shouldn't do that without asking me. Those flea-bitten chickens are only laying half what they were."

"He doesn't need much. What do you think?"

"I think two dozen eggs."

Miles looked up. "Why is everything in twos?"

"I like twos today."

"Okay. Twos it is, then."

"You'll have to fetch the eggs."

"I can do that. He'll be here Friday before the game."

"Save enough for Sunday breakfast," she said. "I hate eating cereal on Sundays. It's the one day I get to splurge on bacon, eggs, and pancakes. Yum."

"You're gonna pump that baby full of cholesterol."

"She can take it. She's tough like her mother."

"At least you're not smoking and drinking. She might be able to handle a weekly shot of cholesterol."

"Give her something to brag about in kindergarten."

Miles shed his socks and shirt. "Do you think she'll go to kindergarten here?"

"Who knows? That's five years and six months away. The world could end by then."

"Tamarack would miss that, wouldn't they?"

"It might. Depends on which way the wind's blowing."

"You're crazy."

"Yeah, but look who married me."

"We're both crazy."

"That's what my parents said."

He smiled. "Did they really say that?"

"Said I'd be barefoot and pregnant, plucking eggs from under lice-infested hens and milking a cow."

"Where'd they get foresight like that?" He shed his last article of clothing.

"It's in their DNA."

"Didn't know your people had any DNA. I'm gonna shower now, so please don't use water anywhere in the house."

"Temperature changes in the shower are good for you. Keeps your skin young."

"What's left of it after freezing and burning."

"Go shower and leave me alone to contemplate the end of the world."

"I'd invite you in but there's not room for the two of you."

"Just don't use all the hot water. We two may wish to shower, too."

Just as Miles closed the shower curtain, Roscoe drove into the driveway and backed his pickup up to the woodpile. While he was throwing tamarack chunks out of the pickup bed, Ele slipped on her outside shoes, took two dozen eggs out of the refrigerator, and deposited them in the front seat.

"Hello, Roscoe. That looks like great burning wood."

"Hello, Miss Ele," he said, doffing his hat. He nodded at the wood. "It's good dry wood. It'll split easy."

"I put two dozen eggs in the front seat."

He nodded twice. "That's just fine. I made a good trade didn't I?"

"We need the wood; you need the eggs. Looks like a good trade for both of us."

He stopped and mopped his forehead with a large red-and-black-checkered kerchief, then stuffed it in his back pocket. "I'll just get on with this."

"You know anything about chickens?"

He stopped with a wood round in his hands, shook his head. "No, ma'am. Not much."

"These used to lay a dozen eggs a day, and now I'm lucky if I get five or six."

"Yup. They'll do that sometimes."

"How do I change it?"

"You just have to wait them out. It'll go back up again."

"How long?"

He shook his head. "Don't know."

Ele turned and walked toward the house. Over her right shoulder she felt the wind pass around the barn and heard it rustle the dead grass by the garden fence, whistling a little even as it purred over the autumn land. She turned to look, but it had passed and the grass stood tall and unmoving against the wire fence and the old tamarack posts that held it up.

CHAPTER 21

MRS. GRANT GREETED TOWNSPEOPLE and parents as they entered the gym, now being used as the auditorium for the Christmas program. Backstage, the grade school kids were on one side and high school on the other. Miles slid the podium to the side behind the curtain and set up his music stand.

When her watch said 7:00 p.m., Mrs. Grant instructed the two seventh grade boys to open the curtain in slow motion while the grade school children sang "Jingle Bells" and two boys dressed as deer pulled a sleigh across the stage through soap flakes. One slipped and fell; the other deer looked at him and everyone laughed.

The grade school choir sang, the high school choir sang, and as they got ready for the remaining two songs, Miles nodded to Tommy and the band members stood down and sat on folding chairs behind the chorus and picked up their instruments. Standing in front of the students, Mrs. Grant could not see what was happening, but she saw some high schoolers leave the chorus formation. Not knowing what was going on, she started into "Deck the Halls" and heard the band join the two choirs; it was a lot more lively than she expected. She searched for Miles, but he was busy studying the music and did not meet her eyes. She directed it through to the end and the audience erupted in applause. She bowed, had the children bow, and turned back for the final "O, Come All Ye Faithful."

Both choirs and the band got through the first verse. Miles quieted the band as the grade school choir plowed on through verses two, three, and four. For the final verse, the band and high school choir enveloped the smaller sounds of the younger set.

The audience began a standing ovation and Mrs. Grant smiled at the students, turned and bowed and asked the children to bow in unison. Miles stepped off the podium, staying behind the curtain and letting Mrs. Grant absorb the full pleasure of the applause. While she was shaking hands and wishing people "Merry Christmas," Miles and Tommy put away the chairs, stand, and podium and were walking out the door when Mrs. Grant called out to him.

"Mr. Foster, would you mind waiting a minute, please?"

Miles turned. "Thanks, Tommy. You go ahead."

She advanced over toward him like a steamer coming into port. "Mr. Foster, I don't like being surprised like that. You didn't tell me the band was going to play."

"No—I didn't. Didn't plan on it myself until yesterday. The choir sounded so much better—so much more alive with the band in the background—that I thought to use it."

"You should have asked my permission."

"I would rather ask your forgiveness than ask permission." He bowed low. "Will you please forgive me, Mrs. Grant?"

She stammered, her hands together in front of her solid middle. "Oh, I don't know what to do." She shook her head, turned and walked off to join Calvin and Winnie, who were seeing the last people out.

On his way home, Miles picked up a cake mix that Ele wanted and a bottle of Jim Beam whiskey. He was going to try a recipe for bourbon balls that Earl Benson had dropped off.

He put the vanilla wafers on the counter top, kissed Ele hello and twisted the top off the whiskey. He sniffed it, then lifted it to his lips and took a swallow.

"Egads—and that's the stuff Donavon drinks all the time? That's poison."

"Let me smell it," Ele said. She recoiled. "Yikes—people drink that to feel good?"

"That's what the label says. I'm going to try it in this recipe Earl gave me. You can sit down and watch the master chef create this wonderful confection."

"Well—don't take all night at it. I've got supper to prepare." She pulled a chair over close to the heater. "Let's go to Portland for a few days during the holidays."

He turned to her. "You want to?"

"Yeah—I do. See our folks and friends."

"I kinda thought we'd have our first married Christmas here in our own home."

She was silent for a moment. "That's nice, but it's lonesome without family around, don't you think?"

"I've got people around me all day while you have only chickens and a cow that are as lonely as you. I'll go to Portland if you wish."

"That's a good fellow. Indulge the bulging bride." She smiled. "I'll call Mom and tell her we'll be over. She'll want to help name the little thing, anyway."

CHAPTER 22

Snow, molded by the constant winter wind, stood in riffles and gullies on the driveway and yard when Miles and Ele got back from Portland. Roscoe had taken good care of the cow and chickens, in that they were all alive and upright.

"It's cold in here," Ele said as she set down a box of groceries. "Would you please build a big fire? Me and the baby are freezing."

"Where do you get off pretending you speak for the two of you?" Miles said.

"I'm in intimate contact with her. She tells me all."

"Has she chosen a name from the two pages your mom gave you?"

"She's working on it."

"Gotta be Samantha."

"Miles, that's so old. She needs a modern name."

Miles crumpled paper, put kindling on top, threw in a cup of kerosene, touched a match to it and slammed the door shut, forcing the smoke and fire up the metal chimney of the Ashley wood stove.

"Do you have to always start the fire like a pyromaniac?" Ele said.

"It works."

"It could kill us all."

"The explosion or the fire?"

"Does it make any difference?"

"No. The autopsy will tell them which."

"That's comforting."

"I'm going to unpack first, and then I'll check the chickens and cow."

"The cow's name is Spot."

"Right. And she remembers that."

"Of course she does. She's a lady with a name."

The chickens huddled around the cracked corn Miles put in the feeder. He bashed the water tray against the side of the chicken coop to get the ice out of it and refilled it from a bucket of warm water. He replaced the burned-out light bulb that added some heat to the coop. There were three eggs.

Roscoe must have picked up the eggs earlier today.

Snow was curved around the corner and into the three-sided barn that Spot chose to lounge in when she wasn't foraging for winter grass that stuck above the snow. She was lying down, chewing her cud, and turned her head to look at him.

"Spot, old girl, how goes it?" He didn't expect an answer. He got none. She continued chewing and looked away. He checked the hay in her box, broke the ice in the water bucket, refilled it, and she didn't look at him again.

Back in the house Miles put the three eggs in a bowl to be washed, threw a log on the fire now roaring like a windstorm, peeled off his hooded sweatshirt and sat in his chair close to the fire.

"Spot didn't give me the time of day," he said.

"That's not her job."

"She could at least get up and acknowledge me when I come into her barn."

"She doesn't think that way."

"She doesn't think at all."

"You see," Ele poked her head around the corner. "That's why you don't get any respect from her. You think she's dumb, and she can sense that."

"She's dumber than my students. They nod or say hello or get up if they are in my way."

"That's social training. She hasn't had that sort of education."

"She is a cow; she is going to stay a cow; and she is not going to get education."

"I'll train her when the baby gets here and needs training too. It'll be good for Baby to have a classmate."

"When's supper going to be ready?"

"I haven't started yet. Probably half an hour."

"I'm gonna have a drink of that Jim Beam with some 7up in it."

"So Spot the cow drove you to drink?"

"You could say that. Where's the 7up?"

"Try the back porch if it isn't frozen."

Miles mixed the drink and returned to the chair by the fire. "This isn't so bad with 7up in it." He took another sip. "I could get used to this."

"I don't think you want to do that. That's called alcoholism," Ele said from the kitchen.

He removed his shoes and stretched his toes. The fire got too hot and he slid the chair back, put his feet on a box, crossed his arms and sat, his mind wandering over all the things left to do in the year. He set the drink down and closed his eyes.

"Wake up, honey. Supper's ready." Ele was rubbing his shoulder.

He popped awake. "That was interesting."

"What?"

"I dreamed the state education department cancelled all of my classes and didn't give the students credit."

"Could they do that?"

Miles shrugged. "Who knows? It was a dream—not reality."

"Did you wash up after the chickens and cow duties?"

He held his hands up. "Yup. Want to sniff?"

"Heavens, no. I believe my husband. Slide your chair up to the table and dig in. You are approved."

TURNS OUT THAT MABEL Kreneke didn't move home from J. D. Wharton's ranch house until two weeks after the Christmas program where they were seen sitting side by side and leaving in one pickup. It was all over town. When J. D. picked up his mail every Wednesday, he just smiled at the remarks cast his way. He agreed to meet Miles in his office, corner booth at the only restaurant in town.

J. D. was digging into a cinnamon roll and a sausage patty when Miles slid into the booth.

"Don't let me interrupt your eating habits," Miles said.

"Wouldn't consider it," J. D. replied. "Besides—you're late."

Miles looked at his watch. "Two minutes is late?"

"The meeting was agreed to at eight, not 8:02."

Miles nodded. "Yes, sir. I agree with that."

J. D. stabbed a piece of sausage on the end of his fork with a chunk of cinnamon roll ahead of it and stuffed it into his mouth. He looked up, slowed down his chewing, and smiled. "What'd you want?"

"I want you to take on educating two boys in history and geography. They need special help, the kind only you can give them."

J. D. put his elbows on the table, wiped his mouth with the paper napkin and intertwined his fingers. "You buttering me up?"

"No. I could, but you're too smart to buy that. No—you're the best hope these kids have to get a passing test score."

"Are they idiots?"

Miles shook his head. "Not at all. They're behind the curve. Had them tested and they came out fine in basic knowledge, but they're slow learners, their parents haven't done anything along the lines of formal education and don't even push it much. I don't want them to go out of here without a diploma. Don't want to give them a social pass."

"Sounds like a lot of 'don't want's on your side of the fence. How about some 'do want's?"

Miles smiled. "I was wondering if they could come out to your ranch couple of times a week and sit down with you and go over the local history and geography, like you did when you came to our class."

"Isn't that your job?"

"It is. But there is nothing preventing me from using local sources."

"So that's what I am? A local source?"

"We can give you any title you'd like. Would you do it?"

J. D. looked across the same street; saw the same things; knew life was changing all over and had his own doubts about the viability of the town in the twentieth century. He rubbed his palms on the napkin and put his forearms on the table. "Miles—I'd give you an arm and a leg if I thought it would help these boys, the school and this town. When I came here we had two mills, a thriving timber business, ranchers were selling short yearlings as fast as they could grow 'em and wheat was moving out of here by the truckloads. The town had four, five hundred people, a CPA and a lawyer, a dentist that came in once a week and a medical clinic staffed with a full-time nurse. We even had a marshal and a jailhouse. The school had maybe a hundred students, but more importantly, the town had a bedrock of 'can do' attitude. Everybody wanted their kids to do better, go farther in life than they had been. We sent fifteen or twenty to college every year." He looked down at his empty plate and threw his wadded napkin in it. "But you know what? None of those college graduates ever came back to Tamarack to live. They didn't come back to work or practice a profession or run a mill or build a business or even teach school. Just for a few years, even— they didn't come back.

"You're wondering where I'm going with this, and the truth is I don't know. I'm just venting, and you're not the one I should be venting at. It should be at the short-timers who come in here, work for a year or so, and then are gone, leaving us to muck up their leavings."

Miles laid a hand on J. D.'s arm. "J. D.—these kids I want you to educate will come back. They're bred and born here—they are the soil that holds the grass roots together and having a diploma won't help them or hurt them working on a ranch or in the mill or falling timber, but knowing the history and geography of this country will be a blessing all their lives. We measure progress by history and knowing the geography will give them a deep-seated feeling for this land, something to build their lives on knowing the creation and evolution of the mountains, the valleys, and the rivers and creeks. You know that. You've lived it all your life."

J. D. nodded. "I'll give it a go. But they gotta be gone by four of a Friday afternoon and no coming around again until Monday noon."

Miles removed his hand. "Mabel will be gone by then?"

J. D. blushed. He looked down at his hands, smiled, and glanced out the window. His lips moved a little but he didn't say anything, just stared out the window.

"Thanks, J. D. You know the boys. I'll send them out with the assignments. Try and stick with the subject matters. They're slow but they're not stupid."

NOLAN AND HIS SISTER, Rebecca Benson, sat together and Shelly, Carla, and Brenda sat in front. They read from the papers on their desks and often took a pencil and filled in a circle on those papers. Miles sat at his desk. It was noon hour, and he nibbled at a sandwich and chips the cafeteria had sent up. It was preliminary test day; a test before a test to determine what the students didn't know before the final state test that all colleges used to determine incoming freshman eligibility.

Miles caught Shelly looking at him several times when she turned pages. She hadn't made an overt move since the barbeque dance, but her eyes spoke volumes when she wanted to pass her feelings along. He hoped she would find a boyfriend and let loose of her fixation on him.

He heard the door open and turned his head. Calvin Brooks motioned him to come out into the hall. He stood up, glanced over the students and walked out.

"Mr. Foster. Mrs. Brooks and I need to go to Prineville for a check-up from the accident. I'd like you to be the administrator while I am gone. We'll be gone just the one day."

"Can I sit in your chair while I'm administrator?"

"Well, do you think that is necessary? It's only for one day."

"Just kidding, Calvin. Sure, I'll do it."

"Fine. Fine." He turned to go. "That will be Friday—this Friday."

Miles nodded.

MRS. BROOKS BROUGHT THEIR lunch up to his office for a change. She asked Calvin if he had appointed anyone to be administrator for Friday.

"Yes. Mr. Foster has agreed to do it."

"You are going to have him do it again after the last incident where he threatened those two students with his belt?"

"It is part of my plan with the Department of Education to hand Mr. Foster enough rope to hang himself."

"My mother always said you ran silent and deep, Calvin. Do you think it will work?"

"I can only hope."

"When do you need to make your recommendations to the board for re-hiring teachers?"

"March fifteenth."

"Are you going to recommend any others be released?"

"No. Not at this time. I'd like to keep the rest until we leave, don't you think?"

She nodded. "They seem a good lot and, of course, the grade school teachers have been here for years."

"Yes . . . I hate for them to be let go if the district fails."

"And it will, Calvin. We already know of eight children that won't be back next year in grade school."

"Yes, and four from high school." He folded up the wax paper his sandwich had been wrapped in and placed it in the brown paper sack, folded that twice, got up and put it in his coat pocket. "I've been asked by the board to make a determination of how many students we need to have from outside of town to afford to make the school bus runs. Everyone is seeing the handwriting on the wall."

Mrs. Brooks put her hands in her lap. "We heard today that the mill is running short of logs and may close."

"We hear that every year."

She nodded. "One day it might be true."

"Just two more years will see us into retirement."

"We could go somewhere else and finish off. Maybe somewhere over on the coast."

"I don't want to leave here, Winnie. I want my last two years to be right here where we know people and the system and the board . . . starting anew is anathema to me." He turned in his chair, elbows on the arms, fingers forming a pyramid and looked out the window over the town and across to the hillside, where the sign for the only motel in town blinked away at the wind that pulsed and rocked it on its flexible steel post. "I just don't want to move again."

Winifred lowered her head, took the white hanky and dabbed at her nose then stuffed it back up her sleeve. "Very well. I hope you've made the right decision on Mr. Foster."

"It will work out, Winnie. There's no one else, really."

Winnie closed the door in slow motion, not letting it slam, and walked down the stairs out the building and across to the grade school. She stood with her feet planted and turned to look back at the high school.

So this is where we end our careers after thirty years. The town is dying; the school is dying; the mill may die . . . and Calvin and I are dying. Everything I see is old except the children.

She swallowed and put her hand on the door handle. It was freezing. As she tugged at it a breeze whistled by, caught the door and swung it open and she went inside. She shivered, turned, and looked out the door glass. The breeze was spinning little whirlwinds in the dirt on the other side of the concrete sidewalk, almost like it was talking to her.

THE SENIORS TEST WENT until 1 p.m. with only bathroom breaks allowed. The five hopeful college bound students gave up their pencils and papers, stood, stretched, and, smiling, left the room in a group. Shelly lingered until the door closed, and then approached Miles's desk.

"I just don't know what I'd give for a good grade," she said.

Miles smiled up at her. "How about a year's salary and a Jaguar XK140?"

She coughed. "That's out of my league, but I have some personal assets."

"I'm sure you do, but they aren't currency in this county."

"We could go to another county . . . "

"No, Shelly." He reached for her paper.

"Spoilsport," she said, as she handed him the paper and walked out. Miles took a deep breath. *Made it past that minefield.*

CHAPTER 23

ELE WAS IN BED when Miles got home and he bent over to kiss her hello.

"What's with the bed routine?" he said.

Ele sat up partway. "I feel lousy."

"You been drinking your water?"

She nodded. "You're going to have to take care of the chickens and cow again. I didn't get it done."

"You're feeling that poorly, huh?"

She shook her head. "This is the worst feeling in the world. If I knew having a baby was going to be this bad, I'd have gone into a convent."

"Calvin asked me to be substitute superintendent while he is gone, Friday."

"That's nice."

"I didn't think he cared for me much, especially after the Christmas program."

"You'll do fine."

"I wonder if he thinks so?" He looked off toward the corner of the room, up in the dark place where the ceiling and walls met and a spider had built a web.

Miles changed clothes, put on his jacket and hat, grabbed the egg basket and milk bucket and forged out into the wind. It bit into his left side as soon as he left the protection of the house.

The wind. Always the wind and always wondering where it was going to come from. Some cold; some dry; some wet ... but wind.

It was almost dark and the chickens had roosted. There was a soft mutter as he entered; a few hens stood up. He checked the nesting boxes and pulled out three eggs.

"Hey, girls, this isn't cutting it. The grain and hard work is worth more than the eggs you're putting forth. Get with the program or face the pot." None of them paid the slightest attention.

Spot was standing up but flailed him with her tail when he moved the milking stool in close. He backed away.

"I can hobble you, if that's what you want."

She turned her head, chewing, her big eyes displaying mock intelligence and went back to the hay. Miles sat on the stool and washed off her udder with warm water. She seemed to like that. He went without the hobbles. When he had milked her dry he looked in the bucket. It was less than half full.

"Spot, where's all the milk? You selling it on the side? Picking up a little retirement money for your old age?"

Back inside he put the milk and egg buckets on the floor, removed his shoes and jacket and walked into the kitchen in his socks. "Honey . . . our livestock is shorting us something fierce. Not enough eggs or milk to be worth it."

Ele replied from the bedroom. "They've been going down."

"I got three eggs and a gallon of milk." He put the eggs in the sink. "How long has this been going on?"

"Last couple of weeks," she said.

"Not a good trade for the feed and effort."

"No, I guess not."

"It appears we agree on that."

"So what are you going to do about it? I've got my hands full having a baby. I can't handle the chickens and cow and laundry and cooking and everything else around here."

"Whoa. I'm sorry. I didn't mean to dump on you."

"You'll have to handle it. I hereby declare you head farmer. Leave me out of it."

Miles sat down on a wooden stool next to the sink. The howl of the fire in the stove took over the house. He glanced at the flames leaping against the glass window.

What a fiery hell. Why anyone would want to be cremated is beyond me.

He heard Ele from the bedroom. "Honey . . . will you bring me a cup of tea, please?"

"You want any supper?"

"No. Tea, and maybe a piece of dry toast."

He put the eggs and milk away, got supper, carried it in on a tray and sat with Ele in the bedroom. The only sound was Ele crunching into the dry toast. She looked straight ahead, her mouth revolving with a rhythm that approached mechanical.

"When we get down to two eggs a day, the hens go. A quart of milk from Spot, and I tie her to her owner's fence and walk away."

"You can't just tie Spot to a fence and walk away."

"You said it was my problem. That's how I propose to handle it."

Ele shook her head, closed her eyes, and slumped down on the pillows.

Miles took the dishes to the kitchen, cleaned up, separated the milk, refrigerated it and stood, hands on the counter, looking out the window at the moon frozen in the sky a foot above the painted hills. A shaking juniper tree caused him to focus on it. The wind had changed direction since he had collected the eggs. It was going to be a cold night. Before going to bed, he put two logs into the stove and shut the damper down and stood a minute collecting the radiant heat into his body. He could take that to bed with him. Maybe it would help Ele.

FRIDAY SLIPPED AWAY FROM dawn to dark with no unusual circumstances. The school did not need a superintendent that day and Miles was secretly happy about that, although he did have his lunch sitting in Calvin's chair looking out the window all by his lonesome.

MONDAY MORNING MILES GOT a call from the testing company. They had evaluated the scores for the seniors and reported that all placed in the top ten percentile. He called the five seniors into the typing room.

"Please close the door behind you, Carla. Everybody take a seat. I have the test results for you."

He clenched his jaw and narrowed his eyes. He waited a minute, then broke into a smile: "Okay . . . you all passed and were in the top 10 percent. Great work."

They leaped up and hugged each other. Shelly hugged Miles. When she finally took her arms from around his neck, her eyes looked like deep pools of swirling green water. His chest felt damp and his thighs hot. He put his hands on her waist and moved her away. "Congratulations to you guys. You did a wonderful job."

"So did you, Teach," Nolan said. "Without you, we wouldn't have made it."

Miles smiled and nodded. "Yeah, you would have. You've all got that thing inside you that makes life work—personal responsibility. I expect you all to do well." He blinked several times, his eyes moist. "Now, get your applications in to your favorite college. I'll sign them and we'll get them on the way. The Pony Express will be through here any day."

CHRISTMAS HOWELL CALLED FROM the mill office asking for Miles. Calvin took the call and asked if he could help him.

"No thanks, Calvin. This is something Miles and I have worked on. I'd rather go through him on this, if you don't mind."

"I'll see if he's free." He went in to Miles's room and up to his desk. "Mr. Howell from the mill is on the phone for you. Something he wants to discuss with you personally."

"Thanks, Mr. Brooks. Do you want to take my class while I answer it?"

"No—they'll be okay." He walked out and into his office with Miles and stood by the window, his back to the desk and phone, his chin cradled in his hand.

"Hi, Christmas," Miles said.

"Miles, I gotta particular situation. My lumber grader has developed a cancer and is going to the hospital for tests and stuff. Wondering if you could spare Billy for a week?"

Miles let his face expand into a smile. "As far as I'm concerned you can, but I'll have to clear it with Mr. Brooks. Hang on."

With his hand over the receiver Miles put the question to Calvin.

Calvin turned, his eyes narrowed. "No, I don't think so. Too close to finals for Billy."

"Mr. Brooks, you and I both know that Billy won't be going on to anything that will require more than having graduated. This will give him a great deal of pride and some practical experience of putting his education and knowledge to use. It's only a week . . . " he trailed off, knowing his argument was not as strong as he would have liked to have made it.

Calvin shook his head.

Miles put the phone back to his ear. "Christmas, we'll have to think it over. I'll get back with you." He hung up the phone and looked at Calvin, who had returned to staring out the window.

This is not the time or place. Think it over; be cool. Return to fight another day.

Back in class, Miles sat upright in his chair seething from the inside out. Everything he had been working for with the three boys was coming to a head. Billy being invited to fill in for the grader was super. J. D.'s adoption of the other two had yet to produce strong results, but there was still time. Spring was coming and that always looked good to young men.

Miles called Billy up to his desk.

He whispered to him. "Billy, can you get your parents to agree to let you work at the mill for a week—I mean, skipping school."

"Dunno," he said.

"Ask them. Get back to me. You want to do it if they'll agree?"

"Will it be okay with the school?"

"I'll figure out a way."

Billy nodded.

THE TYPING CLASS—ALL girls and one boy—had reached 35 words per minute on timed tests with less than three errors. Miles knew it would happen. They were all that good. He could project their upward progress to 50 WPM if they practiced over the summer.

Teaching is so much fun when you've got students you like, that don't mind being in school, that can take direction. Progress—that's it. How differently I looked at this school the first day Ele and I drove up and parked in the lot. It's the people inside this building that make it great. The building just keeps the weather out and the lights on. Now—gotta figure out how to get Billy's week in the mill to happen.

"I'M HOME," MILES YELLED when he opened the door.

"Good. Would you please make us a cup of tea and a toast? We're starving to death."

He hung up his jacket. "Don't you two eat when I'm gone?" He poured water into the teapot, put it on the burner, and got out the toaster.

"We had a handful of dry cereal."

"No milk?"

"Milk makes me puke."

"Spot will be disappointed to hear that."

"Don't tell her until after the baby's born. Anything interesting at school today?"

"Two things. I'm trying to figure out how to get Calvin to let Billy work at the mill for a week. Their lumber grader is going to be gone and Christmas is willing to hire Billy for that week. Problem is, Calvin won't excuse him from school."

"Why don't you have him do it during spring vacation?"

"What?"

"Why not do it during spring vacation?"

"That's what I thought you said. That's pure genius—if Christmas can wait that long." He whooped and clapped his hands. "That's genius, Ele."

"You didn't marry no dummy. When's our tea and toast gonna be here?"

"Coming right up, Madam Genius. I want to make a quick phone call."

Miles brought the tea and toast in on a tray with a five-dollar bill under the napkin.

"What's the money for?"

"For solving the unfathomable problem of Billy working at the mill. Christmas can wait until then and Billy's parents have agreed. No need for Calvin's blessing."

"If I knew you were paying for ideas, I'd have worked harder on them." She lifted the five-dollar bill up by its corner and stretched out her arm. "Please deposit this in my idea account. It will be the first of many. I expect us to retire on this account in the near future, God willing and the Creek don't rise."

"The Creek being Tamarack?"

"No, silly, the Creek Indians. Didn't you read the history that you're teaching to all those vulnerable children under your care?"

"I thought I did."

"Well—Benjamin Hawkins was asked to come back to Washington by the president, and he responded that he'd be there if God was willing and the Creek Indians didn't rise up and scalp every man, woman, and child in the territory. Course by that time, the Creek Indians weren't up to rising up anymore."

"Thank you for that short history lesson."

"You're welcome. Gotta keep the tea and toast people happy around here. We'll have another toast, if you please."

"Coming up."

"And what was the second good thing at school today?"

Miles shouted from the kitchen. "The five seniors in advanced studies passed the state tests in the top ten percentile. They're filling out college applications this very moment."

"Oh, Miles . . . that's wonderful. You made it work."

"*They* made it work, with my help."

"Their parents will be proud, and so should you be. "

"Now—to get Calvin to relax over these things."

"He's got to see that what you are doing is working. That will satisfy him, don't you think?"

"What I think and what he and his wife think could be two different things."

"I heard the toast pop up. Oh, yummy yummy."

MARION STILLSON WAS ADAMANT about it. "I agreed to direct two one-act plays, not three."

"But Marion—there are three," Miles said.

"I don't care. It's your show and I'll do the combined freshman-sophomore plays. You handle the junior and senior play."

"I've got a hundred other things to do..."

"Tough turtle. You planned it, and I'm willing to do two during English classes. But I'd lose what sanity I retain if I went for the third one."

Miles shoved his lower lip up over his top one and stared at the floor. "Did you ever notice how old the boards are in this floor?" He pointed to a joint in the floor.

"I think the Indians built this school before white men came to the valley."

"Naw—they didn't have concrete and planed lumber."

"Well, it might have been a bit later. It's had three changes of furnaces you know."

"This one keeps us warm. I'm happy. Marion... you sure I can't talk you into directing the senior play?"

"Neither love nor money nor extension of my contract."

"But you'll be ready by March thirtieth?"

"You bet."

"Thank you for buying into this. I'm looking forward to it becoming an annual event."

Marion put her coffee cup down and looked into his eyes. "You know, Miles, you're making a lot of extra work for yourself and it isn't going to get you anywhere in this town. Every year, teachers come and go. Calvin and Winifred have been here five years, I've been here twelve. All the rest of you guys are first year teachers. There were eighty kids in school when I started. Now there are forty. If the mill closes, there'll be thirty. The only thing holding this town together is ranchers like us who need stuff closer than John Day or Prineville. If the school has an annual Cinerama or not is not going to change one thing."

"Yes it will. It will give these kids a chance to do something they haven't done. Give them a pride in doing plays and music and get applause and public approval. Look at how the uniforms changed the perception of the band, how townspeople came out and supported the barbeque."

"Sure they did, and they will. But it won't matter when contract time comes around and salaries are pushed against the budget. They'll still buy you for another year for the least they can and the barbeque, the Cinerama, and band uniforms will all be in the distant background."

"I'm not doing it for me. I'm doing it for them."

Marion scoffed. "That's good to say now. But wait until your contract is on the line and the students have nothing to say about it . . . and neither do you."

"Do all teachers get cynical in middle age?"

"Just those that practice reality checks on a frequent basis."

"Thanks, Marion, for doing the two plays. We'll have a lot of fun."

ROSCOE STOPPED MILES HALFWAY to the gym. "How high do you want that hangin' platform?"

"Just so he drops a little. I don't want him to die while we finish the song," Miles said.

"Come look at it. I've got it so it drops about six inches."

The two of them entered the gym and went up on the stage where Roscoe had constructed an artificial tree for the hanging scene from "Tom Dooley." The boys' chorus was to sing it, and the worst singer amongst them was to play the villain, whom the others would proceed to hang as they sang the song.

"Looks fine, Roscoe. Can you make it look more like a white oak tree?"

"Yup," Roscoe said. "Just wondering about the drop height."

"The rope will be hooked into this belt so if he slips he won't choke."

"That'll be good. I'll leave 'er at six inches then, if that works for you."

"That works fine. Thank you. If we ever need to hang someone you can build a higher drop."

J. D. WHARTON AMBLED INTO the parking lot as Miles was shutting down the school bus from the last run.

"Hi, J. D.," Miles said. "What brings you back to school?"

"Evening, Miles. Such a lovely evening, thought I'd bring you up to speed on what the boys and I have been doin'."

"Wanta go inside?"

"Naw. Won't take long." He set a foot on the bumper, rested his elbow on his thigh and took a deep breath. "We—the boys and I—we just got back from doing some geography and history work in the Painted Hills. You know those kids had never seen the hills? Didn't know a thing about them. And them living right here— what, twenty miles from them? Now how can someone expect to understand the geography and history of Oregon if they don't know their own backyard?"

Miles shook his head. "Well—"

"They didn't know they didn't know. And that's the worst thing about living. If a balloon never stretches it doesn't know how far it can stretch."

"That's what I so much wanted you to do, to awaken them. They're not idiots. They know their way around a ranch and a car, but that can't be their whole life."

"Well—what I'm wanting to ask you is if you can get them tested on this local stuff instead of the whole state?"

"I just don't know." Miles looked down at the scuffed boot clinging to the bumper. "I can try. I can ask the Department of Education to approve a testing of local geography and history." He smiled. "Me and the department are not on the best of terms but it doesn't hurt to ask."

"They can't kill you for asking, can they?"

"They haven't killed anyone in the last ten years," Miles said.

"Then you got that goin' for you."

"I'll give it a try."

"Good." J. D. smiled and offered his hand. "See you at the hanging."

Miles shook his hand. "You gotta make sure the rope breaks if they try and hang me."

"I was afraid you'd ask for another favor. Good evening."

"And the same to you, J. D. Say hello to Mabel for me."

J. D. turned around, a large smile on his face. "I'll do that. I'm sure she'll appreciate it."

THE NEXT DAY, MILES took a chunk of time out of study hall and wrote a draft letter to the Department of Education explaining what he thought were the unique circumstances surrounding education in Tamarack; the two boys' IQs and lack of parental support and drive; and how geography and history related to a local area instead of the entire state made sense for the subjects and requested that they be tested on that. Then he added the last paragraph.

"In as much as I am not a member of the Oregon Education Association, I do not expect support from that organization. However, should you require documentation of the efforts these boys have put in and the credentials of J. D. Wharton, who has sixty years of local knowledge and expertise in the geographical and historical background of this county, I can get that to you pronto."

He read it over and then crossed out "pronto" and wrote "immediately" instead.

After typing it and signing it, he went downtown, placed it in outgoing mail, then walked across the street to the General Store and picked up the items Ele had asked for.

ELE WAS SITTING IN the living room when Miles came in.

"Whoa—the birthing lady is sitting up and taking nourishment," he said.

"Good thing you got here to see it. We were heading back to bed. We're pooped."

"You can't count that thing until it's born. It is not on the census rolls yet."

She patted her stomach. "Not long before she starts breathing air, popping bubble gum and wanting to stay out till midnight."

"No midnight curfews for twenty-one years. I was thinking more like ten o'clock."

"The chickens go to bed earlier than that."

"She won't be a chicken, will she?"

"Of course not, silly." She peeked in the sack. "What'd you bring that's good?"

"Everything on your list."

"Good. Please hand me the ice cream and get a spoon out of the kitchen. We girls need a little sustenance."

"Since when is ice cream sustenance?"

"Whatever day this is, is the day it became sustenance."

"And I suppose I'm on milk and egg duty again?"

Ele nodded. "Yes, sir. You gotta carry your weight around here. Earning a living is only half of it."

"I'll see to it, Madam President."

"You didn't bow quite low enough to be excused yet. Try it again."

Miles bowed, touched his toes and then his forehead, nose, chin and heart.

"That should do it. Dismissed," she said as she stuck the spoon into the ice cream.

CHAPTER 24

THE VALIANT WAS A ONE-ACT play that only took six actors. That was the entire senior class. Nolan was put in charge of getting the group to agree to practice times and memorize their lines. The other two plays had three weeks' head start, but the seniors knew they were sharper; they could do it.

Getting the band and choirs up to snuff was easy enough because they had class time for each activity and they practiced in each session. Miles had ordered the music with Mr. Brooks's approval, even though he disagreed on the amount being spent for music that would likely not be used again.

"It will go into the music library," Miles had argued.

"Every teacher wants different materials," Calvin had countered.

"This music is vital to our Cinerama."

"We've never had one of those before."

"It's engaging the entire student body—the band, the choirs; three one-act plays. The plays are being rehearsed after hours with a few exceptions where they can fit into English classes. It will be a fitting summary to the school year. The public will love it."

"Maybe. Are you planning on charging for it?"

"No. It's their tax dollars at work."

Calvin took out the checkbook and, adjusting his glasses, wrote the check and handed it to Miles. "I suppose it could be worth it."

"You'll love it and so will the town."

"If it isn't, don't plan on it for next year."

Miles smiled. "The finale will knock their socks off."

AT BAND PRACTICE, MILES handed out the sheet music to "The Battle Hymn of the Republic."

"I know you haven't seen this before, but I'm certain you have heard it somewhere in your dismal lives. It was the battle music for the Union forces during the Civil War. What year was that war, Carla?"

"1861 to 1865," she said.

"Close enough. Who was the overall commander for the South, Nolan?"

"General Lee."

"Correct."

"And the general for the North, Tommy?"

"General Ulysses S. Grant."

"We've got a lot of smart people here today. Who was President of the United States of America when the war of insurrection began, Shelly?"

"Abraham Lincoln."

Miles nodded. "And when the war ended? Rebecca."

"Abraham Lincoln."

"And what happened to him?"

"He was assassinated by John Wilkes Booth at the Ford Theatre."

Miles shook his finger at her. "Too much information. You ruined my next two questions."

"Brenda, who became president after Lincoln?"

"Johnson."

"And he held what previous position?"

"Vice president."

"Good. Good," Miles nodded his head. "It is good to have a little history with your music class. Now look at this music. It is not difficult. There are no notes in there that you have not landed on before, no timing that is difficult. This will be our finale at the Cinerama, and I want it to rock the rafters. Everybody—look up at the rafters a minute, please. Those rafters," he pointed with his baton. "I want them to come crashing down on the audience. I want the roof to follow, and the walls to cave in when the last note has sounded."

It was silent in the gym. Students looked at each other, their faces grim until Nolan cracked. "Will school be over then?"

"I reckon," Tommy said.

The moment had stretched their emotions. Until then it was the Cinerama, a program they were to put on as a public display of what they had done during the year, a progression for all classes. Now it had been ratcheted up. It had to move people, pass the enthusiasm from the students to the audience; stir in them something that they didn't get every day in the mill or in town or on the ranch. They had to go away with buoyancy that had not been in them when they walked into the gym. It had to carry over into the next day, next week, next month. It had to inspire them to come to the games, to support the school and the dreams of students stuck in it.

The rest of the hour was spent with each instrument group going over their parts. At the end, they tried it together. Miles raised his baton; all eyes came together on the tip of that tiny stick. On the downbeat, Tommy began the muffled distant drumbeat that led into "The Battle Hymn of the Republic." He carried them along as if by magic. There were errors, lapses, and overbearing sections, but the bones were there. They could build on this.

MILES IGNORED THE ROOSTER who was objecting to him collecting eggs. "What have you done to these hens? There is one egg—just one egg from twelve hens." The rooster clucked, fluttered his wings and flew down to the floor of the hen house and pranced around. "That won't keep you out of the pot." The rooster charged at Miles when he closed the door. The latch didn't quite close.

On his way to the barn, he noticed three coyotes jogging along the spine of the rise on the other side of the gully he and Ele called the creek. He picked up a rock and threw it. It landed halfway between them. The coyotes stopped and looked at him. The lead coyote sniffed the ground, then lifted his head and trotted over the rise out of sight.

At the barn, Spot was standing and quiet. He washed her udder, laid his cheek against her warm hair, and milked. When no more milk was forthcoming, he pulled the bucket from between his knees and looked at it. "Spot—that's not enough milk for a family of soon-to-be-three. What's happening on our farm? Are you in a giant conspiracy with the hens to drive us out of the farming business?" He broke the ice on her water bucket, filled it, and dumped hay into her feeder. She looked at him as he started to leave, turned her head to follow him out.

"Okay." He turned around and poured a scoop of grain in her tray. Her tongue slipped out between her lips and took up the grain with a practiced move. Miles nodded his head. "Sympathy is something we humans are subject to. How a cow can make me feel guilty for not giving her grain is beyond me. Teenagers are bad enough."

A loud clucking and screaming came from the hen house. Miles peered through the failing light of dusk. The hen house door was open. Two hens flew out the opening, screaming, flapping wings, feathers scattering. He set the bucket down and ran to the hen house. As he approached the door, three coyotes slipped through the opening, each with a hen in its mouth. They were too fast for him.

"Git . . . git . . . git," he waved his arms and yelled. They were out of reach in seconds. He picked up a stone and threw it with all his might and watched it fall short. He stood and watched them go down the creek and crest the ridge.

"Ele . . . Ele . . . "

She appeared at the back door. "What's all the yelling about?"

"The chickens. Coyotes got in."

She ran out to where Miles stood, spread-legged with stones in his hands, looking at where the coyotes had disappeared. She herded the two hens back into the chicken house and cried, "Miles . . . oh, Miles. My chickens . . . "

He stepped inside. "What?"

Ele was on the ground, pulling dead chickens into a pile between her knees. The rooster was struggling to rise in the corner. "Look what they did."

Miles stood transfixed. He had seen butchered chickens before, but a pile of ripped and torn hens that moments ago had been clucking threw him. Ele was shaking. Little cries came from her until she looked at the rooster. "He won't make it."

Miles turned to look at the rooster, who was standing but limping.

"The latch wasn't closed," she said. "Why would it be open?"

Miles shook his head. "I don't know. I think I latched it."

"It wouldn't come unlatched by itself. A coyote couldn't unlatch it."

"No."

"They got them all."

"All but the two." He pointed to the two hens settling on the top rung of the perch.

"They'll be back. They know there are more."

They walked back to the house. He placed the one egg and what was left of the milk on the counter. "That's it. The hens and that snotty rooster go into the pot and the cow—"

"—Her name is Spot."

"—Spot goes back to her owner."

"The owner isn't back yet."

"Then she goes on half-rations until she kicks in with the milk."

"Miles—that's cruel." She leaned against the counter.

"I'm tired and disgusted and cold and worn out."

"Sounds like you're just plain quitting to me."

He fell into the recliner. "Call it what you want. I'm not feeling charitable tonight." He leaned his head back and closed his eyes.

"Plain to see."

ROSCOE THOUGHT ABOUT IT for two days before he caught Miles between the high school and the gym.

"Miles," he shouted as he left the bus parking area. He jogged over to where Miles waited, his breath causing funnels of vapor to rise and dissipate in the harsh wind that blew across the lot. Roscoe lowered his eyes, scanning the ground before he spoke. "I been meaning to tell you something. I overheard some talk while I was cleaning up last week. Seemed to have a lot to do with you breaking rules and how it was going to get reported."

Miles frowned. "Who was saying this?"

"I'm not 100 percent sure. The voices was mixed, and they was comin' out of the principal's office. But they was sure tearing you apart, piece by piece."

"There was more than one talking?"

Roscoe nodded. "Yup." He rested his hands on his hips.

Miles looked up at the second-floor windows, hoping to see Calvin Brooks peering down, but the glass was vacant. "Were they men and women's voices?"

"Yup."

"You didn't see them when they left?"

Roscoe shook his head. "Nope. I had to leave before they came out."

They stood in awkward silence, each processing the situation through his own filters. Then Roscoe said: "It is what it is."

Miles faced him. "I've always hated that remark, Roscoe. Always thought a person should do something to change what it is to what he wants it to be."

Roscoe scratched his chin. "Feller can't always do that."

Yes . . . that's what a person in his position would say. Good salt-of-the-earth people like Roscoe don't go around changing their circumstances. They live with them. They adjust to them and live with them. I remember Howard, who was proud of being in the working class; spent his whole life working for a company; retired to a small duplex, raised roses and lived out what life remained to him in simple joy and peace. Maybe there is some lesson in that . . . and this.

"Tell you what, Roscoe. Let's don't mention this to anybody, but keep our ears to the ground and see what can find out."

"I already told the missus."

"She won't talk, will she?"

Roscoe shook his head. "Hardly talks to me."

They laughed together.

Miles put his hand on Roscoe's shoulder. "I really appreciate you telling me. I hope it comes to nothing, and I will never tell anyone you told me. Thanks for being my friend."

Roscoe nodded, re-set his baseball cap, and walked off down the street to his rental house.

Miles looked down at his feet. The wind had stacked little clods and broken leaves against his shoes while he had stood there talking. He lifted one foot and watched the small particles take off, each taking a different path as they rolled across the parking lot. Some came to rest against the fence, some went through it and tumbled down the hill to disappear in the grasses that were browned with winter's sleep.

A little like life. Each person takes a separate path to the same end. The final resting place. Man—that sounds fatalistic. And at your tender age, too. Maybe Ele is right—I'm getting cruel and taking on resignation as a fellow traveler.

It bothered him the rest of the day. Names and faces kept running through his mind. People he had seen in and around the school, meeting with Calvin at various times, school board meetings and who hung with him and his wife at various social functions. Finally, after a meeting with the coach and the kids who turned out for the track team, he was able to mentally let it go. He had volunteered to help with the field events during the track season and Roscoe had taken over school bus driving duties.

"Kinda cold to do much today, Coach," Nolan said.

"Don't call me Coach, Nolan. I'm just a helper. Been there, done that, got the T-shirt, so I know a little something about field events."

"What do you want me to call you?"

Miles thought a moment. "How about Junior Field Advisor?"

"Works for me."

"Now, get your butt down and when you spin for the throw, keep the shot-put tight against your jaw. When you're ready to unload it, straighten up and push with your legs and arms. You should hit forty-five feet."

"Yes sir, Junior Field Advisor."

"That's better. A little respect does a lot for an aging man."

Nolan spun, leaped forward in the shot-put circle, and loosed the shot. It sailed over the weeds between the shot-put ring and the normal landing place for the twelve-pound shot that had been chopped up by repeated iron balls landing on it.

"Pretty good for a first throw. Now get serious," Miles said.

"I thought your specialty was the pole vault?" Nolan said.

"I know all things. Do as I say, not as I do."

"That's a good way out."

"Squat and give me another outstanding put. That one won't get you any medals in the district meet."

"Yes sir, Junior Field Advisor."

"I'm beginning to wish I hadn't discovered that moniker."

"It's yours now. Hang on to it because the next one might be worse."

"Your threats do not frighten me."

MILES WENT HOME TO Ele a tired man. He removed his shoes in the utility room and, stocking-footed, made his way to the living room, where he plopped in front of the stove that was kicking out heat from the burning tamarack.

Ele slipped in and kissed him. "Is you too popped to pop?"

"Totally. What's for supper?" Miles said.

"For your dining pleasure, we have corned beef hash covered with two fresh poached eggs, smothered in sausage gravy, hot raisin toast with Spot's butter and juniper honey whipped into a frothy delight. All served on a laminate tray with napkins, flatware, and a drink of your choice . . . which would be . . . ?"

"Beer."

"Would you care for a bottle, can, or tap?"

"Just any beer that is cold, comes to a head and will allow me to forget the trials and tribulations of being a teacher in a crumbling district like this."

"Ah . . . that would be our special for today, Old Milwaukee."

"Great. Bring it on."

"Coming up, Master."

"Somebody has come by and shaped this household up. I like it."

"We try our best, sir."

"I await your culinary delight."

"It requires your cooking it, kind sir. The madam has been busy building a baby girl all day and is stricken with movement paralysis. All the ingredients are placed in their approximate position in the kitchen of this house that you so graciously rented for our use. We will be in the boudoir when the family is ready to eat."

He sat for a moment, letting the heat charge through his stockinged feet. Then he arose and shuffled into the kitchen, letting the heated socks play with his tired feet.

This is just a phase, but a moment in time. I can get through it. Now—where is the jar of bacon drippings?

CHAPTER 25

THE FOLLOWING MONDAY, MILES met with Calvin Brooks in his office. Somehow he had to convince not only the Oregon Department of Education but also the principal and superintendent of Tamarack School District to allow some leniency in the testing of Billy and Don and Warren. If they had to take the same test as other seniors they were dead to the educational system. Asking them to re-take senior year when they had been socially promoted for at least the last six years would fall on deaf ears. Neither their parents nor the kids would hold still for that. They would be loosed into the world without a high school diploma. Not the end of the world, but not much help in a society that more and more required educated people to run the complex systems it had created for its own use.

"Good morning, Mr. Brooks," Miles began.

Calvin nodded. "Have a seat, Mr. Foster."

"Thank you." Miles interlaced his fingers, looked at his legs, then raised his head and looked Superintendent Brooks in the eyes. "How can you help me get the test for Billy and Don and Warren amended to include what they are learning under the tutelage of J. D. and Christmas Howell? You and I know that what they are learning there will stand them in good stead in their life's work and be far more useful than what I'm teaching them in regular history and geography." He looked down at his feet. Calvin sat like a marble statue in the chair, his eyes mere slits.

"You and I also know none of them will come back to repeat senior year. If we can get them an honest test on the local history and geography and the lumber grading information, they can pass it—I'm sure of it. If we go by the test that is based on books they are incapable of reading and my lectures, which they are incapable of taking notes on, they will fail. And as sure as God made little green apples, they will go out into life having failed to graduate with the tag of failure pinned on their chest for everyone in Tamarack to see.

"But . . . if we make up a strong test of what they are capable of reading and comprehending and what they have been studying and submit that as a serious substitute for the state-mandated material, they've got a chance. A chance of being in the graduation ceremony; a chance of walking across the stage with their classmates of twelve years; a chance to hold their heads up when they come to town. And what they have learned will work for them. It really will."

Calvin had not moved. The clock made the only sound in the room as the two men stared at one another until Calvin, his chair squeaking, leaned forward and put his elbows on the desk.

"Mr. Foster. I hired you to teach certain subjects and it was understood that you had some expertise in those subjects and would impart knowledge to the students about them. You knew that the seniors would take an exit exam that is a statewide exam of competence in the subjects they should have learned to a degree that will allow them to function in society or go on to college. Yet you deliberately shunted them off to people who are not qualified teachers, failed to monitor their progress, and failed to report to me that you were doing so. Now you ask me to assist you in getting state approval for an out-of-school curriculum aimed at making these three boys graduates of an Oregon high school. I find that most distressing."

Miles looked at the floor. The clock again took over the silence.

"Have I failed in those regards? Yes. Would I do it again? Yes. Because asking you for approval would have been the death knell at the beginning. And I have monitored their work with both J. D. and Christmas, and I have good reports from both of them—"

"—Unsubstantiated verbal reports from ranchers and mill hands—"

"—We—you and I—can make up tests that will be every bit as tough on those subjects as the ones the state will send out, and I'll put my career up against that."

"You have, Mr. Foster. Not only the Oregon Teachers Association, but also the Oregon Department of Education has your name writ large on their disciplinary action charts. They seek my input before proceeding. Now, what do you think I should tell them?"

Miles swallowed. "I don't care what you tell them, but let's devise a test for these graduating seniors that will prove they took seriously the history and geography that they could read and understand and that Billy got a well-paying job right out of high school because he learned how to grade lumber while in high school. That's all they want—is a chance. They were reading fifth-grade-level books with difficulty when I got here in September. I didn't see any other way of getting them through school unless they were educated. Previous teachers had taught them, but they had not absorbed it. They had to find a way to get interested, and they weren't going to get that reading fifth grade books and taking twelfth grade tests. Will you help me do that . . . for them?"

Calvin slid back in his seat, crossed his arms and looked out the window. "Mr. Foster, my contract calls for me to do certain things but it does not give me the leeway to develop new tests to thwart the state exit exams. The tests will go forward as planned, and the results will be known to the school board and the state board of education in the usual procedure. You pass those students and they graduate just like those before them. I trust I have made myself clear on that point."

Miles nodded. "Yes, sir, you have." He stood up, walked from the room into the hallway, and instead of going to his homeroom went down to the cafeteria and got a coffee with cream and sugar and a cinnamon roll fresh out of the oven.

"Thank you, Martha. I love hot cinnamon rolls and coffee." He chewed the cinnamon goodness, swallowing coffee with it in his own special slurry. It put a cap on the discussion with Calvin Brooks.

MILES SLID BEHIND HIS desk in American History class, coffee in one hand, cinnamon roll in the other.

"You don't look so good," Rebecca said. "Bad night?"

"Bad morning," Miles said.

"Can we eat in class, too?" Nolan quipped.

Miles shook his head. "Only a Master Teacher who has taken at least one beating for his students."

Shelly sat up straight. "Can we see the marks?"

Miles rolled his eyes. "Close your books, put your hands on top of your desks. It's pop quiz time on Amendments to the Constitution."

"Shelly—how many Amendments were originally submitted to the states for ratification?"

"Twelve."

"Right. Rebecca, what are the first ten Amendments called?"

"The Bill of Rights."

"Correct."

By the thirtieth question, Miles had finished the roll and coffee, run the napkin around inside the coffee cup and dumped it in the wastebasket and stood up, kicking his chair back. "Everybody stand up."

He walked back to Nolan and stuck his finger in his chest. "What does the Second Amendment say?"

"'A well-regulated Militia, being necessary to the security of a free State, the right of the people to keep and bear Arms, shall not be infringed.'"

"And why did the states want a militia?"

"To be able to fight the federal government if it tried to take over."

"Was that all?"

Shelly raised her hand. "Also to protect against slave revolts and populists like Shay who started a rebellion from taxes."

Miles nodded. He looked hard at Nolan. "Good. Did every state have a militia?"

"Yes."

"How were they armed?"

"Each man had his own weapon."

"And can each man have a weapon today?"

"So far."

"'So far?' What do you mean by that?"

"Some places an individual can't have a weapon, like Chicago or New York."

"Are you sure about that?"

"Pretty sure."

Miles smiled. "Good enough. How about ammunition?"

"Ammunition isn't mentioned."

"But a gun wouldn't be much good without ammunition, would it?"

"No. Could use it as a club."

"Okay. So it is implied that ammunition will be available. What if Congress or the president decides to tax ammunition or confiscate it? There is no express right to ammunition, is there?"

It was silent.

"Well—is there?" he shouted.

"No!"

"Then how do you defend yourselves if you don't have ammunition?"

"Make your own or keep plenty on hand."

"That should work. You also write your congressman and senators, join the NRA, contribute money to make sure something like that does not ever get into the main thought of America."

Miles sat back down, slumped in the seat and tilted his head back. "You may be seated now." There was total silence.

I just went crazy for a minute. Why did I do that? Where are we, and what's next?

He looked at the ceiling and started to talk. "No other country has a Bill of Rights in their governing documents. It is unique to America. The Founding Fathers did not expect it to last as no other country had been able to avoid being federalized, but it was the hope and immediate prayer of the Constitutional Convention members that the states would ratify the Bill of Rights and this nation could get started being individual states with a loose association called the United States of America." He took a deep breath and leaned back in his chair. "Study your state test for the last fifteen minutes. I'm here for any questions. Thanks for your participation. You're a great class, and don't you ever forget it."

THE ENTIRE BAND PERIOD was taken up with each instrument section's going over and over its part of "The Battle Hymn of the Republic." The repetition was causing rolling eyeballs and robot sounds, but Miles was satisfied with the technical aspects of the piece. To tear down rafters and roofs, it needed to be precise. Then emotion had to be added drop by drop until the right mixture of volume and pacing galvanized the audience into a standing ovation— big smiles on their faces, hands clapping until they were raw.

The choirs were another thing. Sure, the kids had sung before— Happy Birthday, Christmas carols, kindergarten ditties, but memorizing the words and staying on tune with the music was a challenge for kids who spent most of their vocal chords hollering at cows, horses, and dogs or school games. They had glided into a sweet-sounding girls' choir, a dry but husky boys' choir, and a mixed chorus for the finale—"The Battle Hymn of the Republic."

Each play had been rehearsed over and over in English classes and after school. There was not a dropped word, but there would be the night of performance; it was a given that pressure and bright lights would cause lapses. Enough was enough. It was time for the curtain to go up.

WHEN MILES GOT HOME that night, Eleanor looked at the eggs he had brought home in a sack. "These eggs are a different color," she said.

Miles rolled his eyes. "The store doesn't carry colored eggs."

"The store? What about my hens?"

"The hens aren't laying."

"Why not?"

"Ask them. I don't know. I told you I wasn't a farmer. Maybe the coyote trauma turned them off."

Ele sat down in a kitchen chair and rested her head on her forearm. "I can't finish cooking. I'm falling apart. Will you take over here?"

"Sure honey." He slid his hands over her shoulders and massaged in a slow circular motion, the Ohs and Aws dribbling from her lips like canned contentment. Almost asleep, she burst upright. "What are we going to do with them?"

"Butcher them?" he said.

"My lovely hens . . . ?"

"When they don't lay eggs but scarf up the feed and take time and effort, that's when the equation goes awry."

"I'm gonna cry."

He rubbed her shoulders. "We can get some more in June."

"Could we get baby chicks and raise them up?"

"I'm sure we can."

"Good. We're going to bed. Let us sleep for an hour or so before we have supper. I'm shot."

"You got it." He stuck out his hand and helped her stand. "You guys go rest, and I'll see that supper gets served."

"It better not be chicken."

When Ele had vacated the room, Miles sat down, fingers intertwined, staring at the kitchen wall.

How can it go like this? Where does it start and where does it end? Two more months to the end of school, only two. Then the baby. And summer work. I've got to find a job for summer so we can make it. I can do that. Stand up and act like a man. Quit asking stupid questions like that.

She came out and stood, hands braced on each side of the doorway, a sleepy expression on her face. "What about Spot? I just remembered seeing a gallon of milk in the sack, too."

"Spot went to Earl Benson's ranch. She met a lot of nice cows there and will have a good time until she starts giving milk again."

"Poor Spot." She ran the back of her hand across her eyes. "I failed them miserably."

Miles stood up and hugged her. "You did not fail them; they failed you. They quit their side of the bargain; milk and eggs for board and room."

She nodded, turned and headed for the bedroom, then paused. "You know . . . I'm glad they're gone. They were getting to be a burden, weren't they?"

Miles winced. "Yeah, a burden. But when the eggs and milk went away, we had all the work and none of the benefits."

"I'll think about them for a little bit, and then let them go." She closed the door.

Well . . . that's over with. Not as traumatic as I thought. Now—to fix some comfort food for supper. Maybe a hamburger and milkshake, like our first date at the Carnival. Let's see . . . where is the chocolate powder?

CHAPTER 26

Roscoe had set the stage with risers for the choirs to stand on. He had the sets for each of the one-act plays staged in the different corner behind the curtains and the folding chairs and music stands for the grand finale of band and combined choirs leaning against the side wall.

"Roscoe," Miles said. "You have a PhD in organization."

Roscoe nodded. "I try to be ready."

"Well, you did it in spades. Thank you very much. This dress rehearsal will be the last one before tomorrow's presentation."

Roscoe pushed his baseball cap back on his head. "I think it's gonna be a winner."

"You better be right. I've put too much time in on it to have a loser."

"You know," Roscoe said, "you don't always get a good cake even when you mix the same ingredients. There's just times when things go right and times when they don't." He smiled. "I think this one's gonna turn out fine."

Miles clapped him on the shoulder. "I'll take your prediction anytime."

The students started arriving. Some walked, some drove, some had their parents drop them off. No parents were allowed to stay for the dress rehearsal. It wasn't secret, but it was a closed affair.

Marion ran the freshmen and sophomores through their plays. There were a few goofs but in a teenager way, they got through it with good humor and good feelings about the time spent.

The choirs were a different story. Enthusiasm was lacking and even when the boys' choir hung Tom Dooley it seemed wooden, out of sorts and perfunctory.

Miles brought everyone to attention. "Group, listen to me. This is dress rehearsal. Tomorrow night you put this on for your parents and the town. You need to act like you are enjoying this, like this is the culmination of a wonderful year and you're going out with a bang. Put some life into it, people. Okay—get in place for the finale."

Tommy's muffled drumbeat opened the "The Battle Hymn of the Republic." Miles's hand began to sweat. He gripped the baton tighter. The choirs came in behind the opening by the band and in that instant his chest tightened, his breathing labored. His mind flashed back to when he had been one of a 250-member band and a 300-member choir that had performed this hymn in the coliseum in front of 1,000 people. It took his heart out. It dried his mouth and moistened his eyes. He kept the baton going, beat after beat. Chills ran up his back and across his scalp, his nostrils flared. It was taking him, taking him back to his high school, back to singing and playing with hundreds of talented people, making sounds that drove the soul to new heights. He took in a deep breath—held it; the baton went on by itself. The girls came on with their high notes—"*Glory, glory, Hallelujah. Seen Him in the watch-fires of a hundred circling camps*"—it echoed and rolled through his system, setting him on fire. His clothes would burn off, leaving him scorched and branded. "*As He died to make men holy, let us live to make men free, while God is marching on. Glory, glory, Hallelujah, His truth is marching on.*" The band and chorus came together, the rafters vibrated and the last two "*Amen*"s echoed down the hall and back until there was only a stillness that held everyone.

His hand found the music stand and released the baton into its safety. His head came forward and down, his hands grasped the stand. The tears would not hold back; he wept for the whole year, for Billy, and Nolan and Shelly, for them all. They had each given their best and the best had torn his heart out—made it twice its normal size. Blood ran through him like a fire hose.

The students were quiet. Tommy put his drum and sticks on the floor without making a sound. Others followed. The choir left the risers, the band their seats. They filed out the door being held open by Roscoe. At last, there was no one in the gym but Roscoe. Miles looked up from his seat.

"Roscoe ... I ... "

Roscoe put a hand on his shoulder and nodded. "I know ... I know."

WHEN MILES OPENED THE door, the house was cold inside. Two lights bounced reflections off the old hardwood floor from the bedroom and bathroom.

"Anybody home?" he shouted.

"We're here in bed, where the cold and wind can't get us," Ele replied.

He hung up his coat and caught the scent of a dead fire. He opened the stove, the cold handle interrupting his thoughts of a warm hearth and home. He reached for paper and kindling.

"Where did you put the kindling?" he said.

From the bedroom came a weak sound. "Burned it."

"All of it?"

"Yes."

He rested his arms on his knees, his head drooping.

Why would anyone burn all the kindling?

He sat for several minutes, thinking about what had brought them here, how they had felt when they first saw the house, the town. How exciting everything was, the new cow and chickens, getting food from the yard, living with the juniper, sagebrush and wind and building roaring fires that heated the house and brought the soul closer to the surface.

He put on a Levi's jacket and gloves, pulled a wool cap over his ears, and slouched out the back door to the woodpile. The wind cut into him as he lifted a pine round to the chopping block, the ever-present juniper scent mixed with occasional whiffs of sagebrush assaulted his nose, freezing his nose hairs and closing his nostrils. The axe sang when it split the frozen wood.

I wonder if an axe ever got so cold it shattered in the cold and wind? How cold would it have to be?

His next swing, the axe missed the center of the block and glanced off the side, cutting off a small chip, bounced off the frozen ground and into his shin. He dropped it and grabbed his leg. The pants were cut through. He pulled up the material. There was a thin red line with a visible trace of blood, clotted and frozen in place. He walked around the woodpile several times. His leg seemed to work, but he knew it would start to pound as soon as the nerves came back to life. He finished splitting enough wood for several fires, hauled it in, dumped it in the wood box, sat down and started the fire-building process.

When he had good flames he closed the front door to the stove, closed the damper a quarter of the way, and went in the bedroom. He peeled off his pants and looked at the cut on his leg.

Ele lay with her head propped up on a large pillow. She managed a smile. "Sorry," she said. "I just couldn't go out and get more wood. What happened to you?"

Miles blinked and grimaced. "Sent the axe into my leg. Not bad."

Ele came up on her elbow. "Miles, you need to have that looked at. It's bleeding."

"Yeah, so what? It just means I've got a heart somewhere."

"It could get infected."

"Not in this cold. No bacteria could handle that."

"Get me a wet cloth and I'll clean it and dress it for you."

After Ele had cleaned and bandaged his leg, Miles sat on the edge of the bed in the silent room, the cold creeping around his feet.

"I'm just shot," he said.

"You, too?"

He nodded.

"Poor baby. Come here and let me hold you."

He lay beside her on the bed and she stroked the side of his face and his forehead. His eyes closed. They lay like that for some time until something brought Miles up short and he sat up.

"What was that?" he said.

"I didn't hear anything."

"The fire must have popped. I'll go look. What would you like for supper?"

"Soda crackers and milk. Maybe a banana."

He put some more wood on the fire and got supper. They ate in the bedroom, Miles sitting on a chair.

"How did practice go?" she asked.

Miles nodded. "Good. It was really good. I can't believe those kids. How they can put out so much when you ask for it."

"There're good kids."

"Yup."

SATURDAY DAWNED COLD AND clear, the wind quartering out of the southwest whispering out of the mountains down the ravines and past the school buildings into the center of town to break up on the hillside across the creek. Townspeople turned up their collars when they stepped out into it. Signs were up in the windows of every business in town—the Cinerama would be held tonight at 7:00 p.m. at the Tamarack High School gym. A night of entertainment with three one-act plays, choirs, and band. Come one, come all.

Miles slept in late. Ele was mixed up in her blankets when he awoke and crept in to rebuild the fire, put the coffee on and stare out the window toward the east where the clouds split around the lifting sun. It was not the weather he had hoped for, but it was what he got. He could hear Roscoe saying, "It is what it is." The saying built defenses inside him, caused him to rebel at anything that dogmatic. When he hit a wall he either went around it, under it, or over it. Life was too short to accept what was. You changed things; changed what was, you did not have to accept it. *So where had that gotten him?*

The coffee pot began puffing. He poured two cups and carried Ele's in to her. She was sitting up, looking out the window.

"I don't want to have our baby in the cold."

"You should have thought about that before you lured me into your bed."

"I wasn't thinking nine months ahead."

"Next time use a calendar instead of passion."

"Maybe." She took the cup. "Thank you."

They drank their coffee in silence, each contemplating the day stretching out before them.

Ele looked up. "Tonight's the big night."

MILES WENT TO HIS classroom first. He wanted to get in the schoolteacher mode, and that always did it. The quiet, the books lined against the back wall that served as the library for the high school, and the smell. Linseed oil from the floors that Roscoe coated them with every month leaked up from the edges of the room, along with the burn smell of the wax that made it shine. Dust from the blackboards and the soft taint of a banana skin someone had thrown in the wastebasket after Roscoe had emptied it. Two fruit flies were hovering around the peeling.

On his desk was a letter with only his name on it. He opened it and started reading.

> Mr. Miles Foster,
>
> Please be advised that any efforts to change or replace the state tests for outgoing seniors will be a matter of utmost concern to me, the Tamarack school board, and the state Department of Education.
>
> If you have any further questions regarding this, please see me in my office.
>
> Sincerely yours,
>
> Calvin Brooks, Superintendent

He looked out the window toward the gym, windows so clear he thought he could smell the Windex that Roscoe had used to clean them. There, in a couple of hours, he would direct the end of the semester's efforts in music and drama. Then another month of school, Ele's having the baby, spring coming up from the valley and the summer breather. He wadded up the letter and threw it in the wastebasket.

Roscoe was placing the scenery for the first play. He had already set up the band chairs and choir risers and greeted Miles with a smile and a nod.

"Good evening, my good man," Miles said. "I see the crowd has not entered yet and the police are expecting several thousand, so I got here early to avoid the mash."

Roscoe frowned for a second. "If there's several thousand, we're in the wrong place at the wrong time."

"Humph. So you don't believe that the ads in the *Portland Oregonian*, the *New York Times*, and *Wall Street Journal* will draw them to the desert? O ye of little faith."

"It ain't faith, Miles. It's knowin' who comes in and goes out of this town. I doubt you'll even draw in people from John Day or Prineville."

"So there won't be any Hollywood contracts for the actors nor Boston Pops' offers for the musicians. Not even a well-dressed crowd to fill the box seats?"

"'Fraid not. They'll be in jeans and snap shirts but they'll be clean and their boots won't have any manure on them."

"Well—that's a blessing, isn't it?"

"Yes, sir."

Miles climbed the stairs to the stage and looked out over the seating arrangements. He counted a hundred chairs. It would accommodate half the town.

That should do it. Okay . . . let's start this thing.

The students started arriving, some in clothes that looked like they hadn't been worn in some time.

"Evening, Tommy. You're looking good," he said.

"Good evening, Mr. Foster. Looks pretty good, doesn't it? It was my dad's when he graduated. He kept it in the closet all this time."

"Neat. Check the tension on your drumhead, will you. It could sound better at the entry to the 'Battle Hymn.'"

"Yeah. I'll check it. Are you excited?"

Miles nodded.

Shelly came from behind the curtain. She looked like a Rose Bowl Princess. Miles was taken aback.

"Like it?" she said.

Miles shook his head. "Shelly, it's a knockout."

"Is your wife here? I want to show it to her."

"No. She's staying home tonight. Baby on board and all. Someday, you'll know that feeling."

"She's not here for your big night? Do you want me to substitute?" She put her hand on his arm. Her eyes, how she could make them convey meaning.

"Not fair, Shelly."

She moved inside his arms and hugged him. Hugged him until he lifted his arms up and returned the hug.

Nolan was standing by the instruments. "You only hug the girls?"

"You big lug, come over here."

Nolan danced around the instruments on the floor and opened his arms around Shelly and Miles. Then Tommy walked over and joined in. Carla and Brenda saw it coming together and got in. Twelve people stood, arms entwined, feeling the warmth and energy of the group.

Roscoe looked around the curtain.

"Come over here, Roscoe. Get in this group."

Roscoe shook his head. "No, sir. Don't believe I will." He ducked behind the curtain and hurried down the stairs.

Townspeople started filing in and taking seats. Greetings were being exchanged all over the floor. Some studied the printed programs they got at the door and pointed at the kids they knew in it. The noise of talking and laughing filled the empty gym, seeped up and poured over onto the stage.

Marion had a basket on her arm full of makeup items and hurried to the dressing room to get the first play in place.

Miles stepped on stage in front of the curtains. He found Superintendent Calvin Brooks and Mrs. Brooks, and met their eyes. Calvin had his arms crossed over his chest, but he was smiling.

"Ladies and gentlemen," Miles began. "Tonight, we present to you a Cinerama. Part drama, part music, and all great entertainment. There will be three one-act plays, the girls' chorus and boys' chorus will sing between the plays, and the finale will feature the mixed chorus and the high school band. Sit back, relax, enjoy the evening . . . and thank you for coming."

Roscoe was standing at the edge of the curtain, his hands resting on the cords.

"How many do you think are here?" Miles said.

"Almost a hundred. I counted about fifteen vacant chairs and some of those have filled up."

The ninth grade actors took the stage, Roscoe dimmed the lights, and Marion took a chair at the side of the opened curtains.

The plays and the choirs came off without a hitch, until the boys' chorus enacted the hanging of Tom Dooley. Billy slipped on the plastic bucket they used for him to stand on, the rope to his belt tightened, and he almost completed a real hanging within sight and sound of the entire town. Nolan gave him a bear hug and held him up to prevent the rope from closing off his throat. There was a round of applause as Billy turned around and shook Nolan's hand.

The band played three numbers and then the finale was at hand: "The Battle Hymn of the Republic," with band and mixed chorus and the end of the evening. Miles took his place as students adjusted their instruments and choir members moved in a little closer on the risers. He nodded to Roscoe and the curtains parted once again. The crowd drew silent.

As if from a distance, Tommy's muffled drum beat broke that silence. Then the trumpets. The choir picked up the first strains and the band held the volume even as the choir sang "*Mine eyes have seen the glory . . .*" until after the first verse. When the girls started with the second, "*I have seen Him in the watch fires of a hundred circling camps,*" Miles signaled for more volume and brass and voices blended. His shoulders lifted. "*In the beauty of the lilies, Christ was born across the sea with a glory in His bosom that transfigures you and me.*" Sounds blended and vibrated and bounded back and forth between the walls, the rafters shook, a door shifted open. *"As He died to make men holy, let us live to make men free, while God is marching on."* Miles was not there at *"Glory, glory, Hallelujah."* He was alone, soaring above the audience. When the choir hit the first *"AMEN,"* every throat in the audience was tight. Moisture welled in Roscoe's eyes as his arms hung on the curtain cords. Nolan looked up at the rafters.

And Miles—Miles's soul was astride his sleeve. The baton was not his to guide, it was stirring a vessel of sound that climbed off the stage and poured over the audience. The singers in their youth, as intent as angels. Shelly's eyes riveted him, emotion boiling from them. He looked away. He could see Rebecca, Jay, Richard, Carla, Brenda smiling big as he looked at their eyes, and they all knew it came together just right, just now, tonight, and throughout their lives they would remember this hymn, this night, and that it was all worth it. The work, the other things they had missed, the time spent learning music—it came together like it was welded by God and nothing, nothing would ever dispel the rapture of this moment. Nothing. The last *"AMEN"* hit Miles Foster in the chest, shutting off his breath.

Miles put down the baton. He blinked his eyes several times, standing with hands on the music stand, nodding to the students, moisture in his eyes. Applause erupted from the audience. J. D. Wharton stood up, then Mabel, and Christmas and Earl, and as they looked around, everyone rose from their chairs applauding. The noise filled the auditorium.

The students rose one by one, put away their instruments, walked down the stairs to meet their parents and turned to walk out, some looking back, eyebrows raised, smiling and waving as they passed through the door. Miles walked into the crowd, smiled, shook hands, talked with Marion and Coach Russell and Calvin Brooks, who stood at the exit like a pillar with his wife, smiling and thanking people for coming. Miles could hear the congratulations to him from townspeople and hear the pride in his responses. Miles nodded and passed by them and walked out in the spring evening. He looked up at the sky, bursting with stars it could barely hold.

I'm a lucky guy. A very lucky guy.

ELE WAS AWAKE WHEN he came into the house. A good fire was going and the oily, hot, buttery smell of popcorn caught his senses.

"How did it go, Maestro?"

He threw his coat over a chair. "Splendid." He shook his head. "I couldn't have asked for any more."

"There's popcorn and hot chocolate in the kitchen. Would you please get it?"

"My delight. Thank you."

"Pssh . . . it was nothing."

"Thanks for making the effort, anyway."

He brought the items in, set them down, and hugged Ele. She held him close to her, stroking the back of his head and neck. The fire popped in the stove. The wind came up, whistling over the top of the vents and chimney. It was a warm wind. Ele looked out the window. The grasses were bending. Maybe spring was just over the hill. The next week would start the last month of school. The hard stuff was done. Now the ending—the part they each had to do right to button up a good year.

CHAPTER 27

Monday morning there was an envelope taped to Miles's home-room door. He tore it off and read it. He unlocked his desk, took out his lesson plan book and headed for the office of the superintendent. He knocked once. Calvin lifted his head and nodded.

"Good morning, Mr. Brooks." Mabel Kreneke was seated in the guest chair, hands in her lap, her face unreadable.

"Good morning to you, Ms. Kreneke. You wanted to see this?" He laid the three-ring binder on Calvin's desk in front of his face, covering up whatever it was that Calvin was working on, and stood with his feet apart.

"Yes. Good morning, Mr. Foster. Thank you for coming in so promptly. There has been some question about the trajectory of your lesson plans and classroom study leading to the graduation process. The board has asked me to look into it." He nodded to Mabel Kreneke. "Ms. Kreneke has been appointed by the board to assist."

"What do you want to know?" Miles said.

Brooks shook his head, his lower lip protruding a bit. "Nothing particular, just the general direction and adherence to lesson plans," he kept nodding.

"You and I know it is difficult to stay right on course. The plan is always subject to alteration when it faces facts."

"Hmmm," Mabel said. "Facts such as . . . ?"

Miles held up his left hand and extended his first finger. "Fact one: The senior class has three members who are reading at fifth-grade level and incapable of understanding and carrying through on oral or written lesson schedules." He raised another finger. "Fact two: The material prescribed for seniors is of average interest. This class has five members who would be bored stiff with the suggested lesson plan material and are in fact doing college sophomore level work that I've assigned them. Fact three: the education the lower three members are getting from J. D. Wharton and Christmas Howell is far superior to what the state, this school, or I can teach them and will benefit them much greater in life after Tamarack High School."

Calvin had met his eyes while he talked. Now he looked down at the binder before him, touched it with both hands and leaned back in his chair. "Thank you. That will be all."

"You intend to keep the lesson plan book?"

Calvin nodded. "For now. Good day."

Miles was halfway to his homeroom when Roscoe came up the stairs.

"Boy—that was some evening," he said, nodding. "Some evening." He smiled. "I hear people talking about it all over town."

"Thank you, Roscoe. You're my eyes and ears around this town."

"Yup." He looked down at his shoes. "I don't know that I've ever had my eyes wet so long." He looked up at the ceiling. "It was almost like I was lifted out of that plain old gym and put on some cloud or other."

Miles clapped him on the shoulder. "Glad you enjoyed it."

Roscoe turned to leave, then turned back. "I heard something I don't like though. There was talk the mill might close."

"Who said that?"

"Oh, it was just general talk."

"I'll call Christmas when I have a moment and see what I can find out. That could put a crack in this school."

"Sure could . . . Yup."

When Miles got to his room the seniors were huddled in one corner and with teenage conspiracy, they shoved Nolan out of the group toward Miles. Nolan, a shy grin on his face, standing three inches taller than his teacher, walked over and handed Miles a box. The group reassembled around Miles and Nolan.

"Open it," Shelly said.

Miles set it on his desk, cut the twine and tape and pulled back the cardboard flaps. Under the top packing he pulled out a red and black box.

Surely this is camouflage. Can't be . . .

He lifted the lid and stared at a new Ruger .44 Magnum single-action revolver. He looked up at them gathered there, smiling so hard their faces were going to crack.

"I don't know what to say," he said, shaking his head.

Being the least bashful, Shelly took the lead. "You're the best teacher we've ever had and we knew you couldn't control us with anything smaller." She moved around Nolan and hugged Miles.

"That's enough, Shelly," Carla said, rolling her eyes. "We're all in line."

When the hugging and laughing and wiping of eyes was over and each student was intent on their assignment, the revolver lay in the box with the lid open on Miles's desk. He couldn't take his eyes off of it. It lay in its molded bed like a stallion in a stall, waiting for the bridle and saddle and a rider to carry over the hills across the creeks and into the high country.

When the noon bell rang, Coach Russell and Marion slipped into Miles's room to admire the revolver.

"That's a monster," Coach said as he picked it up, sighted along the nine-inch barrel and hefted it several times. "What do you shoot with that cannon?"

"Anything you want to," Marion said.

"Not quite," Miles said. "People are off-limits for now and the season is short."

"Impressive gift," Marion said. "See you at lunch . . . in the room."

Miles caught her eyes and saw that there were words left unsaid.

He slid the revolver in the box, put it in a drawer and locked his desk. On the way to get his lunch, he passed Shelly in the hall.

"How did you guys get the money together and get someone old enough to buy that cannon?"

"Earl Benson helped us. He was smiling all the way through it. He thought it just might kill from both ends."

"I'm sure it will kick plenty, but I do believe I can handle it."

Shelly put her hand on his biceps and squeezed. "Ohhh . . . I think that will do it."

Her hand on his arm and those magical eyes stunned him for a moment. "I've got lunch with the faculty," he excused himself, not trusting what he might say next.

Miles sat across the two-foot plank that served as the lunch table in the faculty room. Partway through the Reuben sandwich Marion cleared her throat, put her elbows on the table, and broke the dam.

"You have probably heard there is talk of the mill closing, but I overheard a conversation between two board members. There's talk of closing the school as well." She swallowed, her head bobbing as she quit chewing. Her brow furrowed, her eyes searched Donavon's and Miles's eyes. Miles looked at Donavon.

"I don't care," Donavon said. "After the seniors leave, it'll be three years before this school can mount a challenge to any other team." He took another bite, his eyes roaming from Marion to Miles while he chewed.

"What about the other kids?" Miles said.

Donavon pursed his lips and shook his head.

"When does the board offer us contracts for the coming year?"

"April—late April," Marion said.

"Then we'll wait till then . . . won't we?"

The other two nodded.

Miles looked at the wall. "I wish there was a window in this room."

MILES SLAMMED THE CAR door and walked across the gravel driveway to the front door of Earl Benson's house. It was a Wednesday afternoon and Roscoe had taken the bus route for him. He knocked and heard voices and scuttling. Earl opened the door, a grin on his sunburned face.

"Come in, come in," he bowed and held the door open. "Wanta beer?"

"Earl, you know I don't often drink decayed vegetable matter."

"This is good stuff. Gotta big head on it, too."

"Okay. I'll try it."

"Good. I knew you would. Sit down, I'll get you one."

Miles picked up the magazine Earl had left open on the table. Scientific American, *an unusual magazine for a rancher.*

Earl set a frosted glass in front of him, suds drifting down the sides. "Lick that off—it's good stuff."

Miles stuck his tongue on it and tasted. "Still tastes like decayed vegetable matter."

"You'll get used to it." Earl took three big swallows, licked his lips, then brushed his shirtsleeve across them. "What's on your mind this afternoon?"

"I want to thank you for helping the senior class get me that Ruger."

"That's a great gun. Kills from both ends." He smiled and took another swallow. "But you're welcome. It was interesting to see them wrestle with getting you a present. I don't think any of them had ever gotten a present for a teacher before. When the Caldwell and Kenkey boys said you had let them deer hunt from the school bus, they zeroed in on a pistol so fast it stunned me."

"Well—I like it a lot. Looking forward to coming out here and shooting at something."

"Something moving or something still?"

"Either or both."

"Let me know and we'll set up a little range and then go chase rabbits. There's a whole passel of them in the upper meadow. They'll make good running targets."

Miles took a drink of the beer and made a face. "I don't know that I'll ever get used to this."

"Sure you will."

Miles looked at the glass of beer then up at Earl. "Earl—you know the school board members. I heard a rumor today that they are thinking of closing the school."

"Yeah—that's been talked about."

"What's it come from?"

"Mill might close. That'd take out fifteen to twenty students. The finances are teetering as it is. Losing that many would make it unsustainable." He put both hands on the beer glass. "These board members are good citizens and pretty good ranchers, except for Mabel, who is kind of a wild spark. She can go either way and be very vocal about it."

"Will she listen to J. D.?"

Earl shook his head. "She doesn't listen to anybody but her own muse. She's been on the board so long I think she's cemented in. Gets a lot of town votes."

"I've got a battle coming up, I think—on lesson plans and what I've been doing to educate the students."

"You remember the first time I met you, and I asked if you were going to teach them or educate them?"

Miles nodded.

"And I've been asking my kids what they're doing in your classes. You're educating them—and that's good; that's very good."

"Glad you like it, but Calvin Brooks is not impressed."

"He's just a man. You're far and away a better teacher than he ever thought of being. Just keep educating them and it'll all come out in the wash." Earl looked at his empty beer glass. "Want another beer?"

Miles held his up. It was two-thirds full. "Naw. I'll just suck on this one."

"Suit yourself."

When Miles went out to his car he stopped and looked up the hillside. The evening breeze was coming down, cool and smelling of the sweet scent of buds bursting on the alder trees along the creeks. Pretty soon, the alfalfa would be adding its perfume to the air.

THE LIGHTS WERE ALL on at the house when Miles got there. He came in the back door and shed his shoes in the laundry room. "Hello," he hollered.

"I'm in here," Ele said.

He went into the living room and kissed her hello.

"You smell like beer," she said.

"That's what happens when you drink beer. I went up to Earl's place to have a pow-wow with him on the school situation, and thank him for helping the seniors get me this gift." He laid the revolver on the coffee table.

"Wow—what's that for?"

"Keeping chickens, cows, and wives under control."

"Do you shoot them or hit 'em with it?"

"I hear tell it works either way. Haven't tried it yet, but I'm thinking it will do the job."

"I'm the only one left to use it on."

"You're exempt until after you have the baby."

"That's comforting to know." She snuggled up to him. "Will you heat the soup and get some crackers and honey for supper? I'm totally beat."

"From what—turning on all the lights?"

"I cleaned the house and left the lights on so you could see my success."

"Well then, I'll put the soup on to heat, get my white gloves, and make the inspection official."

CHAPTER 28

ON MONDAY MORNING, MILES found his lesson plan book on top of his desk. No explanation, no note. He put it in his bottom drawer and prepared for the first class.

Nolan and Carla came through the door together. "Did you shoot the gun yet?" Nolan said.

Miles shook his head. "No cartridges in this town."

Nolan looked at Carla, then laughed. "We should've thought of that."

Carla punched Nolan on the arm. "Get a box when you go to Prineville."

"No," Miles said. "I need to take Ele to the doctor for her pre-birthing exam—I'll get a box."

Carla took her seat. "I'm as ready as I'll ever be for this test today. I know everything about anything. Just ask me."

Miles smiled. "The questions will be on the test. You just smack 'em down when they come up."

The other students filed in, some laughing, some silent. Billy took his familiar seat at the back right of the room, crossed the cowboy boots attached to the end of his long legs, and intertwined his fingers behind his head. The class was ready.

From the papers Miles handed out, nobody could tell there were five different tests—one for each level of education the student had reached. Christmas Howell had worked with Miles to make up a test that would go through the information Billy had studied and then a little beyond to know where it stopped.

Don and Warren had soil, ranching, farming, and local geography and history tests that J. D. Wharton had worked on for the whole semester, adding questions to it as they reached each level. The top five got tests sent down from Oregon State University, with the caveat that the completed tests be sent back to the University for grading and evaluation.

The middle group took the standard test devised by the textbook author, which was almost as boring as the actual textbook. Fortunately, band and chorus did not require exit exams; their performances were their tests. In two weeks, the district jazz band festival was to be held in John Day. That was to be a graded affair for which Tommy had been practicing a drum solo interlude that would knock the socks off the judges.

The classroom quieted and only the shuffling of feet and the turning of pages competed with the hum of the fluorescent lights. Miles sat at his desk looking out at the greening hillside. Usually the time between the beginning and end of a test afforded him thinking time, but today he sat slumped in his chair just looking. Several times he goaded himself to plan something, to define his argument with Calvin Brooks, to plan on a rebuttal to the school board if the need should arise. His usual self-determination flagged and a half-smile came over his face as he sat there, as he would have said to his friends, contemplating his navel.

When the hour was over there were no smiles, no laughter. The students filed out, dropping their test papers on Miles's desk.

Must have been tough for all of them. I don't see much joy in Mudville today.

He picked up his lunch tray, filled it, and headed for the faculty lounge. Marion and Donavon were in their chairs.

Interesting how people choose a chair or place at a table and that is theirs for life. They don't move. And it's uncomfortable if you interrupt that pattern—uncomfortable for everyone—the interrupted and the interrupter.

"Well, my happy warriors," Miles said. "What brings you to our luxurious accommodations?"

Marion looked up. "Lunch."

Donavon smiled. "A break."

"Fair enough. Let us partake of this grand menu and deal with the mundane problems of life here and now."

"I'll give you one," Marion said. "I got my letter renewing my contract for another year in the mail today. My husband called and said it arrived."

"That's good. What about our coach of the year?"

Donavon swallowed. "Haven't checked my mail yet today. I was hoping to get an offer from Portland. How long can we put off agreeing to a contract if we're waiting for another one?"

"Two weeks," Marion said.

Donavon lifted his spoon and looked at the contents. "Are these your chickens in this soup?"

Miles looked up. "Nope. Coyotes got 'em all."

"Oh, that's terrible," Marion said.

ROSCOE STOPPED MILES ON his way back to the cafeteria. "You get your contract renewal yet?"

Miles shook his head.

"Oh. Let me know when you do."

"Sure. You wanta come over and hear the jazz band practice for the contest?"

"Naw ... I've got a restroom to clean up. Someone got sick in it."

"Was it from the chicken soup?"

Roscoe shook his head. "No—it was before lunch."

"Good."

MILES COULD HEAR TOMMY'S drum beat twenty yards before he opened the gym door. Three of the students were standing around Tommy as his arms and drumsticks whirled like an octopus gone mad. The concussion was terrific just before he hit the cymbal at the finale. Tommy was all smiles, holding the sticks together in both hands.

"Holy cow, that was loud," Miles said.

The students turned to look at him, smiles broadening their faces. "Wasn't that great?" Carla said.

"Absolutely vivid," Brenda said.

Shelly raised both arms, forcing her sweater to mold around her breasts. "That should knock 'em dead."

Miles blinked, then chuckled. "It'll do . . . it'll do."

Miles got out the jazz band music, set up the stands, and waited for the rest of the ensemble to get there. They were scheduled to play two numbers at the festival. "The Chattanooga Shoe Shine Boy" had the featured drum solo and Tommy had added some drama to it, and "The Darktown Strutters' Ball." Tommy smiled like his face could not change, that come winter or summer, rain or shine, he would bear that image from now on.

They ran through the two numbers, stopping here and there to smooth out transitions.

"Sounds good," Miles said. "Everyone ready?"

"Yes," they shouted.

"Okay. Meet here with your instruments and uniforms Saturday morning at eight o'clock. We'll take the school bus to John Day, play our two numbers, bring home first prize, and have a wonderful weekend. Practice, practice, practice. Other than that, see you here Saturday morning."

After school, Miles swung by the post office and picked up the mail. On top of the catalogs and bills was a letter from the Tamarack County School Board. He started to tear it open, thought about it, and stuffed it in his briefcase. He'd open it at home, with Ele and some hot chocolate and a fire. He had big plans for next year. Courses of study that would branch out from the current curriculum, allowing the brighter students to specialize after conquering the basic information for the state test; an organized mill and woods class with Christmas Howell and field trips up into the mountains to study the actual formation for a bit of geology, along with geography and history and people—how the people came to be here in this valley along this creek, punching out a living from the plateaus and forests that surrounded them. He and Ele would get some young chickens and a cow that was fresh and there would be three of them to see next winter through. It was good to see the hills, smell the creek and hear it bubbling behind the post office. And the sun . . . .

He picked up the grocery items Ele had on her list and drove home with his thoughts bouncing around about what his salary would be for the coming year.

"Ele," he shouted. "Get the hot chocolate out and pop some popcorn. The contract is here."

She didn't respond. He opened the kitchen door. "Ele?"

A weak voice replied. "I'm in the bedroom. Please don't turn on the lights. I have a raging headache."

"Oh, sorry."

He put milk on to steam, got the chocolate, and popped some corn. Then he put it all on a tray, along with the letter, and delivered it to the bedroom with a dimmed light coming in from the hallway. He took a chair and eased it up beside the bed.

"I'm so sorry you feel punk. Everything else okay?"

"I guess . . . but everything right now is this baby in my stomach and this ache in my head. I can't wait to get back to normal, if there is such a thing."

"There is, I promise you that. Here's some hot chocolate."

She shook her head. "You drink it. I don't have any room left down there for it."

He took a sip, set it down and slipped his knife blade under the flap of the letter. The twice-folded letter was typed on official letterhead. Miles started reading. "'Dear Mr. Foster. The Tamarack School Board has declined to renew your contract for the coming school year. We thank you for your . . .'"

He dropped it on the floor.

"Oh, Miles," Ele said. Her face turned into a frown. "I'm so sorry. Maybe they made a mistake."

Darkness came over his eyes, as if the hall light couldn't shine into the bedroom. He pursed his lips and folded the letter. "Well—they have spoken."

"What are you going to do?"

"Right now, I'm going to sit here and let the feeling go away. I'm half-embarrassed and half-mad, and I don't know which is going to win out."

The chocolate got cold. The butter on the popcorn returned to a solid state. Miles opened the blinds and they both stared at the horizon as it darkened and then lightened, as the moon began to rise behind the hills to the east. Neither spoke as Miles returned to the chair and sipped the chocolate and the moon rose above the hills to cast moving shadows in the room—a juniper tree, the clothesline posts.

Miles woke up mad. The sheets were moist and twisted in his legs. Ele lay still as a log on the other side.

I'm not going to let them do this to me. What are they thinking? They need to know the truth about the things Calvin has probably been feeding them.

Donavon was smiling and joking as he took his familiar seat in the faculty room. He arranged his lunch in front of him on the plank, then pulled an envelope out of his pocket, unfolded it and read.

"'Dear Mr. Russell. The Tamarack County School Board is pleased to extend a contract for your services for the coming school year at a salary of...'"

"Yeah—how much?" Miles said.

"I'm not saying. It would make you both jealous, not to mention Calvin."

"Shoot—Calvin knows. He sits with the board."

"I'm not accepting until I hear from Portland, though." He crossed the fingers on both hands.

"What about you?" Marion asked, looking at Miles.

"Declined. No renewal."

Marion and Donavon exchanged glances.

Marion put her fork down and looked Miles in the eyes. "That's crazy."

"Right," Donavon said.

"Well—I read the letter often enough to get the point. The operative words were 'We are *not* renewing your contract for the coming school year.' It was plain English."

"What are you going to do about it?"

"I haven't decided yet."

"You could get a good job in Portland," Donavon said. "None of this country style breathing down your neck in the classroom."

"I'd like to know what it was that forced them to make that decision."

"Don't worry about it. There'll be plenty of teaching jobs available."

"That may be, but I want to teach these kids, live in this town, smell these hills."

"You'll get over that."

Marion stretched out her hand and laid it on his arm. "I'm so sorry." She shook her head. "I don't know where to start."

"I do," Miles said, and stood up and walked out.

Calvin was having lunch with his wife in the third-grade room, so Miles took a seat in the superintendent's office and waited. At 1:00 p.m., Calvin Brooks walked in the room, saw Miles in the chair. He nodded, then proceeded to put papers in his briefcase, sit down, fold his hands on top of the desk and look at Miles.

"What may I do for you, Mr. Foster?"

"Tell me why you're not renewing my contract."

Calvin shrugged his shoulders and moved his head. "The board found your services unsatisfactory."

"In what manner?"

"Oh, I don't know. Probably in general."

"Can you be specific?"

He nodded. "Yes. Insubordination. Disobedience. Impulsiveness. Unprofessionalism."

"And who told them that?"

"Mr. Foster, I'm not going to argue with you about what the school board did or did not do. It is their prerogative to hire and fire teachers. You were not fired. You were not re-hired."

"The result is the same."

Calvin was silent while his overlaid index finger tapped the arthritic hand beneath.

Miles looked out the window. "When is the next school board meeting?"

"The board meets on the third Wednesday of each month."

"I would like to be on the agenda."

"I'll make a note of that and ask the secretary to post it."

"When will I know?"

"When everyone else knows. Now, if you will excuse me, I have to go my next class and so do you."

"What if I don't go? You gonna fire me?"

Calvin looked at him a moment, then picked up his Civics book and left the room.

Miles followed him. "Why did you make me assistant superintendent twice if you thought I was insubordinate, disobedient, impulsive, and unprofessional?"

Calvin did not reply. He opened the door and disappeared into the classroom.

MILES ENTERED HIS CLASSROOM to confront the tall smiling Nolan.

"Hey, Teach, you're looking down in the dumps. Did we all flunk the test?"

"Naw. My contract didn't get renewed."

"Fired? You?"

Miles jerked back. "Is that so hard to understand?"

"Well, yeah."

"Well, get used to it. I'm outta here in thirty days."

"Where to?"

"Who knows? Foreign Legion maybe. Me and my Ruger .44 Magnum."

"But you've got no shells?"

"I'll get some on the way there."

"I can't believe this . . . just can't believe it." Nolan shook his head.

Miles grabbed him by the shoulder. "Look, Nolan. It is true. It is real. The school board did not renew my contract. End of story."

"Except you're gonna fight . . . right?"

"Of course. I love teaching here. Girding up now for the battle."

Nolan nodded and backed away, a twisted look on his face.

CHAPTER 29

THE JAZZ BAND WAS all set up and waiting for him when Miles entered the gym. There was no horseplay, no joking and laughing.

"Why is everyone so glum in here today?" Miles said.

Tommy spoke up. "We heard you were fired."

"True story. But that isn't the end of the world."

"It's the end of ours."

Miles tipped his head back, looked down his nose. "Naw . . . come on, you've had teachers before me and there will be teachers after me."

"We didn't do this good under them."

"We didn't do this *well* under them," Miles said.

"Oh, right . . . yeah."

It was silent for a moment. "You know . . . you guys need to learn how to work with many teachers. Each teacher presents material in a different way. They each have a personality you can learn to live with, and it will stand you in good stead when you go out from here and start working with new people. I'm just one of many you'll have had when you look back on it."

Miles reached down for the baton and looked at the music. "Let's see if we can raise ourselves up with some good jazz. Take 'Darktown Strutters' Ball.'" He raised the baton: "Ready . . . one, two . . . "

There was no life to the piece. Sounded to Miles like a dance band in a retirement home with an *oompah, oompah* sound. He put the baton on the stand and crossed his arms over his chest.

"Where's the enthusiasm? Where's the fire? The judges are going to go to sleep if they hear that." He pointed at Carla. "Can you put some life into that clarinet solo?"

"I could if you weren't leaving."

"You're graduating—you're leaving. Folks—this isn't the end of the world." He shook his head. "I was looking for a job when I found this one. There'll be others."

The silence ate into everyone like a worm in a late fall apple. The band sat on their chairs, instruments in laps, eyes staring at the music.

"We're not getting anywhere, are we?"

Most of the students shook their heads.

"Well, let's not force it. I'm going back up to my room. I wish you guys would practice together or separately until you know the music note by note and can bring it out of you and into the audience and judges. We want them to not be able to avoid leaping out of their chairs and dancing." He turned to Tommy. "Tommy, would you please put the stuff away."

"Sure."

Miles walked down the stairs and out into the parking lot. Two crows were playing on the wind coming down the hillside behind the school. He smiled. "Yeah, well, you guys have to work seven days a week for your food." They were unimpressed by his declaration and dropped a wing to turn and coast over Tamarack, heads scanning the earth for edibles.

Instead of going to his room, he followed the crows. Out the gate onto the road and down the hill to town. He waved at J. D. Wharton at the post office and kidded with Ralph on his way to the restaurant. He sat in a booth looking out the plate glass window onto the main street of Tamarack and ordered a coffee and cinnamon roll, hot with butter on it.

"School out?" Pamela asked.

"Don't think so," Miles said.

"Just wondered. You here and all . . . ." She set his coffee down. "Roll will be hot in a minute."

He crossed his arms and looked across the street at the tire store. Two generations had run that place, putting tires on everything from cars to tractors. He felt glued to the booth, glued to the town, and yet with one letter they had asked him to move on.

Cupping his hands around the mug, he lifted it and sipped the top of the coffee. Good, strong, tasted like camp coffee. Pamela set the roll down and, with a sideward glance, backed off without further conversation. He watched the butter melt into the groves in the top of the roll, knowing that after years of enjoying this treat he knew exactly when to cut into the roll to let the melted butter run down the inside before he took a bite.

He finished the roll and coffee, looked at the wall clock, paid the bill and walked back up the sidewalk and up to the school. Fifth period would start in a few minutes. Tommy would have seen to closing up the band room and, fortified with coffee and roll, Miles was ready to take on his added class of Typing 101.

It was silent except for typewriter chatter when he entered; all eyes were on the typing books perched on the holders. He thought back to the assignment and wondered what to do. Confusion had not stunned him before. He sat in a chair in the back corner, crossed his legs and sat as silent as the students. Finally, they began to run out of typing to do, and one by one the machines fell silent. Still they looked straight ahead not talking amongst themselves or looking at him.

"Okay," he said rising from the chair. "Let's get this out in the open and crush it. Let me start by telling you I have enjoyed my first year of teaching more than you can imagine. Love it here; love you guys and gals and can't imagine any better starting place for a teacher. You and the town have been wonderful. But—there is a system that needs to be served by the entrenched bureaucracy, and they don't put up with mavericks."

Carla turned in her chair. "You're not a maverick, Mr. Foster. You're an excellent teacher."

"Right." "Yes." Several sounded out.

"Thank you. I've tried my best—probably broken more rules than I know about—but I've always had you guys and the town in my sights and I wanted it all to be better. Not to end like this."

He tucked his chin down and glanced at Shelly. "Go to page sixty-five and let's do a five-minute time test. We'll start when the big hand hits the twelve. Are you ready?"

There was nothing to do when the class was doing a time test. They did their own correction and words-per-minute calculation when it was done, so really all he had to do was think, ponder, walk around, check on techniques and gaze out the window. At least this room had a window in it.

RALPH LIFTED HIS HEAD from writing in his ledger when Miles opened the door. "Mr. Foster, good to see you today."

"Thanks, Ralph. Same to you. I need a few things from your emporium."

"Absolutely." He stood up, brushed his hands off on the apron he wore every day in the store, and met Miles in the baking goods section.

"What may I help you with?"

"Baking powder."

Ralph picked it up. "Big or little box?"

"Little will do. No sense moving it with us to the next town."

Ralph's face dropped and he lowered his voice, although there was no one else in the store. "Miles," he shook his head, "I don't know what that school board is thinking. I think it's terrible. You've done more to make that school worthy of being called a school than . . . ."

"Thank you, Ralph. Didn't know it was getting around. I can't take much more of it."

"Too close to the skin?"

Miles nodded.

Ralph put his hand on Miles' shoulder and squeezed. "You'll do alright. I know you will."

Miles took the baking powder and a two-pound bag of sugar over to the cash register. "I better start paying you instead of running a tab. I'll be out of paychecks pretty soon."

Ralph smiled and waved his hand. "Forget it. I'll put it on your tab. You can run, but you can't hide."

"Thanks, Ralph. I've really appreciated knowing you and being here."

"Same here."

"Oh, by the way, would you come to the school board meeting and put in a word for me?"

"You bet—you bet. Just let me know when it is."

ELE WAS LYING ON the living room couch when Miles got home. She was pale, her hair struggled to find a pattern on her head, and one arm hung down toward the floor. Miles kissed her, her lips as soft as ever.

"Got the baking powder and sugar," he said.

"Good. Although I don't feel like cooking right now."

"That's fine. Your day go okay?"

"Yes. Mrs. Howell came by to see how I was and visit some. She said Christmas told her to start thinking of another place to live because more than likely they'd be moving at the end of summer logging season." Ele smoothed out the comforter that spread over her lower half. "Another interesting thing . . . she said the school board did not renew the Brooks' contracts."

Miles stopped on his way to the kitchen. "Are you kidding?"

Ele shook her head. "That's what she said. I questioned it too."

"Cleaning house. Close the mill and fire the superintendent. Next thing you know someone will want to close the post office and the General Store."

"That's the way she talked. Nobody's gonna commit until they know for sure, but Christmas said the log deck is way down and contracts for new logs are few and far between—not enough to keep the mill running."

Miles sat down on the couch, rubbed her thigh and looked out the window.

"Well—we're looking for a new place, too. I doubt any schools around here will hire me after getting fired here."

"Oh, Miles . . . I'm so sorry. I wish I could have done more to help you."

"Honey, it wasn't your fault. Your only fault was marrying somebody who is disobedient, impulsive, insubordinate, and unprofessional."

She rubbed his hair. "You forgot wonderful, smart, fun, creative, sexy . . . ."

" . . . And a good cow milker and chicken feeder."

"That, too."

"So the mill really is closing? Hard to believe," he said.

They stayed that way watching the light leave the day, together, touching, feeling the warmth and electricity of touching each other's skin.

CHAPTER 30

THE TAMARACK JAZZ BAND arrived in John Day in the small school bus, unloaded their instruments and spread out to listen to other bands. Miles got the band registered, found out their playing order and hustled back to the group meeting place.

"Cripes, there are some good bands here," Tommy said.

Carla frowned. "I don't like their music choices, though. Too stiff."

"We're on at one-thirty, so eat early and make sure you brush your teeth afterwards. No plugging the reeds with ham sandwich," Miles said. "Meet here at one o'clock sharp."

Miles sat down to listen to several of the bands perform.

Good precision but lacking spirit. The talent, but not the heart. We've got to get the heart into it. He looked around for some lunch and settled on a barbeque pulled pork sandwich. Glad he didn't have to brush afterwards. He wanted the barbeque sauce to stay with him all the way through the New Orleans jazz.

EVERYONE WAS LOOKING SHARP in his uniform, anxiety dancing across foreheads like an invisible lightning bolt.

"We're up now," Miles said. He rearranged the chairs from the previous band, pushing them closer hoping for a more unified sound in the large gym. He took out the music, laid it and the baton on the stand and crossed his arms. Every member looked up.

"Heart," he said. "You know this music and you're good musicians. Play it with all your heart and soul. Be one of the people in the song—in the music—be a participant—each of you." He looked down, then back up. "I love you guys. Do it. Do it for us."

They smiled. He reached for the baton and lifted his arm. The first strains of "The Darktown Strutters' Ball" burst into the air. Carla hit the clarinet solo with a clear punch, and Tommy covered her with a drumbeat that took the chorus and they were all in. The notes came off crisp. They pulled the trumpet from note to note as Nolan swung it back and forth, eyes half-closed, fingers dancing on the valves. There was an invisible skin covering them all—they were one giant organism that leapt and sang and danced. Several students at the back of the hall swung into a dance, the music taking them out of convention and into invention. It was over too soon. The audience rose as one, clapping and hollering. They had felt it. It had entered their bodies and their minds had let them go—let them do what they felt like, and they felt like moving.

When the last of the clapping cascaded off the walls Miles turned the page, lifted the baton and "Chattanooga Shoeshine Boy" burst out of the instruments. The dancers slipped their feet over the floor grabbing hands, swinging their partners, constant movement. Some of the dancers wore the band uniforms of other schools. The beat was increasing, and the people standing were moving in rhythm. Some swung their arms like they were shining shoes. It rose, it fell, it moved up and down the hall and then ended with Tommy and a drum score that Miles had not heard before. He looked at Tommy but his eyes were closed and the drumsticks rose above his head. The other band members turned toward him, stood up and played the chorus again. It was out of Miles's hands. Tommy had taken over the finale. Every person in the audience was standing, clapping, some dancing, and the judges were smiling back and forth amongst themselves.

They practiced this. The buzzards—they're gonna ruin this.

He put the baton down, a smile on his face as big as all outdoors. He turned to the clapping, yelling audience and bowed, then pointed to Tommy and each of the members in turn. They each bowed.

Well—their hearts went into that sucker. Come on, Miles—smile more.

Everyone was seated when a judge took the microphone on stage. The audience quieted.

"Ladies and gentlemen, thank you all for coming and for supporting the jazz bands from your schools, your students, band leaders and your communities. This is the first time we have had a unanimous winner. All three judges voted number one to Tamarack High School jazz band. Mr. Miles Foster, please come up and accept the award."

Miles stood unsteady, his eyes moistening. He looked at the band members who were cheering and clapping beside him. He smiled and nodded to them and made his way to the stage.

The judge handed him the trophy, a bronze trumpet atop a plaque where each member's name could be inscribed. He held it and looked out over the audience.

"Before they played, I asked them to put their hearts into it. To forget the people and the town and the place," he pumped his fist, "Be a part of the music. They did. I'm so proud of them I could bust. Thank you for this prize."

He walked down into the audience and handed the trophy to Nolan for all to see. He made his way to the dressing room and alone sat along the wall and let every emotion come out. Let it wash his soul. He sat hunched, happy and sad at once.

They did it. They did it again. How can they wring this much out of me? They're kids—just kids. They're smiling, happy, and I'm sitting on a hard bench crying like a baby. But what an outpouring. They knew it, too. They expected it. Man, that was great.

Nolan walked in. "You alright, Teach?"

Miles shifted his feet, nodded. "I'm okay."

Nolan turned and walked out. Tommy came up to him. "Is he in there?"

"Yeah. He wants to be alone."

"At a time like this?"

"Especially at a time like this. Come on, let's get the girls and get something to eat before we catch the bus back. It's late."

Tommy turned. "I'm with you, boss. Lead on."

ON MONDAY, THE SCHOOL was alive with smiles and pats on the back as the jazz band collected accolades for their weekend performance. Tommy could hardly get out of a crowd who would pen him in against a wall to hear him tell the story again. When he finally got to Miles's class he sauntered up to the desk, head down with a slight smile on his face.

"Couldn't help it," he said. "It just came out of me."

Miles chuckled. "Oh, I doubt that. It was too good for impromptu. You and the whole jazz band practiced that little maneuver and slid it right by me. I was standing there with the baton in my hand knowing the piece was over and there you were, eyes closed, head bobbing, drumsticks flying like a herd of geese with the wind behind them and the rest of the people chiming in. Just came out of you? I think not. Planned, rehearsed, and I might add—beautifully done."

Tommy's smile widened. "You liked it, huh?"

"It was beautiful. Thanks for taking the chance."

"That's what you taught us—take a chance and see where it takes you."

Miles pointed at Tommy's chair. "Hmmm. It takes you to your seat . . . now."

Tommy smiled. "Yes, boss."

Miles stood and opened the textbook. "If you remember, this is U.S. History class. Please open your books to page two seventy-five and let's get into small groups to discuss the forming of the United Nations after World War II and the effect it had on the United States and the rest of the world. Groups of three, pick your own moderator and come back the last fifteen minutes of class with an answer to this question: Did the forming of the United Nations release America from post-war obligations to assist previously colonial countries?"

"What's that have to do with Tamarack?" Tommy asked.

Miles assumed a George Washington-type stance, shoved his hand inside the front of his shirt. "Tamarack is a colonial outpost controlled and managed by the timber company, the mill, and the school district."

Nolan held up his hand. "I hear the mill is closing."

Miles nodded. "That's the scuttlebutt. Anybody know for sure?"

Billy slid down in his chair, his mouth partially open. Miles looked at him.

"Billy?"

He shook his head.

"You don't know, or you won't tell?"

"Don't know."

"Okay. Let's get back to it. Get into your groups and get this point debated and ready for group answer. You've got twenty minutes."

There was one extra student who was not in a group. It was Billy, and Miles motioned to him to come outside in the hall.

Miles put a hand on Billy's shoulder. "You gonna be okay if the mill closes?"

Billy nodded.

"Good. What have you planned?"

"I applied in Prineville and John Day."

"That's good thinking, Billy. Let me know how it goes."

Billy nodded and they headed back into the classroom.

CALVIN BROOKS STUCK HIS head into Miles's classroom. "Your wife asked you to come home."

Miles looked at the clock. It was 2:45. "Now?"

Calvin nodded. "I'll take over your class."

When he got home, there was a suitcase sitting inside the door and Ele was on the couch. One arm was across her forehead and the other hand on the child within her.

"It's time," she said.

"Oh, holy cow. Let me grab a sandwich and we're off."

"We're off now—no time for a sandwich."

Miles swung around. He helped Ele off the couch, grabbed the suitcase, and out the door they went.

The highway to Prineville was vacant this time of day, before the last log run and before homeward-bound traffic or going-to-town traffic. Ele leaned against the car door, eyes closed, and before they got to the Ochoco Mountains gave a couple of short cries and clutched her extended belly. Miles leaned over and touched her.

"You okay?"

She nodded. "If you can hurry—hurry."

He looked at the speedometer—they were doing sixty-five. Too fast in the fading light of the pine forest with deer going to feeding grounds, but he kept it there.

Miles pulled into the EMERGENCY entrance at the hospital and had the door open and Ele partway out when the emergency staff showed up with a wheelchair. They went in, registered, and Ele got prepped for childbirth.

Man alive. We're about to be parents. We couldn't keep chickens laying or cows producing milk. Wonder how we'll do with a baby? Gotta be some natural knowledge granted to women about this stuff. Chickens and cows are not as important as a real live child.

The nurse ushered him out of the room. He found the snack shop and devoured a day old ham and cheese sandwich, along with a cold apple.

Not up to Tamarack High cafeteria standards, but edible.

The OB/GYN doctor bounced through both double doors, outfitted in a long green robe with matching head cap and a smile under his tired eyes.

"Mr. Foster," he extended his hand. "Eleanor is progressing nicely and I expect a short time before you become a daddy. Excited?"

"Yeah—I guess so."

"You know it's a girl?"

"Yeah, well, my wife had that figured from the start."

"It's like they say, women know these things," the doctor said, as he turned. "The nurse will let you know when you can come in and see your wife and baby."

"Thank you," Miles muttered. "I'll be here."

"Yes—I guess you will," he said, and burst through the double doors again going the other way. Two orderlies scrambled to miss being hit by the doors.

He must have slept, because he awakened with a start when a nurse touched his shoulder. He looked at the clock. It was 7:35.

"Mr. Foster? You may go in now."

Ele looked like she had been swimming in the surf—hair askew, face blotched, but with a smile that showed her perfect teeth.

"Meet Little Miss Foster," she said.

"Love her already," Miles said. "She's darling . . . and asleep. No chickens to awaken her and no cow to milk, she'll have a grand life."

"What about me?" Ele said.

"You too—lovely . . . spent but lovely."

"Yeah well, I did all the hard work."

"You surely did, my dear. Now that you've seen her, what do you want to name her?"

"I really like Alexis. You okay with that?"

"We can call her Lexi for short" Miles nodded several times, letting his eyes wander. "I like it. You rest and I'll be back in the morning to take you girls home. She's beautiful. You did a fantastic job."

Ele managed a smile. "Thank you. Good night, darling."

CHAPTER 31

THE TAMARACK SCHOOL DISTRICT board meeting opened at 7 p.m. on the third Wednesday of May to a packed audience. The school board members whispered to each other and cast glances at the audience before they took their seats and kept their eyes on the papers in front of them. Calvin Brooks sat at one end, his head moving from the papers to the board members to the clock and back to the papers. Milton Waterman, the chairman, called the meeting to order. Roll was called; all were present.

"I'm aware of the reason for this huge turnout," the chairman said. "We generally don't have enough people in the audience to keep the room warm."

He shuffled the papers in front of him, making them into a perfect pile. "We'll dispense with the usual order of business and take up the issue for your turnout tonight." He turned to Calvin. "Would you please give your report on Mr. Miles Foster."

Calvin adjusted his tie, scooted his chair back and stood up, holding his report in front of his face.

"Upon the recommendation of extending contracts for the next school year to the existing teachers I recommend 'No' for Mr. Foster. The reasons are his disobedience, insubordination, his impulsive nature and unprofessional attitude toward other teachers, the Oregon Teachers Association and the curriculum espoused by the Oregon Department of Education." He sat down. The audience stirred.

The chairman looked out over the audience—he knew every one of them. "With that recommendation from the principal and superintendent, the board members did not extend a new contract to Mr. Miles Foster. Now I will take questions."

He pointed to J. D. Wharton.

"Milton," J. D. began. "You and I have known each other for over fifty years. I've never known you to ride roughshod over a good act to serve some authoritarian principle. This teacher, Miles Foster, is not only a good act but he is a breath of fresh air in this stilted educational system that has been allowed to fester under state rules that apply more to cities than rural communities like Tamarack."

There was general clapping.

"And isn't it true that the board also did not offer a contract renewal to Mr. Calvin Brooks? Yet the board is taking his recommendation to get rid of Mr. Foster? How do you square that with common sense?" J. D. looked at Mabel, but as soon as their eyes met, she looked down.

Clapping burst out. "What? What?" several people shouted. "You fired Brooks?"

Milton held up his hands for quiet. "We'll not have outbursts like that in this meeting." He tugged on his belt with both hands before starting over. "Mr. Brooks is not in question here. Please confine your remarks to Mr. Foster."

"Well, answer the question," someone said.

Milton looked at the other board members. "The board is not in touch with individual teachers and looks to the principal and superintendent to keep it advised of their actions and to make recommendations on their retention. Mr. and Mrs. Brooks have not been retained. Next question."

Christmas Howell put his hands on his knees and shoved himself upright. "Mr. Chairman, my name is Christmas Howell . . . "

"We know you, Mr. Howell," Milton said.

"For the last six months, I have been working with one of the students to become proficient in the lumber mill business. It is not a regular course subscribed to by the Oregon Department of Education, but over the course of time that student became an extremely valued employee and shows promise to rise to higher levels of management. He passed the test Mr. Foster and I devised; he passed the state board test for lumber grading, and is working part-time at the mill. He may not meet the criteria for high school graduation according to the Department of Education, but he sure became a fine person and a fine employee with Mr. Foster's tutoring."

The audience burst out clapping.

"Now," Milton said. "I said no more of that."

"Milton," J. D. said. He stood and waved his arms over the audience. "These people are your friends and neighbors. You work for them in the running of this school. I believe you can let them express their displeasure or satisfaction with anyone's remarks, rather than ride down on them like you would a green bronco."

The clapping began before he finished. J. D. stayed standing. "Would you or any member of the board like to give us an example of this referenced disobedience and insubordination Mr. Brooks is referring to?"

Milton looked at Calvin Brooks. "Mr. Brooks?" he said.

Brooks stayed seated. "Mr. Foster purchased band uniforms without my approval. The funds were not in the budget. He sent an NSF check for a deposit and another for full payment. He put the school's credit at risk."

Earl Benson stood up. "You know, I don't like to get embroiled in someone else's decision-making process, but this case is different." He shook his finger at Milton. "Miles Foster and the band put on a whale of a dance and barbeque with the help of several members of this audience and paid for those uniforms. They hang in the band closet now, and they were *not* paid for with school funds."

The clapping erupted and sounded like a rainstorm on a tin roof.

"Not only that, but I know for a fact that he prepared five different lesson plans for each of his classes so as to challenge the least to the most capable at whatever educational level they were in when they were passed along to him." He shifted his feet and smiled. "The first day we met—at the teacher presentation in the gym—I asked him if he was gonna teach our kids or educate them. He got it. He not only taught them, he educated them. This board action stinks and I'm ashamed to say I voted for all of you at the last board election."

People jumped up. Some were clapping and others smiled and waved at friends in the audience. It took Milton several minutes to quiet them down.

"Any other questions or comments?" Milton said.

The crowd, sensing they had prevailed, was silent. Earl, J. D., and Christmas had made their case.

Then Ralph stood up. "There was a mention of insubordination against Mr. Foster. I am aware that twice he was made the assistant superintendent for a day while Mr. Brooks was away. It's hard for me to believe he was insubordinate to Mr. Brooks, and yet have him appoint Miles as superintendent when he's not there."

The crowd fired up again and clapped.

Milton turned to Calvin Brooks, who looked smaller and smaller in the chair at the end of the table. "Mr. Brooks, would you care to address that?"

Calvin cleared his throat. "Mrs. Grant was placed in charge of the Christmas Program, which Mr. Foster and the high school choirs were a part of. Classes were to memorize all verses to sing in the finale, but Mr. Foster would not have his choirs learn all verses."

"What did he do?" Ralph asked.

Calvin hunched his shoulders before he spoke. "He had them learn the first and last verse and hum the others. Said he could not take time in his classes to teach them when they needed to learn other materials."

"And you spoke to him about that?"

Calvin nodded. "Yes—I did. And so did Mrs. Grant. We both asked him to do it."

Lyle McKinley stood up, hooked his thumbs in his overall straps, and said: "This is a bunch of poppycock. You get a good teacher in here. He does a royal good job and for little snipping things that don't amount to nothing, you fire him. And besides that, you fire him on the word of the superintendent that you just let go. Just don't make sense to me."

Again the clapping arose.

Milton looked out over the crowd. "Any other questions?" He glanced around.

"Seeing none, I close the general meeting and call for the vote of the board. As to the question of not renewing the contract for Mr. Miles Foster, say 'Aye.'"

All board member's lips moved. "Aye."

"Those opposed by the same sign."

The silence stretched into the audience, unbelieving and disappointed. Several stood up and walked out of the room. Milton curled his papers into a roll, pushed his chair against the table and exited out the side door. He was in his car and through the gate before the audience filed into the parking lot.

J. D. CALLED MILES AFTER he got home. "Miles—we didn't do you any good. They hung to their decision. Looks like they had decided beforehand what to do and, despite the good words on your behalf, they voted down the line."

"Even Mabel, too?" Miles said.

"Yup—even Mabel. We haven't talked about it and I doubt we will. She isn't back here yet, but I think it'll be one of those things that just isn't mentioned around here. She's a strong woman and I like her company, but I just can't agree with her on this."

"J. D., thank you for your support . . . "

"Well . . . it didn't do any good but we gave 'er the old college try. Sure got a lot of people out—largest school board meeting they've ever had in this town." He coughed. "How's the little girl?"

"Alexis is just fine. She eats, burps, pees, and sleeps."

"That's what babies do. It ain't a hard life—yet."

"Thanks for calling, J. D. Please tell Mabel no hard feelings. I'll find other work."

"I'm sure you will, Miles. I enjoyed working with the boys this year. I'll miss them, but they said they'd write if they found work."

"Yeah—as if they'd actually write a letter."

"Exactly. Well—good night, Miles."

"Good night, J. D."

CHAPTER 32

ON SATURDAY MORNING, BILLY was in the General Store trying on new Levi's when Miles came in. Miles waved and yelled "Hi" to Billy, who was clear at the other end of the store. Ralph poked his head around the corner, wearing his usual broad smile.

"Good morning, Miles. What brings you in so early on a weekend? Your young'un short of something?"

"Hi, Ralph. She's not short. It's Ele and I who are short—of sleep. That child eats every two hours."

"Kids are like that. Ours kept me and the missus up night after night. You get used to it and about that time they start sleeping all night."

"Isn't that the way of it? I need some flour and grapefruit juice—you have any grapefruit juice?"

"Oh, sure—right over here." In ten seconds Ralph had flour and juice stacked on the counter. Anything else?"

"No, that should do it. How much?"

"I'll put it on the tab."

"Okay. But you'll have to catch me before we leave town."

"That was a miserable meeting, wasn't it? I thought the townspeople would bring you through that, but . . . " he shook his head.

"Ralph, don't worry about it. I'll find something. Jay and Richard got jobs falling timber—making three times what I got paid and they're just fresh out of high school."

"Not many a faller makes it to retirement, but lots of teachers do."

"Well, there's that."

Billy walked by with two pair of Levi's in his hands. He laid them on the counter and took a step back while he took out his wallet.

"What are you slicking up for, Billy?" Miles asked.

"Got a job in Prineville. Start the day after school is out. Grading lumber."

Miles chuckled and got a big smile on his face. "Billy—that's wonderful, just wonderful."

"Thanks to you and Mr. Howell."

"You had the talent, Billy. All we had to do was find it and blow on the coals."

Billy paid, took the sack with the Levi's in it, and walked out the door.

Ralph nodded. "Now there goes a boy nobody thought would do much. He'll be leaving our town, but he'll be back and he'll be remembered. You did him a big favor."

"Hope so," Miles said. "Right now I don't feel like I did anyone a favor."

"Well—I've found that time smoothes those things out."

"You could be right. I'll have to wait and see. Thanks, Ralph."

Miles put the sack in the car and walked across the street to the post office. There were the usual advertisements, catalogs, and three letters from towns around Tamarack.

That's strange. Why would towns be writing me?

He opened one. The letterhead read Grant County School Board.

Dear Mr. Foster:

Our school board would like to offer you a contract for the coming school year to teach History, Geography, Music, and assistant coach. If you are interested, please call us at the below number to set up an appointment to meet with the principal and superintendent for an interview.

Sincerely yours,

Rachel Longbaugh

Miles looked up from the letter. He stood immobile on the sidewalk, clutching the envelope. Ralph saw him from across the street and, apron flapping, trotted over and put his arm around Miles.

Ralph looked him over. "You okay?"

Miles nodded but could not speak. He lifted the letter up and Ralph took it.

His eyes scanned the typed letters and a big smile spread across his face. "See," he said. "I knew you'd be appreciated around these parts. That's great . . . just great."

Miles looked at him. "I gotta get out of this town. I'm starting to cry all the time."

Ralph put a hand on his shoulder and shook him. "Yeah—but it's a good cry. Nobody objects to that."

"Calvin might."

"Let him. You've got a bright light to follow now—a clear path." He looked at the other letters in Miles's hand. "What are those?"

"I don't know."

"Well, look at the return addresses. They're all from school districts. Come on . . . open them up."

Miles stuck his thumb under the flap and ripped the envelope open.

Dear Mr. Foster:

We have become aware of your release from contract at Tamarack Creek School District and would like to offer you a position in our high school at Prairie City. You would be responsible for U.S. and World History, U.S. Geography, Civics, Music, and there is an opportunity to assist in the Physical Education department. We would like to discuss salary and conditions as soon as you are available. Please contact me at your earliest opportunity.

Walter Houston
Chairman School Board

Ralph motioned to the third letter. "Open it, too."

Dear Mr. Foster:

We learned of your availability this morning and wanted to quickly get notice to you that the Mt. Vernon school district would be pleased to consider your application for employment for the coming school year at a salary and with duties approved by both parties. I enjoyed meeting you at the John Day Jazz Festival and was pleasantly surprised with the music your group provided and your winning first prize.

Please call me at your earliest convenience at the number below.

Sincerely yours,

John Windsor
Chairman, Mt. Vernon School Board

Ralph stood back, the lower half of his apron flapping in the breeze that tumbled down Tamarack, widened out when it got to town, and tussled with the dust that lay next to the curb. Miles lifted his head; the breeze smelled warm and frosted with juniper berries ripening in the longer days of sunshine.

He looked in Ralph's face with the wrinkled forehead, crow's feet stretching out from the ends of his eyes, smiling for all he was worth. "It's a good day," he said. "A good day," and hugged him.

"I'M HOME," HE YELLED when he came in the front door.

"Take off your shoes if you're coming in the front door. We don't want cow dung on the carpet where Alexis crawls," Ele said.

"We can replace the carpet." He held up the three letters. "Where would you like to live next year, my darling?" He dropped the sack and thumbed the letters. "There's John Day, there's Mt. Vernon, there's Prairie City."

"What?"

"Offers of a contract, that's what."

"To teach?"

"No. To feed chickens, collect eggs and milk a cow. Of course it's to teach."

"They're willing to hire you?"

He slapped the letters. "Here's living proof in these fine letters."

"Oh, Miles. I'm so happy. And so is Alexis—look at her smiling."

"Must mean she's getting ready to throw up. I've seen that smile before."

"She is not. Lexi is very happy for you and so am I."

"That makes me happy." He sat down, took off his shoes and threw them toward the utility room. "Just think—getting fired wasn't the end of the world, but the beginning of a new one."

"Isn't that always what happens? Something ends and something new begins? I had just broken up with Bill Rogers when you came along. You weren't a teacher and now you are. And now you're teaching somewhere else. It all works to the benefit of the world."

Miles blinked. "That's a pretty grand explanation for getting fired and re-hired—benefiting the world."

"Every little thing works toward that goal. Remember the Bible verse the pastor quoted when he married us and we didn't think about it then? I've been thinking about it for the last few weeks. You remember it?"

He shook his head. "No."

She took an oratorical stance. "'As you do not know the path of the wind, or how the body is formed in a mother's womb, so you cannot understand the work of God, the Maker of all things.'" She put Alexis in the crib. "It's from Ecclesiastes."

Miles nodded. "Seems strange now, but it rings true, doesn't it?"

"Absolutely." She put a blanket over Alexis, looked up at him and smiled. "Can we have chickens and a cow in any of those towns?"

THE END

Other Square One Titles of Interest

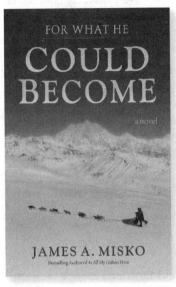

For What He Could Become
James A. Misko

When Bill Williams, a half-Irish, half-Athabaskan Indian, left his native Alaskan village after a disastrous bear hunt, he left behind not only the only home he had ever known, but also the girl he loved. It was then that the true adventure of his life began. He worked on a Yukon riverboat, searched for gold, and took a job building the Alaskan Highway. When the country became involved in World War II, Bill signed up to fight and was immediately sent overseas. The experiences of war were devastating and the trauma left him with deep, indelible scars. After surviving the Battle of the Bulge, Bill returned home only to discover that his girlfriend was married to his brother and the village was no longer a welcome place for him.

At this point, Bill's life takes a downward plunge into a world of alcoholism, unemployment, and homelessness. But an unlikely series of events suddenly sheds a beacon of light on the hopelessness of his life, and he is given a second chance at love and happiness—but only if he rises to the challenge.

$16.95 • 384 pages • 5.5 x 8.5-inch paperback
ISBN 978-09640826-1-8

As All My Fathers Were
James A. Misko

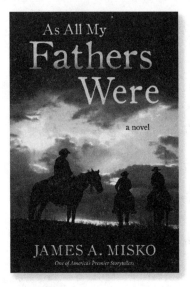

Ranchers Richard and Seth Barrett are devoted to running the family ranch on Nebraska's Platte River. It is their intent to keep doing so the rest of their lives; however, the terms of their mother's will requires them to travel by horse and canoe along the Platte River, to understand why their maternal grandfather homesteaded the ranch three generations earlier. From the grave, she commands them to observe industrial farming's harm to the land, air, and water.

A ninety-year-old bachelor farmer, with a game plan of his own, butts in and threatens to disrupt and delay the will's mandatory expedition. A conniving, wealthy neighbor seeking to seize the property using a gullible hometown sheriff and a corrupt local politician thwart their struggle to keep their ranch and meet the will's terms.

The Platte River, "A mile wide and an inch deep," becomes its own character in this turbulent novel and lives up to its legend as being "too thick to drink and too thin to plow."

$19.95 • 416 pages • 6 x 9-inch paperback
ISBN 978-096408264-9

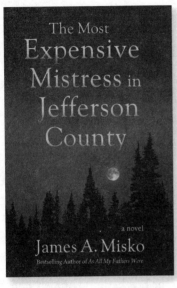

The Most Expensive Mistress in Jefferson County
James A. Misko

What would you do to earn 10 million dollars? Would you be willing to compromise your principles? Hawkins "Hawk" Neilson is about to find out in *The Most Expensive Mistress in Jefferson County*.

The United States Forest Service, Fish and Wildlife Service, Bureau of Land Management, and other government agencies have signed a contract—along with 130 ranchers, farmers, and the Nez Perce Indian Nation—to exchange over $400 million of property in the largest land deal in Idaho history. Hawk has drained his bank account and borrowed more money to close this transaction. Can he make it through the last week before closing? When the Indians suddenly demand an additional million dollars for one of their properties, Hawk explodes. Now he must deal with a situation that could change his life forever.

$15.95 • 208 pages • 5.5 x 8.5-inch paperback
ISBN 978-096408262-5 • December 2016

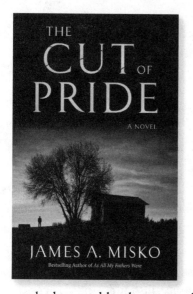

The Cut of Pride
James A. Misko

"In his novel *The Cut of Pride*, Jim Misko does something that is rare in modern literature: He writes about hard, brutal, unpleasant physical labor. And he does so with such vivid detail that the labor itself becomes one of the story's major entities. His cast of complex, dysfunctional characters—owners and employees of a mink-raising farm in coastal Oregon—is nearly destroyed by the seemingly endless toil. Maintaining a sense of human worth is a constant struggle. The brotherhood of men who work well together, like the brotherhood of fellow soldiers, is shown through the friendship of old West Helner and Jeff Baker, a young hired hand. Slaving alongside each other, both are nearly unmanned by Rose—West's domineering wife and owner of the mink enterprise. Here is a story with unforgettable characters, whose pride, distrust, and bitterness make for grim yet gripping drama." —James Alexander Thom, author of *Follow The River*

$15.95 • 208 pages • 5.5 x 8.5-inch paperback
ISBN 978-096408262-5 • December 2016

For more information about our books, visit our website at www.squareonepublishers.com